RIDE

A BAYONET SCARS NOVEL

JC Emery

Dani,

Enjoy the ride!

JC Emery

Series & Titles by JC Emery

Men with Badges
Marital Bitch
The Switch

The Birthright Series
Anomaly

Bayonet Scars
Ride

Ride

a Bayonet Scars novel
by
JC Emery
Copyright 2013 by Left Break Press
ISBN-13: 978-0615911687
ISBN-10: 0615911684

Find JC Emery on the web!

http://www.jcemery.com
http://twitter.com/jc_emery
http://www.facebook.com/jcemeryauthor
http://www.goodreads.com/jc_emery

Cover Design by Brenda Gonet at Gonet Design
http://www.facebook.com/gonetdesign

Edited by Rachel Bateman at Metamorphosis Books
http://metamorphosisbooks.com

Praise for JC Emery's *Ride*

For my mother,

The toughest broad I've ever met.

Acknowledgements

This book was a serious whirlwind that couldn't have been possible without the incredible people who have stepped up and made this book possible. Books, you've once again tolerated and indulged me in the writing and publishing journey. I hate to remind you, but NaNoWriMo is once again upon us. Please, be tolerant. Mandie Jones—I love you, buddy! Thank you for helping out and struggling through the romance! Adrianne, and all my girls at Indie Ignites, thank you for your support. Nazarea Andrews at Inkslinger PR, you pulled some strings and worked your magic getting this book out there—thank you! Rachel Bateman at Metamorphosis Books, thank you for putting up with my comma splices and misplaced modifiers. Your ability to deal with my constant lateness is admirable. Brenda at Gonet Design, you've outdone yourself this time. That cover is HOT!

To everyone on my beta team: Kristina Amit, CR DeStasi, Julie Deaton, Danielle Plane, Mindy Smith Stickels, Judy Ruiz, and Amber Vaughn. Your support and encouragement has been simply amazing. I hope to see each and every one of you along for the ride once we start Thrash. And finally, Dawn Johnson. You started as a reader, who became a friend, who has become one of my most valuable assets in this world. You're more than a PA, you're a lifesaver. You're the one who's up with me at 3am running through plot twists, dialogue issues, and full-on freak-outs when I'm convinced everyone is going to hate Alex and Ryan.

And finally—Mom. I've tried to figure out how I can thank you for not only giving me life, but believing in my dreams so fully, I'm almost convinced I can achieve them. You are a never-ending source of love, encouragement, and utter ridiculousness. Without you, I couldn't do what I do every day. I thoroughly enjoyed your company and input along this journey. You know I'm going to need you for Thrash, right? Many women say that their greatest fear is becoming their mother. My greatest fear is *not* becoming my mother. You may not see it, but you are the toughest woman I've ever met. You deal with shit that would make other people throw in the towel, and you do it with grace and love. I love you beyond words. You kick some serious ass.

MAY

Prologue

When you're drowning, you don't say "I would be incredibly pleased if someone would have the foresight to notice me drowning and come and help me," you just scream.

- John Lennon

THE HOUSE IS dead silent except for the quiet murmurs coming from Ma and Pop's bedroom. When Pop called and told me to get my ass over here as soon as possible, I thought he was fucking around. He wasn't.

We've known that shit could go down for a long fucking time—or at least Ian and I have—so it shouldn't be this big of a surprise. But it is.

"You good, brother?" I ask, looking down at Ian, who's sitting in a chair at the kitchen table. He hasn't said anything since he showed up a few minutes ago. The way he is now—wavy, light brown hair slicked back, skin pale, a thin sheen of sweat on the ridge of his brow—takes me back to when we were kids. We'd been brothers all of five minutes when the kid freaked the fuck out over Pop throwing his boot at the wall in a moment of frustration. He was so skittish and fearful of every fucking thing. He looks up at me, jerks his chin at the chair across the table, and then lets his eyes fall back down to the table top. I pull the chair out, cringing when it creaks and squeaks as I drag it out from under the table. Everything's so goddamn quiet right now that the noise feels invasive.

"Just fucking with my head, ya know?" he says in a gravelly voice. His face is carefully blank, and his posture gives away nothing, but I know him too well to think this shit isn't sending his ass sideways.

I nod and lean my elbows on the table and say, "I get that."

"What Pop's about to do? You good with that?" he asks.

I pause to consider the question. Am I good with it? I'm not entirely sure. I never stopped to wonder if I was or not, because I know how much this means to Ma. In my mind, she needs this, so we do it.

"Doesn't matter," I say. Because it doesn't. Pop made a promise he shouldn't have fucking made. But he did, and here we are. I'm not about to let Ma suffer for Pop's bad call. Ian looks up at me, an eyebrow raised, a look of disbelief on his face.

"Look, the shit that went down? The promises he made? It happened. Nothing I can do about that. The kid's family," I say.

With a nod of my head, I meet the man who I consider to be my brother in the eyes and say, "What we're doing here is righting a wrong. It's about fucking time that Mancuso got his."

Ian's face hardens at the mention of the man who once gave him nightmares.

"We run into him and I got a clear shot?" he says. I nod my head and smile wide because now he's finally thinking shit over.

"You get a clear shot, you wound him," I say. My body warms at the idea. "And carve out his eyeballs with your fingers."

Finally, a smile spreads across his face, and a smirk plays at his lips. If anybody deserves the kill the guy, it's my brother.

"You got it, brother," he says. Feeling better about where Ian's at, I stand from the table and stride through the living room and down the hall on the opposite end of the house, toward Ma and Pop's room. The door to their room is at the end of the hall, just past Ian's old bedroom and the hall bath. The door is open, giving me a good line of sight to what's going on inside. Ma's curled up in the center of the bed with Pop hovering over her. The last time I walked in on an intimate moment between the two of them, they were both naked and I had to blow a grand on coke just to numb the images of Ma getting drilled from behind. If I hadn't made the mistake of telling Duke—that fucker—I might not be reminded of it on the regular.

"It's okay, Mama," Pop says. He kisses the top of her head and smoothes down her wayward hair.

"Should I talk to them?" she asks. He lets out a stilted laugh and groans.

"Nah, they can unload their shit on me. You step in the room, they don't do it now, and next thing ya know I got guys losing their shit and getting themselves killed."

"What if they say no?" Ma asks. I bite my tongue to keep the grunt that's burning in my throat. Pop, Ian, Wyatt, and I already discussed this. If the club votes against it, then the four of us will go alone. It's not ideal, but it's better than the kid ending up dead.

"What did I promise you?" he says in a harsher tone than he was using just a minute ago.

"I know," she says with a sigh. "It's just…"

"No, fuck that. It's not just anything. I make you a promise, I keep it. I ever give you reason to doubt me?"

She shakes her head and pats her eyes dry, saying, "No."

"Then stop doubting me now. I'll walk through fire for you, Mama. You know that," he says and kisses her cheek. No matter how many loving moments I've been witness to between them, it still amazes me how much they love each other. Love like this, that stands decades and fights—that stands despite separations and parenting two bratty fucking punks—love like that? It's as real as anything fucking gets. That kind of shit makes a man almost believe it can be replicated.

"Fucking pervert," a deep voice says from behind me, and a heavy hand slams on my shoulder. I jump in place and throw my fist back without even looking to see who's there. Spinning around, I see Wyatt, the club's vice president, blocking my swing. He bursts into heavy laughter. Ma and Pop scramble from the bed and hurry over to us.

"Damn," Wyatt says, looking Ma up and down. He whistles and smirks at Pop. "Your pervert son was standing here. Damn shame you're dressed, babe."

Pop laughs and looks over at me with a disturbingly happy smile on his face. Sick fuck. "Dude. She's your mom," Pop says.

I shake my head and throw my hands in the air. Ma pats me on the check and shakes her head. There's a coy smile tugging at her lips.

"Don't be such a grouch, Ryan," she says.

I turn on my heels and leave the house, shouting behind me, "Come on, you nancies. We got Church."

Despite the laughter and easy going demeanor when we leave the house, the moment we're on our bikes and heading for the clubhouse, the mood shifts. Wyatt's mouth forms a thin line, and his eyes harden. Pop is quiet pulling down the long dirt driveway and then he's quiet as we enter the clubhouse. Ian is pretty much always quiet when we're about to discuss club matters, so that's nothing new, but there's a fucked-up vibe emanating from him.

I round up the brothers as Pop and Wyatt head straight through the main room of the clubhouse and dart to the right down the long hall and to the chapel at the very end. All they know is that Pop's called Church, but they don't know why. We had our weekly meeting yesterday, so they know something's up.

Inside the chapel, the boys are restless. Their eyes are darting around, and a few of them have figured out who knows what's happening and who doesn't. I keep my head down as I cross the room and take my seat next to Ian—the club's treasurer—and Diesel, who doesn't hold an officer position. Across from me is Duke—my best friend and our secretary. His eyes are wide when they land on mine, and he mouths, "What the fuck?" I try to ignore the question and let my eyes skim around the table. I would have said something to him had I the time, but I didn't.

On the other side of Ian is Grady—the club's sergeant at arms. He's leaning over the table, hands clasped. His brows are drawn together. And across from him is Wyatt. As the head of the table, Pop sits closest to Wyatt and Grady. Neither Ian nor Wyatt are meeting anyone's eyes, either. I hate this shit. It's as uncomfortable as all get out. But Pop asked that we keep it on the down low until he's made his speech so his men can hear from him first.

"I know you're all sick of looking at my ugly mug," Pop says from his seat at the head of the table. His grayish black hair is in need of a cut and keeps falling in his face no matter how many times he tucks it behind his ears. Even though the dude's over forty, he's still got the same build and coloring he had back when I was a kid. Ma has a theory that the reason he stays so young looking is because he's mean and has practically pickled himself in being an asshole. By that same thought, she's told me more often than I should be proud of that I'm never going to age beyond twenty-five. Don't know what it says about her that she loves such assholes, but that's Ma. The ornerier Pop gets, the more she falls in love with him. God only knows why.

"Years back, before half of you were even patched—back when Rage sat in this chair—I asked my brothers for something on behalf of my woman. She was a good woman then, and she's a damn good woman now. I don't regret taking on her shit and asking the club to shoulder that burden, and I'm fucking proud to wear this patch. Made a promise to Ruby, and in exchange for the club helping me to keep that promise, I did any fucking thing asked of me. Some of it fucked me up for a while, and some of it's still fucking me up. But I did it. I've done my time, which took me away from my kids." Pop's eyes fall on me and then Ian before he looks over the room again.

"I've always put the patch first. My old lady, my boys—they understand that—but now it's time I put them first. I gotta call in that marker."

I look around the table to find that everybody is nodding, or at least mostly resigned to what they think comes next. It's no secret that Pop put that marker in, and it's no secret why. When each of us patched in, we knew the score. Each brother has certain things he needs. He takes care of his shit, does his time, and if he needs it, he can call in a marker, too. A member needs something, the club takes care of it. That's just how we operate. But this shit? This shit's out of our playbook.

"Ain't no thing, Pop," Bear says from the other side of the table. "Just tell us when and we'll be locked and loaded."

"We got this shit," Grady says, nodding. Pop's silence is unnerving. The boys are all starting to talk amongst themselves now. Chief's gotta let Barbara know he's going to miss Izzy's choir performance and Stephen's parent-teacher conference. Grady's thumping the table, asking Chief if Barbara can watch his daughter, Cheyenne, because his mom is going to be out of town for most of the week. The rest of them are already talking firepower and logistics. All of them except for Ian, Wyatt, Pop, and me. Even Duke, who's half-past pissed, is talking things over with Diesel.

Pop thunks down the gavel just once. His face is paler than it was minutes ago, and his shoulders are dropped, almost in defeat. The boys quiet down and turn to give him their full attention. He clears his throat and says, "There's a complication."

Family or not, my brothers aren't exactly cool with the shit Pop's asking of them. As Pop explains the situation, the tension in the room only increases. After a moment of pure silence and stillness from the room, absolute chaos erupts. Chairs get shoved back, fists get slammed into the wooden table, and insults are exchanged.

From across the table, I can feel Duke's eyes on me. He shakes his head and mouths, "Prick". His shoulders roll with anger, and his eyes look straight-up fucking deadly. Duke's my brother almost as much as Ian is, but he wouldn't understand this—the risk we're willing to take and why. He wouldn't be down with it, and judging by the way he drags his hand down his goatee with his blue eyes glaring at me, he doesn't get it now.

"How's that look?" Chief asks from my left. He leans back in his chair and looks around the room, carefully skipping over Pop. Voting down something this personal fucks with a club, but if the club decides it's too dangerous, Pop has to respect that. Shit won't be easy to let go, but we will.

"Blood," Grady says. "That's how it looks."

"Since when did you grow a pussy?" Wyatt asks, look across the table.

"Ain't about being a pussy, brother. It's about being smart. This ain't smart," Grady says.

"She's a kid," Chief grunts out. "A fuckin' kid."

"I'm not good with this shit," Grady says.

"If it was Elle…," Chief says, trailing off as he references his eldest daughter. "Nothing else would matter. I'd want my girl safe."

"It's not Elle," Grady grumbles.

"And if it was Cheyenne?" Wyatt says, speaking up from beside Pop. Grady's body stiffens, and he shoots up in his chair with Wyatt doing the same right after him. Fucking pissing contests.

"It ain't Cheyenne. It ain't ever gonna be Cheyenne," Grady barks out. A few of my brothers look to Grady and nod their heads.

Beside me, Ian clears his throat. Slowly, he lifts his head and meets everyone's eyes. He lowers his gaze to the table and lets out a heavy breath. One word falls from his lips and it's the only thing he needs to say—and the only thing I know he can say right now.

"Please," he says. His voice booms with the pain of his request. I want to pat his back, but he'd damn sure feel like a bitch if I did. Instead, I mean mug my brothers, daring any of them to say shit to him. As Ruby's biological son, he's got a special place at the table right now because this vote is really fucking personal for him. It takes the brothers a minute before they calm down enough to start asking questions about Mancuso and his boys, and how this is all going to go down if we vote yea.

After a long, drawn-out discussion, and a lot of fucking bitching, the vote comes in. Ten votes, and all we need is a majority. It's no surprise that Grady votes nay, but what does surprise me is that so does Duke, and Diesel. I breathe a sigh of relief when I mentally tally the votes. With Wyatt, Chief, Fish, Bear, Ian, and Pop and me—we got the club's vote. Pop slams the gavel down, and I stand. Grady, Duke, and Diesel look pissed, but it's over now. As I stride out of the room, I let the tension roll off my shoulders.

"Hey, Fucker," Duke shouts from behind me. I stop in place, knowing better than to assume he's not talking to me. When I turn around, I see that he's got his arms crossed over his chest and he's fixing me with a hard glare. "Good job giving me a head's up about this shit."

"Didn't have time, brother," I say.

"Fuck you," he says. "You rode off without a fucking word. We're supposed to be bros and this is how you do me?" He's used to being in the loop, and obviously being out of the loop pisses him off. Truth be told, I wasn't fucking thinking about giving him a head's up. I had other shit to attend to. I still have other shit to attend to. We leave in six fucking hours, and I gotta take the van with Wyatt up to Willits to get more ammo and then get back here. It's gonna be a long fucking night, and this dickhead wants to sort his shit out.

RIDE

When Pop came to me tonight, asking where I was coming at with this thing with Alex, I didn't even think about it. She's family even if she doesn't know it. Ma's been telling us about her for as long as I can remember. She's important to Ma, and that makes her important to me. But instead of preparing to go up against Mancuso and his men, I'm standing here having a fucking bitch fest with this asshole.

Duke's attention drifts across the room, but his body remains still as his eyes shoot daggers at Nic, one of the club's pickiest—and meanest—whores. He shakes his head at the sight of her, sitting at a bar stool in tight-ass jeans and a flimsy tank top.

"Don't get pissed at me because you're hard up and Nic won't give you the time of day," I say with a smile. His eyes flash in anger as he strides toward me. We're nose to nose now, and my temper kicks in. My entire body tenses and prepares to throw down. "It's all good, brother. She's Grade-A fine with a side of crazy, but she sucks a mean dick."

He reaches up and pounds his fist into the side of my head. My vision blurs, and it takes me a moment before I can see straight again. A hand flattens itself on my chest and puts pressure, moving me backward. I shake away the blurriness to see Wyatt standing between us.

"We're going to need everybody in one piece," he says to Duke. "Go ahead and get drunk. You just earned yourself a spot in the van."

"Fuck you," Duke hisses at Wyatt, who just shakes his head.

"Not helping, brother. You already got bitch duty. Keep it up," Wyatt says. I turn and walk away, to which

Wyatt shouts after me, "And where the fuck are you going?"

"Check on Ma. Meet me at the house with the van," I call out as I walk through the door and out into the cool night air. It's gonna be a long fucking week, and I need to let Ma know that it's a go. As I pull out of the Forsaken lot, I force myself to calm down. We've done a lot of shit in the time I've been patched, but nothing like this. Don't think we've ever taken on anything this fucked up. Taking on the Italian mafia is no fucking joke. I just hope this girl is worth the risk we're taking.

Alex

Chapter 1

A woman's place in public is to sit beside her husband,
be silent, and be sure her hat is on straight.

- Bess Truman

THE ROOM IS packed full of Italians to the point where I think the walls might explode. This many Armani suits and Versace dresses in one house can only mean one thing around here: somebody is dead.

Across the room, my best friend, Adriana Thomas stands, looking as bored as I feel. I catch her attention, and with a head nod and eyebrow arch she knows exactly what I'm looking at. She puts her hand over her mouth and giggles, making me giggle, too. It's so ridiculous. Sidled up to the dessert table is my Aunt Gloria. She has one of Uncle Emilio's giant cannolis in her mouth, the cream filling all over her face, not even noticing the mess she's made of herself. Uncle Emilio will not be pleased if he catches sight of this. He's been trying to calm Aunt Gloria's appetite for years.

My father's hand, wrapped around my forearm, tightens, and I remember that I'm supposed to be paying attention to the conversation before me. I turn back to my father, Carlo Mancuso, and smile apologetically. I'd forgotten my place for a moment there. Across from my father stands one of his soldiers, Leonardo Scavo, who—as always—keeps his dark brown eyes on me. A blush forms on my cheeks and I look away, smiling. Leo's just barely twenty-three and is quickly rising in the ranks on his way to becoming a Capo. He's smart, good-looking, and my father trusts him, which meant he has some serious earning power. I try to remind myself that I could do much worse than Leo Scavo.

"Alexandra!" Aunt Gloria shouts from across the room, wiping her face clean of cannoli and striding toward me. Ever since my mother died a few years ago, Aunt Gloria has taken it upon herself to teach me how to be a woman in this world. I smile despite my grouchy mood. If Aunt Gloria thinks something is wrong she'll never let me hear the end of it until she knows exactly what's up.

It's not that I don't like my aunt; it's more like she makes me uncomfortable in public. She's so loud and always shouting about something or other, which embarrasses Uncle Emilio to no end. It's not a secret that if Gloria wasn't Joseph Mancuso's daughter—and Carlo Mancuso's baby sister—Emilio Vescovi never would have married her, nor would he continue to parade her around in public. The woman is a drunk half the time. But she's also the closest thing to a mother that I have.

My father releases my arm and allows Gloria to slide in between us. I'll give her one thing, she knows me well. She knows how much I hate being dragged around by my father like I'm some sort of prized show dog. And because she grew up in this lifestyle, she also knows I don't have the ability to do anything about it. I lean over, kissing her cheek. She returns the kiss and wipes the smeared lipstick off my cheek.

"Carlo." She greets my father with an enormous smile. She kisses his cheek and he kisses her forehead, as is tradition in the family. My mother explained it to me once—a kiss on the cheek is a sign of respect, which is why Uncle Emilio, my father's underboss, always kisses my father's cheek in greeting before a sit down—not that

I'm supposed to know that. A kiss on the forehead is a promise of protection.

"Have you been good to my girl?" she asks. My father locks his jaw in frustration. Gloria, while oblivious, is disrespecting my father—or at least that's the way he sees it. Despite being born into the family and having married a family man, Gloria never really watches her tongue. Somehow, she gets away with it. If I were to try it, my mouth would be swollen for a week.

"Ask her yourself, Gloria. She's standing right next to you," he says, swirling the single malt scotch in his cognac snifter before knocking it back. Gloria looks to me, but says nothing. Loud and abrasive, sure, but even she knows her limits. Asking my father if he's been good to me suggests that he is incapable of caring for me, that she doesn't trust his judgment. If there's one thing you never question in this family, it's the boss's judgment. It doesn't matter if he's your brother or not, and it's really unwise to do so in a room full of his men.

In an effort to ease the tension, I ask my father if he wants me to get him some more scotch. Without even looking at me, he shoves his glass in my direction and focuses his attention on Leo.

"Let's talk, Son," my father says, clapping Leo on the back and leading him toward his office. My breath catches. A few heads turn suddenly, surprised to hear his declaration to Leo. Calling him "Son" publicly is my father making him a promise, a promise for my hand. I look at the ground, refusing to meet anyone's eyes as I make my way to the wet bar in the game room and remind myself—again—that I actually kind of like Leo.

Adriana beelines from her place next to her mother and catches up to me just as I turn the corner into the empty game room. She whisper-shouts, "What the hell was that?"

I look around to make sure we're alone and say, "You *know* what that was. Daddy Dearest pretty much just sold me to the highest bidder."

"I can't believe this shit. I'm so sorry," she says, giving my back a gentle rub. I try to shake it off, but it's difficult. "I thought you were going to talk to him?"

"I *did* talk to him. He gave me some bullshit about making sure I'm taken care of, making sure I'm not being used, et cetera."

"At least Leo's hot," she says, giving me a wicked smile.

"Yeah, he is."

"Well, I'm here all summer. We need to hang out before you get so wrapped up in Scavo dick that you forget all about your best girl."

"Sure thing," I say and wave her comment off, watching as she shuffles back to her mother's side. Best friend or not, I kind of want to slap her right now. She has no idea how lucky she is. For graduation last year, she got a new BMW to take with her to Vassar. I got a trip to see my nonna in Cusio, Italy, where she spent three months trying to train me to be the perfect house wife. I don't know why she bothered. Her efforts at turning me into the perfect Principessa kind of failed.

Watching the door to my father's office from my place in front of the wet bar, I wonder what my father has to talk to Leo about that is so important they had to have a meeting in the middle of Sal's wake. Business is never to be discussed during a wake, but that kind of respect is rarely reserved for rats like Sal. Nobody talks about it because Sal was a Capo and that would be disrespectful

RIDE

to him and his widow, Caterina, but the bullet-hole in the center of his throat tells everybody the truth: Sal talked.

The only access on the first floor to my father's office is through the game room, which is off the center hall and has limited visibility from the other rooms in the house. When my grandfather ran things, years back, he'd sealed off the entrance from the main hallway at the front of the house after some crazy teppista barged in on him. As my father tells the story, my grandfather had seen the guy coming from the bay window. Had the guy been a moment faster, it might have been grandfather with the bullet hole between the eyes. To this day, we don't know what the guy came here for. Now, my father likes a little more time to be able to react and has since sealed off that door.

Curiosity gets the best of me, so I set the cognac snifter down on the wet bar as quietly as possible and tip-toe toward the office door. Unlike some of the bosses whose homes I've been in over the years, my father doesn't have a camera on his office door. He refuses to be a prisoner in his own home, he's said. And thank God for it, too. I've spent hours of my life in front of that door, listening to conversations I never should have heard. I can't help myself; I just want to know what it was they all keep so secret.

I crouch down in the doorway to steady myself and press my torso as close to the locked door as I can without touching it.

"Such a pity, the thing about Sal," my father says casually. Leo agrees stiffly after a moment. "Relax, Leonardo. My house is your house, or at least, it might be one day." As I hear the words from my father's mouth, my stomach sinks. This is exactly what I've been afraid of. It's not that my father hadn't chosen well, it's that he's chosen at all. Despite having known for years that my father would play a big part in my betrothal, I didn't realize that he would actually be the one making the choice until recently.

Headstrong and in denial, I always thought I had a say in the matter. I was so very wrong. I wipe the tears from my eyes and take in a shaky breath. Neither one of them has bothered to consult me in this little arrangement. This is obviously the only way I'll find anything out about what they've planned for me.

"A man in my position, he looks for certain things in a family member. Do you know what I mean, Leo?" my father sounds like he's smiling, something he doesn't do a lot of these days. I miss the sound of his voice when he's smiling.

"Yes, Padrone," Leo says.

"Oh no," my father laughs lightly, "don't call me that. That's my father." Leo gives a choked laugh. "Are you nervous, Leo, because there's nothing to be nervous about. It's just Carlo and Leo, that's all." Leo laughs again, this time more relaxed.

"I'm just grateful for your consideration, sir."

"I see the way you look at Alex. That's what we're here to talk about, Leo. Today is not about business, it's about pleasure. I want my daughter taken care of, and I know you can do that. Especially with your own crew—" my father is cut off by Leo's stuttering.

"My own crew?" he asks. Carlo chuckles.

"Not today, son, but do you really think I'm going to let my little girl marry a Soldato?" They keep talking, but I can't hear any of it. The pounding in my heart drowns everything else out. The rhythmic thumping gets louder and louder until it makes my head swim. I blink, my vision blurry from the tears that come, forcibly streaming down my face and neck, wetting the collar of my cardigan. The game room feels like it's getting smaller with every breath I take as a thick humidity settles in, making the tips of my ears and fingers red and hot to the touch. I realize after a moment that I'm sweating. I have to get out of there.

On shaky legs, I stand and tip-toe away from the door and out of the game room as silently as I came in. I round the corner down the center hallway and race for the stairs. At the top of the staircase on the second floor, I slam into something. For the first time since leaving the game room, I look up, and nearly fall backwards at what I see. It's Caterina, Sal's wife.

"Alex," she says gently, reaching out a wrinkled hand and touching my cheek, wiping my tears away. "What's wrong, Miele?" I shake my head, not wanting to tell her. After everything, she's still calling me 'honey'. She's mourning her husband—like I should be. Sal had been in the family since before I was born. Before everything went south, my father had me calling him Uncle Sal. The moment my father instructed me to just call him Sal I knew what was coming. We all did, but there was nothing we could do about it.

My father could have given Sal a pass—he did for Emilio's younger brother. He just chose not to. It hadn't made sense at the time, but I understand it now. He was making room for Leo, to give him his own crew. My stomach turns. Getting rid of Sal because he was a rat is one thing; doing so in order to promote another is disgusting.

"I miss him, too," she says, her voice low. I nod. "But let's not worry ourselves over that, okay?" She cups my face with her hands and wipes my tears away. I gave her a small smile.

"I'm okay. Really," I lie. When my father told me not to call Sal "Uncle" anymore, I knew the same went for Caterina. She isn't exactly out, but she'll never be back in either.

"We make our choices in life, Miele. Remember that." She smiles sadly and looks up, her entire body going stiff before retreating down to the first floor. I look behind me to find my twin brother, Michael. I let out a heavy sigh and start for my room, ignoring his footsteps behind me.

"What's got you so upset?" he asks. I wave him off and enter my room, only to have him follow. "You want me to call Tony?" I plop down on my bed and cover my head with my pillow.

"Okay, I'm getting Tony," Michael warns. I scream into the pillow before throwing it at him. Tony is our cousin, Gloria and Emilio's son, and he is a total hothead. He's a few years older than us and, once he got his button, pretty much taught Michael everything he knows about the family. It isn't really allowed—talking to someone outside of the family about business—but we are a different kind of family than the one my father runs. We're a family linked by blood and kept together by love. But Tony joined *the* family, so I guess he doesn't really belong to us anymore.

"Leave Tony out of it." I narrow my eyes at him. Michael is what Adriana calls "beefy"—tall and muscular. He's my twin brother, sure, but whatever similarities we had went out the window once he hit puberty. I stayed short and gangly, while Michael started looking like the spitting image of our father. By the age of thirteen, he was more man than boy, and my father started treating him as such. Meanwhile, he wants me to be the girl who never grows up. There is no such thing as fair in the Mancuso household.

"So then tell me what's got you upset," Michael says and sits down beside me. I shrug, not wanting to get into it. Michael used to understand me, but lately he's all about the family. God forbid I complain about something. He tells me that's just the way it is and I need to get used to it. But that's easy for him to say, being a guy. I didn't have the privilege of being born with a penis and will probably pay for that for the rest of my life.

"Come on, Al. Tell me."

I let out an exasperated sigh. If I don't tell him, I'll be hearing about it all summer long.

"I overheard Dad and Leo talking," I mumble. Michael smiles wide. That just pisses me off. Michael and Leo get along well. I guess Michael figures I could do worse, too.

"This is a good thing, Alex," Michael says encouragingly. "Dad could have picked one of those stupido princepes for you, ya know." I roll my eyes.

"Oh yeah, you're one to talk. You're a princepe yourself, dumbass." I smile and elbow him in the gut. His smile makes me feel better. It always has. He's a good brother, no matter how much I complain about him.

"Anyway," I say, "It's not about that. I just thought I'd have a choice, ya know? I knew Dad would have to approve and all, but I thought that I'd at least get a chance to date someone and decide for myself whether I like him or not." Michael's smile falls and he nods.

"I get it." He put his arm around my shoulders and pulls me into him. I lean in, taking whatever comfort I can get. "You want me to talk to him for you?" My eyes light up, hopeful. He scoffs and starts laughing so hard I think he's going to choke on air.

"You think I'm going to talk to 'The Iceman' for you?" He snorts, using the name my father's men call him. Yeah, Michael is a real bad ass using different mafia-related nicknames when my father can't hear him, but to his face it's all "yes, sir" and "no, sir."

There are two hard knocks on my bedroom door. My father. When the door opens, I see his tired face staring back at us. He walks in and slumps into the chair by my vanity, a faint amusement in his eyes.

"'The Iceman', huh?" Carlo says. Michael's face falls. He looks at his feet and starts wringing his hands together. "If you're going to talk about people, son, you need to be brave enough to say it to their face."

I don't like this. I've seen it before with Tony. My father's grooming my brother so when he's ready to earn his bones his attitude will command respect. My eyes dart away in discomfort. This is not what I want for my brother.

Michael is so smart and has such a big heart. Our mother wouldn't have wanted this for him, and she wouldn't have wanted it for my future husband, either. If she were here, she'd rein my father in, in her own quiet way. She would distract him from all of these little lessons he's trying to impart upon my brother. She would be so much better at it than I am.

"He called you 'The Iceman' because I called you 'The Godfather'. I'm sorry," I rush out, staring my father in the eyes, unable to stand the silence and Michael's fidgeting. My father nods his head.

"You see, Michael, your sister—a girl—has the guts to be honest with me. Right now, this little girl is being more of a man than you are. I know you want to show me that you're ready to be a man and all, so start showing me now. What did you say right before I came into this room?" His tone is light, but I know better than to assume that means all's well. Michael stands up and faces our father, squaring his shoulders.

"Sir, I called you 'The Iceman'," Michael says without a hint of nervousness. My father stands and walks toward him. Before I can shield myself from it, he's got Michael by his throat. Michael doesn't move a muscle; his eyes don't waiver. I know my father's grip around his neck isn't very tight. He's making a point. My father leans in and touches his nose to Michael's.

"As your father, inside of this house, I find the childish jokes funny. I enjoy your sense of humor. But outside of this house, if you come to work for me, that can't happen. If you want me to teach you what I know, if you want me to guide you so that one day your own smart ass kid can call you bullshit names while you're trying to show him the ropes, then you need to watch your tongue. I want to leave this to you, son, but in order to do that, you have to want it. I'll always be your father, but that won't matter if you join my family. I just want you to be prepared for that."

He lets go of Michael's neck and takes a step back. I keep my eyes trained on my paisley bedspread, rattled that my father has let me be witness to this conversation. He's always very careful to skirt the lines around me, never saying too much.

"It's time you learn about this side of the family, Alexandra. One day you'll have a husband and you'll have his children. You need to know what you're getting into. I just wish your mother were here to help guide you." He trails off at the end. I nod. He wants me to know my place as a wife and mother so I'll know what I'm marrying into. The problem is he's overlooked the fact that I was born in it. It doesn't matter who I marry. I'm already in the life, and there's no changing that.

"Hey, Dad?" Michael says, relaxing to his normal self. For a moment I think he's going to keep up the tough guy look in front of our father, and I worry that means he will always keep the tough guy look when he's around. Staring at my father and brother, so much alike and growing more alike every day, my heart aches. It's like being faced with Michael turning into somebody he isn't before my eyes.

My father smiles at him. "Hey, Mike."

"Tony's having a party tonight. Am I clear to go?" I wait for it—the moment where my father tells Michael he can take off. The verbal acknowledgement of the disparity in treatment between me and my brother. Maybe I should be more excited about being married off. I wouldn't have to deal with my father's gross injustices any longer. No, then I'll have to deal with my husband's—a husband I didn't even get the chance to pick.

"You know the rules," my father says, pointing his finger at my brother with a proud smile on his face. We're not kids anymore, both nineteen now, but with me being a girl I don't step a toe out the door without permission. Michael, however, unofficially works for our father. He's on call 24/7 and not really confident enough to stop asking for permission to go out and do stuff.

"I'll do you proud, Old Man," Michael says. He smirks and blocks the playful punches my father throws at him, while throwing out a few of his own.

"Okay, have fun, ragazzone. Avvolgere tuo uccello," my father says as he walks out of the door. He turns around and looks at me and rubs his neck. I know what he said, and the expression on his face tells me he'd forgotten I was still in the room He wouldn't have told my brother to use a condom had he remembered I was sitting right here.

"Why don't you go check on your Aunt Gloria, and lock up the liquor while you're at it. It's about time all those sciocchi go home anyway." It's not a request. My father disappears down the hall, and the moment I know he's out of earshot, I turn on my brother.

"Yeah, ragazzone," I say in frustration. "Wrap your fucking dick." I turn away from Michael's grin and flip him the bird as I stand up and leave the room.

Chapter 2

This life of ours, this is a wonderful life. If you can get through life like this and get away with it, hey that's great. But it's very unpredictable. There's so many ways you can screw it up.

- Michael Castellano, suspected Colombo family associate

DOWNSTAIRS, THE CROWD'S thinning out. First, I lock up the liquor cabinet, then find Aunt Gloria and kindly take her glass of wine from her. She's actually pretty awesome when she's sober; sharp as a tack, and more guts than half the men I know. Unfortunately, she's usually sloshed, and that means her natural charm rarely makes an appearance.

Once I have her in her coat and Uncle Emilio ready to go, I see the rest of the guests out. They all know that once Emilio leaves it's time for them to leave as well. I don't see Leo go, and actually, I'm pretty grateful for it. I don't know how I'm supposed to talk to the man who was bargaining for my hand with my father not a half hour ago. Being a family man I guess it's never occurred to Leo that his intended should be with him because she wants to, not because her father sold her down the river.

The front parlor is a mess; so are the dining room and the kitchen. I steel myself for the task of cleaning everything up. Somehow all these people get the pleasure of coming over, creating a mess, and then leaving. There are splatters of meatballs under the dinner table, stray noodles stuck to the floor, and even a few plastic forks strewn about, half broken.

"Pigs," I mutter.

"Tell me about it," a deep voice says from behind me. I scream loudly and jump up so fast I nearly pass out from the head rush. When I regain my senses, I realize it's Leo. I feel my face heat immediately. I don't want to marry the guy or anything, but I don't want to make a bad impression either; I was raised to mind my manners. He smiles kindly at me despite the spastic look I just know I'm giving him.

"I didn't mean to startle you," he says, putting his hands in the air.

"Not the first time you've done that, is it?" I ask, motioning to his raised hands. I regret it immediately. Despite my comment, Leo smiles even brighter.

"You're a lot mouthier than Carlo lets on," he says. I stand frozen, not sure what he expects from me. Am I supposed to smile and flirt back, or am I supposed to play the obedient little principessa? That's why Leo's interested in me, isn't it? Because I'm obedient? That I'm Carlo Mancuso's daughter? That I'm his ticket up the ranks? He doesn't even know me. Clearly, I'm a business deal, and above all, that pisses me off. I'm used to being seen for who my father is and not who I am, but this still bothers me. I could get stuck with this guy's ring on my finger, my body in his bed, and my belly full of his kids. I cringe at the thought of my entire life being planned out for me. No surprise, no option, no choice.

Leo bends down and picks up the trash that's at his feet. He walks into the kitchen and pokes through drawers until he finds where I keep the trash bags. He's got two out and hands one to me before he opens the other for himself. I mean to tell him that he doesn't have to help. I want to tell him to stop helping, but I can't get my lips to move. Here he is, one of my father's favorite *soldatos*, wearing an Armani suit, picking up trash in my dining room. As he bends over, I notice the gold Desert Eagle gun at his hip and stifle the sigh that threatens to break through. He's on the job. He'll always be on the job, and when I get stuck married to him, I can't expect anything less.

"You don't—" I start, but stop the moment I see my father come into the room. Leo looks up at my father from his crouched position and stands immediately.

"What's going on in here?" Carlo asks, looking confused. I open my mouth to speak, but I don't know what to say. None of Carlo's men have ever helped me clean before.

"I wanted to help Alexandra clean up, Sir. Then I was going to ask her if she would like to go for dessert with me, since you said I could ask her out and all," Leo explains. My mouth still isn't working, but a strange feeling appears in my stomach. It's like a hundred butterflies have settled in my belly and are trying to take flight. Nobody has ever asked my father for permission to take me out before.

My first boyfriend and I snuck around as much as we could, which didn't amount to anything. After we'd dated a few months and I'd given him my virginity, he had the nerve to ask if my father was looking for any new runners. That was the first time I'd ever seen Michael fly into a rage—it was terrifying. I made it a point after that to never tell Michael when someone broke my heart. As much as I like to see the softer side of him, my brother has a violent streak just like our father. He believes in an eye for an eye. To this day I don't know what Michael did to the guy, but he put him in the hospital—something about his heart.

"*Si vuole veramente colpo su di lei, non è vero?*" my father says, asking Leo if he really wants to impress me. For whatever reason, anytime there's something my father doesn't want me to hear he'll say it in Italian, as though I'm not fluent. Leo responds in Italian, telling my father that he does want to impress me. I blush again, not sure I can take much more of this—them talking about me right in front of me.

"*Gelato mi impressiona,*" I say, telling them that gelato impresses me. Leo raises his eyebrows, and my father smiles softly. He walks over to me and kisses my forehead gently. "In case you've forgotten, Daddy, you're the one who taught me to speak Italian."

"Forget? No," my father says. "Sometimes, though. I do like to forget that you're no longer a little girl." My father walks toward the game room before turning around and staring at Leo. "Leave the mess, son. You've got a girl to impress. Just have her home by eleven." He leaves the room without turning around.

"That was a little awkward, wasn't it?" Leo asks. I blink at him before regaining my composure.

"What? Oh, no. My dad sold me to a Turk down the street for two sheep last week," I deadpan. I'm loosening up around Leo, and I can't decide if I like that or not. On one hand, I want to hate him and refuse to get to know him based on principle. On the other hand, he's offering gelato and the chance to ditch cleaning duties. Once the smile brakes out on Leo's face, I decide that this doesn't have to be so bad after all. I just have to give him a chance.

"Seriously? I just paid three sheep. I think I've been ripped off," Leo says, laughing. I can't stop the smile that comes to my face.

RIDE
34

"Whatever." I wave him off, setting the trash bag on the dining room table. "I'm going to let you take me out for gelato. That is so totally worth four sheep."

Leo leads me down the center hallway and out through the front door. We walk up to a black Mercedes sedan. He comes around the passenger's side and opens the door for me. I climb in; when he's settled in the driver's seat, I look to him.

"Mafia Black, how original." I smile teasingly.

"Hey, it's standard issue. You know, your father didn't tell me how big of a smart ass you are."

I roll my eyes. "I'm sure there are a lot of things he didn't tell you," I respond. This conversation is making me uncomfortable. I don't like discussing my father with people I don't know very well.

"Is that so?" his eyes seem to darken as he looks at me, like he'd discovered something new and hidden. I wiggle in my seat, growing uncomfortable with the intensity in his eyes.

"Well, I am nineteen," I defend myself.

"Nineteen, right," he says and starts the car. The rest of the drive to the gelato shop is silent. I choose not to overanalyze it and instead just enjoy the quiet. Just as we are pulling up to A Taste of Sicily, I speak.

"You're twenty-three, right?" I ask. Leo confirms what I already know. "So why are you interested in a nineteen-year-old?" I stumble over my words, trying to make the question sound better, less insinuating, but no matter how I phrase it, it sounds insulting.

His frustration is palpable as he clenches and unclenches his grip on the steering wheel. Parking the car, he unbuckles himself and turns his large torso toward me. "I'm not interested in *a* nineteen-year-old, Alexandra.

RIDE

I'm interested in you. And you'll be twenty in a few months anyway. I'm not that much older than you." Leo's voice has taken on a darker note. He doesn't sound nearly as pleasant as he did earlier. He quickly composes himself, his face relaxing, and he's back to being Mr. Charming.

"I didn't mean for it to come out like that," I say apologetically. He shrugs and gets out of the car, comes around to the passenger side and opens the door for me. He has manners, I'll give him that. I get out of the car and turn to the street. I've been to this place a hundred times or more. It's not far from the house, but is even closer to Tony's place. This is the closest I'll be getting to Tony's party tonight. I don't think I want to be there, knowing what goes on and all, but I hate knowing I can't make that decision for myself. Mr. Muscles with the gold gun will see to it that I don't step foot in that direction.

Slick black sedans race down the street toward Tony's house—all of them Mercedes—completely indistinguishable from one another. They're going well above the posted speed limit, which is unusual. My father's men know better than to break traffic laws for no apparent reason. It draws attention to them—puts a spotlight on the organization.

An ear-piercing, feminine scream rings out in the night air, and sounds of shouting follow. Leo stiffens immediately and wraps his hand around my upper arm, putting his body between me and the madness down the street. It isn't often that this kind of trouble happens around here these days. It's pretty rare in fact. Since my father scooped up two other families, the competition's been down, and his family has become too strong to really mess with.

More screams, more shouting—and then the screaming stops and there's only a deep male voice yelling over the others. "I'll kill you, Fortino!" Michael.

I don't think there will be a time when I'll ever not know his deep baritone screams. My stomach sinks. We don't say those words unless we mean them.

The boom comes first to silence my thoughts. Every part of my body freezes. Leo's large body swings around as he wraps me in his arms and rushes into the gelato shop. Stuck in a tunnel of panic, all I can hear is the heavy thud of my own heart. All at once my senses come back to me, flooding my entire body.

Leo runs out of the gelato shop as the screams start up again. This time they're more guttural. I wish I didn't know what those screams sound like. They sound like death. I rush out after Leo. He's at the street, unmoving, unaware that I've followed him. More gunshots ring out and more shouting, but the only voice I can hear is Tony's. Words twist in agony, a voice about to break, Tony screams through sobs. He keeps screaming "dead" again and again and again.

Michael.

I run past Leo at a sprint. I can vaguely make out his shouting from behind me, but I'm too fast. For all that muscle and length, he can't catch up to me. I run toward the large crowd that's wrapped around the agonizing screaming. The pounding in my ears grows louder and louder until I can't hear anything else. I push my way through the crowd. Elbows try to block me, arms shoot out, but I'm determined.

Michael.

I break through to the center of the crowd to find some young guy I don't recognize pointing a Glock

RIDE

toward the ground in front of him. I follow the line of his gun to Tony, lying on the pavement, propped up by one elbow, his other hand over his gut, which is drenched with dark red blood. The man with the gun forgotten, I race toward Tony and slip behind him so I can support his weight.

Not Michael.

I breathe a selfish sigh of relief that it's not Michael.

Rough hands grab at my shoulders, but I fight them off. I can't turn away. The man with the gun redirects the Glock from Tony's gut toward my head. I grew up around guns and was raised to not fear them, but all of that goes out the window when I have one pointed at me. Still, I refuse to leave Tony. He's hotheaded and twisted from the inside out, but he's always been good to me and Michael. He's the one who showed Michael how to cover up that mess he'd gotten himself into with my first boyfriend.

"Put the gun down, Junior!" Michael shouts from beside my ear. Startled, I now feel Michael's presence behind me. If he's trying to pull me away, that means he's safe. He's okay. Michael isn't dead. A weight lifts from my heart, and I say a silent "Thanks" to God that he's okay. But then I remember the man with the gun and realize that this could change.

Looking around the crowd, I notice for the first time that this guy before me, the one Michael called Junior, isn't the only one with a gun out. Junior has at least five guns trained on him, ready to fire were he to take another shot. Behind Junior stand two men, their guns pointed the same direction his—at me. I pivot my head around to see Leo, chest heaving in anger, directly behind Michael. His eyes are narrowed at me and his Dezzy, the gold Desert

Eagle, is in his right hand with his finger on the trigger. I've walked into a gunfight and only realize it now that it's too late.

"Get out of the way, girl!" Junior yells, his gun trained on my forehead. I shake my head from side to side and clutch to Tony even tighter. He's paling, his body growing cold. "Or do you want me to shoot you, too?" Tears stream down my face as the fear finally kicks in. I take several shaky breaths to calm myself down, trying to remember the lessons my father taught me. A guy knows whether or not he's going to shoot you before he even gives you warning, my father says.

"You would shoot the principessa, to what, make a point?" Leo asked. Junior's eyes are wide with a new fear. He didn't recognize me—that was his first mistake. From behind me a gun fires, so loud it makes my ears ring. The shot hits Junior right between the eyes. His body crumples to the ground. I'm not sure what he's lost his life for—shooting Tony, or for pointing a gun at me.

Shots ring out in all directions. I hold tight to Tony, whose body has gone completely limp, and feel the protective arms of my brother wrap around me, shielding me from the gunfire. It's only a matter of seconds, but it feels like an hour has passed. The women scream and run away as quickly as they can. Their men mostly stay behind, draw their own guns, and fire. I squeeze my eyes shut and sob into Tony's neck. This is too much, all of it. I don't want to be a part of the Mancuso family anymore, let alone *this* family. I shouldn't be here. I shouldn't be seeing this. But I am, and it's one of those things you never forget.

Michael screams in my ear, and warm liquid trails down my shoulder. I try to turn to identify what it is, but

I'm unable to. He grunts and holds me tighter. The sobs come harder, more violently, when realization strikes—Michael's been shot. My throat burns from the exhaustion. I'm screaming, crying, putting on a display of emotions that might almost match how I feel inside.

I can't live like this. It's too much—the guns, the screams, the blood. It's not the first time I've seen a gunshot wound. But it is the first time I've had a gun pointed at me. No matter how hard I try, I can't force the sobs to stop; they keep coming, assaulting my body in uncontrollable tremors of panic.

Michael pulls away, and a sharp gust of humid air hits my back. It's not quite chilly, but not quite warm, either. I open my eyes, seeing the crowd has parted, people running in all directions. It's now that I hear the sirens and see the flashing lights. Panicked, I look around for Michael, finding him rushing to grab a discarded gold gun from the pavement. I cry out at the sight—Leo is lying on the pavement on his side, a bullet wound in his abdomen—and bury my face in Tony's neck as I rock myself back and forth, holding Tony to me tightly.

"Listen to me, Alex," Michael says, crouching down in front of me. I nod to signal that I'm listening. I just can't stop the rocking. Stopping means sitting in stillness, and stillness means death. Tony can't be dead. Leo can't be dead, either. And Michael can't be shot.

But they are, or likely are, I don't really know.

"The cops are on their way. Take care of this, okay? And do not talk to anybody. Not anybody, you hear me? I'm heading to Fortino's," Michael says, kissing my forehead. I don't want him going to Angelo Fortino's place—I know what that means. I know the guy's name, but can't remember what he looks like. I don't give a crap about Angelo Fortino. I care about what Michael's about to do. But I have to focus on what I'm going to tell the cops right now.

Michael's about to start earning his bones and then there's no going back. There's no way to stop him from becoming one of them. That is, if he doesn't get himself killed first. The thought is unimaginable. I nod again, unable to do much else, and rock harder, my hands clinging to Tony as best I can. The blood is everywhere, making him slippery, but I can't let him go. I could never let him go. I have to focus on Tony right now. Michael is okay enough to stand and walk, I tell myself. As he runs off into the darkness, I try to convince myself that he can't be that bad off. Michael's okay. He has to be.

The flashing lights descend, the sirens squealing in my ears. Officers step out of their cars; a few have their guns drawn and pointing to the pavement. The very sight of more guns sends me into a deeper panic. I start screaming again. They approach, putting their guns away. One officer bends down before me, and I recognize him as a man who has come to the house a few times. He's always walked in looking nervous and left looking relieved.

"Ms. Mancuso," he says gently, "I'm Officer Adam Davis." Davis—I know that name from somewhere. And then it comes to me: I'd met his wife at the wake. Rebecca Davis, formerly Rebecca Scavo. I just stare at him, wanting to speak. One of the reasons Leo got his button so quickly is because he was able to provide one of the most important assets a man in my father's position could have: a meat eater—which was just their way of saying he was a dirty cop.

"Listen, you know me, right?" I nod. "You need to tell me where Michael went so I can protect him. Shit's happening and if he's going where I think he is, it might be too late." I think about what he's saying. He wants me to tell him—an outsider—family business. I can't do that. I just left the wake of a man who had done that very thing. But then, I've seen Officer Davis in and out of my father's house a few times, going into his office with him alone. I can trust him, right? Am I willing to risk Michael's life? Am I willing not to? It's never a question. My father has his family and I have mine." Angelo Fortino's warehouse on Dock 47," I whisper. The tears come again, less violently, still powerful. I'll never be able to take it back. I've just shot everything I have ever known to hell. It's this moment my life comes crumbling down—the moment I become a rat.

Chapter 3

*Nobody ever did, or ever will, escape the
consequences of his choices.*
- Alfred A. Montapert

SEATED IN THE emergency room at Lutheran Medical
Center, cold and covered in dried blood, I wait. My eyes
are sore; pained from all of the tears I've shed. We
arrived at the hospital what felt like hours ago, and still I
haven't heard anything. I wrap my arms around myself
and scan the E.R., relieved when they fall on a familiar
face.

Aunt Gloria and Uncle Emilio stand at the entrance,
glancing around the room. They both wear emotionless
masks. When Gloria's eyes meet mine, her stone face
softens and contorts in ways that looks painful and tears
rush out. I run to her, unable to stand the distance, and
throw my arms around her midsection. We cry together
there, at the entrance of the emergency room. It all feels
so surreal. We shouldn't have to pick up the pieces of our
lives every time something goes wrong. We shouldn't
have to live this way.

Uncle Emilio reaches over and lightly pats my back
before walking to the nurse's station. I break away from
Gloria, who's calmed her tears much faster than I have
mine. Emilio speaks with one of the nurses for a minute
before ushering us toward him. To my surprise, a nurse
escorts the three of us through the intake area and down a
long, sterile hallway past several rooms.

"Upon arrival, Anthony was unresponsive and had lost a lot of blood. He's stabilized now, but before he arrived, he had stopped breathing and we're not yet sure what effect, if any, the loss of oxygen has had on his brain. We have him sedated so his body can heal without interruption. He may be groggy and appear confused. Try not to push him to interact just yet." The nurse, whose name I don't get, walks away and leaves us in front of an open door. Inside are a standard-issue hospital bed and a few machines with tubes going all over the place. I look at the patient file—handwritten on the information sheet is ANTHONY VESCOVI.

Emilio enters first, followed by Gloria, and then myself. I keep to the corner, out of their way, and the pair of them tentatively approach and reached their hands out toward their son. Sure, he's full grown, over six feet tall and built like a boxer, but to his parents, he'll always be their little boy. And for me, no matter how big and mean and bossy he's gotten over the years, I still see Tony as the boy who would sit beside me during Sunday school and fill in his coloring book so neatly in the lines. I never could keep such great control of my crayon, the colors shooting out all over the place.

I choke back a sob at the sight before me. The man lying in this hospital bed doesn't look like *my* Tony. My Tony always has a tan, but this man's face is so ashen it's frightening. His fingers twitch at his side as he slowly moves his head from side to side to look at his parents. Gloria bends down and places a gentle, lingering kiss to Tony's forehead as he has done to her many times over the years. As a man, especially a Made Man who's sworn his life to the organization, he's to protect the women in his life. But this is his mother and, as mothers do, she'll always stand in for him in the face of danger, whether he likes it or not.

At that thought I let the tears fall down my cheeks. I miss my own mother so much. And though she wasn't like Gloria in her bravery and commitment to her family, she was my mother. Esmeralda Mancuso had her own way of going about things. When Tony started to earn his bones, Gloria threw a fit. She wasn't just upset, she was enraged. She didn't want her boy to be a murderer. My own mother would have just distracted Michael as best she could, but she never, *not ever*, got in the way of my father's business.

"Emilio Vescovi," a hard voice says from the doorway, breaking me from my thoughts. A short, round man in a suit holds up a badge identifying him as F.B.I. Uncle Emilio turns around, keeping his annoyance at bay as best he can, and nods his head at the door.

"Agent Wilks, why don't we take this into the hallway? These ladies have had a tough enough night," Emilio instructs on their way through the door. Agent Wilks casts a suspicious glance over his shoulder as he steps out of the room.

Slowly, I approach Tony's bed and brush his hair back from his face. It's short, but stuck to his damp skin.

"Dav," he says in a gritty, pained voice. His eyes bore into mine. It's like he's trying to tell me something that's gone over my head. What is he trying to say? I ask him just that, trying to understand, but his voice gains strength in his anger. He repeats "Dav" again and again. Nothing makes sense. Gloria looks at me with worry.

"Maybe I should get the nurse," she says and reaches for the button. Tony's arm shoots out and stops her. He shakes his head from side to side, telling her not to get

the nurse in broken breaths. Gloria pulls her arm back
and wrings her hands with worry.

"Come here," Tony says in barely a whisper. He's
sweating now from the exertion of attempting to interact.
I lean in close to his mouth so that I can hear him. Then, I
think, maybe his words will make sense. With his lips at
my ear, Tony says the one thing I hadn't expected: "You
stupid little girl. Sei morto per me"

I pull away, shocked and confused. I take a step back
and shake my head again and again. *Davis*. Tony must
have heard me tell Officer Davis where Michael was
going. But why would that make Tony so angry? Officer
Davis is on our side. I'd overheard his conversations with
my father numerous times. Officer Adam Davis was on
the take.

*Take care of this, okay? And do not talk to anybody.
Not anybody, you hear me?*

Michael told me not to talk to anybody, and I did it
anyway. Had I done something wrong? It didn't feel all
that wrong in the moment, but the way Tony is glaring at
me I think I made a mistake. Maybe I shouldn't have said
anything to Officer Davis.

I back away into the corner of the room, tears falling
down my face. Gloria catches onto the sudden change in
my demeanor. Standing before me, concern lacing her
aging features, she asks me what's wrong. I don't want to
tell her, but I have to figure a few things out and she
likely had more answers than I did in that moment.

"Who is Angelo Fortino?" I ask in hushed tones. Her
eyes go wide and she leans in. My father and Emilio have
had several conversations in his office about Fortino's
warehouse and the money they've been making. He must
be important.

"How do you know that name?" she says.

"I hear stuff," I say, about to leave it at that. But there's something in Gloria's face that tells me I can trust her with this. "Michael said he was going to Angelo Fortino's place. He was shot and I..." I can't finish the sentence.

"Oh God, Alex. No," she pleads, her hand on her mouth. All I can do is nod my head. I did. Whatever she's formulating in her brain is likely right. What other reason would Tony have for telling me I'm dead to him? For what other reason would he disown me?

"Angelo Fortino oversees the meth lab, Alex, as part of your father's newly-acquired business." My blood runs cold with her words. *Meth lab?* I thought that the rumors about my dad getting into the drug business were all talk. I didn't know that he had really gotten mixed up in that junk. I never could have imagined it. So why is Michael fighting with this meth guy?

But that doesn't matter now. What matters is that I gave an outsider the location of the meth lab. Even if I hadn't known what information I was handing over, I talked. Images of Sal, lying in his coffin with the bullet hole in his throat flood my mind. I reach up and place my hand over my throat protectively. They can't kill me for this, can they? I'm the principessa—mafia royalty. Surely, my father won't allow it.

I stumble out of the room, sick to my stomach. Gloria hovers behind me. In the hallway, Agent Wilks has Uncle Emilio in handcuffs and is handing him off to another agent. I scream loudly and run forward, but am held back by Gloria.

"Fighting them won't do any good. Just don't say a word. We'll figure this out as soon as he leaves." I nod at her instructions. Agent Wilks says a few words to the other agent and then turns Emilio and walks toward us.

"Mrs. Vescovi, Miss Mancuso," he greets us, looking a bit too eager. "Emilio Vescovi is being held by the F.B.I. in an investigation relating to the cooking and distribution of methamphetamine, along with Carlo Mancuso and Angelo Fortino, and Michael Mancuso is being held as an accomplice."

"What, how?" I yell. My hands shake in fear as I fight back the frustrated tears that threaten fall. Beneath the fear and frustration is the realization of the consequences of my choice.

My father was arrested once, but that was before my mother died, years ago, and I didn't really understand what was going on then. The arresting officers were very professional and didn't even handcuff him in the house. It wasn't until I sneaked a peek out of the living room window that I saw them put handcuffs on him and load him into the back of an unmarked police car. Until then they had told me he had a business meeting to attend. And I had believed it.

"Mr. Fortino has found himself in a bit of trouble and so have his associates—Mr. Mancuso and Mr. Vescovi. The kid was on site when we pulled up." Agent Wilks smirks. He leans forward and claps his hand on my shoulder. "Tough break, kid," he says and walks off.

My knees give way and I crash to the floor. The sudden impact sends a throbbing pain through my legs up to my hips. Sobs rack my body, making it hard to breathe. In and out, it's that simple, and yet my lungs can't manage it. My breaths come in short, hyper pants, my lungs strain to keep up. I'm not prone to panic attacks, but I imagine this is what one would feel like—my chest constricts, my lungs burn, and I feel like I'm going to come out of my skin. Or just stop breathing entirely.

Gloria peels me off the floor and uses her body as a prop to keep me upright. It can't have been easy; my frame feels like Jell-O.

"Oh Alex," Gloria whispers into my ear, "What have you done?" *What have I done*? Through the pounding in my ears and the caustic screams that die in my throat, I can barely make sense of the world around me. Then it hits me—*I did this. I brought this on the family. I'm the reason that Gloria's husband is being arrested.*

I focus on my breathing, forcing it into even patterns, and steady myself on my feet, pulling away from Gloria. I scrub my face with my hands and wipe away the remaining tears. I have to pull it together. I can't keep acting like this. Gloria grabs me by my arm and drags me down the hallway. We round a corner and continue down another long, sterile hallway. I do my best to keep up with her long strides, but she's steadfast in her determination. I just let myself get pulled along, realizing my Aunt Gloria might be the only person I can trust to get me out of this mess alive.

Suddenly, Gloria pulls me into a small room that appears to be an informal office with a heavy wooden desk, two tall filing cabinets, and a chair on either side. With a quick look around, Gloria closes the door and takes several deep breaths to calm herself. Her hands are shaking just slightly, her breaths coming in strained pants. She leans back and rests against the desk. When she's calmed herself down sufficiently, she speaks quietly and in Italian.

"What did you do, Alex?"

"I don't know," I say. I have to be honest with her, but when my brain tries to extract the words from my lungs, it all comes out as a lie. I cover my mouth with my hands as if I can wipe away the lies, the truth, and everything that has happened in the last six hours.

"We can't have this conversation in English, Alex. It's too dangerous," Gloria says in Italian. Right, *dangerous*, I think. But who makes the conversation itself dangerous— the police or the family? Because as I see it, considering most everybody who matters is fluent in Italian, it doesn't matter what language I speak in. But it needs to be said, and I'm not about to argue with the one person I think will help me.

"Officer Davis," I squeak out in hushed tones, my Italian fluid despite the tremor in my voice. Gloria keeps her face stern as I do my best to relive the events from earlier. I tell her about overhearing my father talking to Leo about me, but purposefully omit how I'd overheard it. I tell her how I thought Michael had been hurt or worse and how I ran to save him, despite having no way of doing so.

I tell her everything right down to the most awful truth of all—when I told Officer Davis where he could find Michael, and how Tony had obviously overheard. I may not have known what giving Officer Davis Angelo Fortino's name would do, but it doesn't matter. My father and Uncle Emilio are in custody. My brother has to have been treated for his gunshot wound, but he's in custody, too, I guess. My biggest problem, however, is Tony. He isn't just angry with me; he's disowned me. Tony having overheard me talking to Officer Davis is beyond bad.

Gloria takes a few moments to let it all settle in. She looks half set to strangle me and half set to walk out of the room as though she's never heard anything. There's nothing more I can hope for—that much I know.

"Oh, God," Gloria finally says. She shakes her head and wraps her arms around her torso. A minute or two passes before she speaks again. "Some things have to happen, Alex. None of it is going to make any sense, and I can't explain." She's imploring me with her eyes, willing me to understand. But I don't.

"You're scaring me," I whisper, tears wetting my cheeks. She clears her throat, walks to me, and hugs me to her chest. I fight back the flood of tears that I don't think will never end.

"And you're scaring me, Alexandra. There is only one thing I have ever told you not to do. One thing that I was wholly serious about, just one thing, Alex—and you did it anyway. You spoke to someone outside of the family about family business." I deserve her judgment. She deserves this moment to scold me for my epically poor behavior, but her words make my blood boil.

"I thought I was protecting my brother," I defend, the words coming out in a frenzied, jumbled combination of Italian and English, which happens regularly when I'm upset.

"There is nothing further you can do, sweetheart. You must trust me. I'll take care of this. Can you do that?" I nod. It's not too much for her to ask. "Go back to the waiting room, miele. Wait for me. Do *not* go anywhere."

"Is Michael here?" I blurt out, distracted. I don't want to go to the waiting room if I have a chance to see my brother.

"It's too dangerous," she says. Her mouth turns down in apology. I start to object, but she shakes her

head. "I'm sorry, but no. This is non-negotiable."
Everything, it seems, is too dangerous now. I walk down
the hall like I've been instructed. I keep my eyes on
watch for any familiar faces. Down the hallway, just after
the turn down the other hallway that leads back to Tony's
room, stands Officer Davis and Agent Wilks. I approach
silently, intent on listening to their faint conversation as I
pass.

"The girl, she gave up the location," Officer Davis
says, pride evident in his smug voice. My stomach churns
at the sound of it.

"Did she know what she was doing?" Agent Wilks
asks.

"No. She's seen me at her father's house a few times.
She thinks I'm on the take." Davis claps Wilks on the
shoulder and walks away. Agent Wilks stands in the
hallway a moment before a large smile paints his face and
he walks down the hall after Officer Davis. I wait until
they're both out of sight to follow behind them, praying I
won't see either in the waiting room. Aunt Gloria could
have stared at me all day with her looks of pity and fear,
and I'd much prefer it to Agent Wilks and Officer Davis's
proud voices. What I did was make a horrible mistake,
but I suppose for them my greatest failure is their greatest
luck.

Chapter 4

The hardest thing to learn in life is which bridge to cross and which to burn.

- David Russell

WE FINALLY GET back to the house. Gloria pulls up in the driveway and slams on the breaks to avoid hitting the garage door, she was going so fast. The outside is eerily desolate, which is unusual. We don't always have men guarding the house, but with both my father and brother elsewhere for God-only-knows how long, we should have guards keeping an eye on things. Gloria seems to notice that the lack of bodies around the house have captured my attention.

"I sent them away, miele," she says. I follow out of the car, fumbling, after her. She races up the drive and dives into the side door that welcomes us into the kitchen. I'm a total disaster, not knowing what else to do but follow her. She moves fluidly through the kitchen to the mud room. I wait by the door as I watch her open the cabinet where I keep the laundry detergent. She throws the laundry supplies aside and pulls out a gun. For a moment I let my imagination wander as to where else my father keeps weapons in this house.

Gloria shoves past me and makes her way across the main hall and into the game room. My stomach lurches when I realize she's headed right for my father's office. We aren't supposed to be in there—nobody is—not without my father. Oh, Gloria is going to get it this time. There's only so much Carlo Mancuso can put up with from his sister. This woman is insane. Still, I follow her as she bursts into his office. The house is strangely silent.

I don't feel safe being here and it's amplified the farther Gloria gets away from me. She looked around for a moment and then storms back out.

Gloria says nothing as she sets the gun down on the counter and pulls a clean glass out of a cupboard and grabs an open bottle of scotch from the dining room table. She pours herself two fingers, drinks it, and then refills her glass.

"Do you remember what we talked about at the hospital?" she asks, downing the contents of her glass. I haven't forgotten, and I tell her as much as I watch her refill her glass twice more. She lean over the kitchen counter, hands splayed apart as she stares out the window into the backyard. She reminds me so much of my father in this moment—calm, calculating, and aware of everything around her.

"Good," she says. "Now go get some sleep." I want to protest, but I'm too tired. I leave her in the kitchen and go upstairs to my room. I stand before the full-length mirror in my room and notice for the first time that my clothes are covered in dried blood and my eyes are cracked and swollen.

I force myself into the shower and scrub my body as vigorously. It doesn't matter how much soap I use or how hard I scrub, I don't feel clean. I'm not sure I'll feel clean ever again. Eventually though, I give up and dry myself off. I dig through my drawers until I find what I've been looking for.

The old, ratted nightgown I pull out and shimmy into was my mother's. It was the one she wore just before she died. My father thought I was sick and nearly sent me to a hospital because I wore this nightgown for a week straight after she died. I didn't even clean it. I just pulled it on and wrapped myself in her smell. I needed the comfort then just as much as I need it now. Only now her smell has long since faded and been washed away.

I give up on my nap after only a few hours. I'm not sure if it's the sunlight that keeps me up or the horror that fills my mind when I close my eyes. I can't stay still, my body thrashing around with the thoughts of the night. The small amount of time that I did sleep, I remembered that Leo Scavo was also shot, and awoke with a twinge of guilt for having forgotten about his injury.

I lie awake for what seems like hours more, at first numb to the terror that fills my heart and mind, then so uncompromisingly aware of it that I can do nothing but scream.

My throat gives out eventually, and I succumb to a coughing fit. I know Gloria hasn't left me alone in the house, but still she doesn't come to check on me. Never once in the hours I've been in bed does she offer me an ounce of comfort. More than anything, I need her to tell me it will all be okay, but I know that is a lie, and lying is one thing Gloria hates to do.

When I can't stand wallowing in my own sorrow anymore, I get up and walk downstairs. I can hear Gloria on the phone in the game room. Mumbled words filter through the hall: safety, death, take her now, please, please, please. I know I should try to break myself of the habit of eavesdropping. It never ends well, but eavesdropping, it seems, is the only way I can gather information. They all see me as a child and never bother to tell me anything, especially if they think I might argue. And I like to argue. A lot. The one word that sends chills down my spine is "tomorrow." Gloria ends her phone call with, "yes, tomorrow." I pray tomorrow will never come.

RIDE

I rush back up to my room, uninterested in overhearing anything else. Under my bed is a bottle of my father's nicest scotch that Tony procured for me a while back. I pull it out and crawl into bed, drinking until I can't think clearly enough to care anymore.

When I wake the next morning, the overwhelming despair sets in again and I drink until well into the afternoon. When my stomach revolts at the idea of more scotch, I pull myself out of bed and spend the rest of the day wandering around the house in my mother's nightgown, just looking everything over. Gloria's packed a small bag for me: a few personal items from my room and the gun she found in the laundry room and a wad of cash she got from God-only-knows where. I ask her, without trying to be a brat, what she's up to, rifling through my stuff. The things she puts in the bag seem random at best. I figure if she is packing a bag for me I should have things I actually need, like clothes and maybe a hair brush.

Gloria throws together some pasta for us for dinner and doesn't even bother to clean up after we were done. I start to, but she stops me. "It doesn't matter, baby," she says.

We spend the rest of the evening in the family room on the sofa, looking through family albums. Earlier, she was so cold and factual. But now she's more solemn than anything. She insists on a night of bonding, which is nice, but it also feels too much like goodbye—like we're doing something that we both should remember. It feels important.

When we've gone through all of the photo albums from my and Michael's birth on, Gloria pulls out an album I've never seen before. It's nondescript enough to blend in with all the others, but this one has my mother's name on the spine. It's dusty, as though it hasn't been touched for years, and from the way she's gripping it so tightly, I guess that my father doesn't even know it's here.

"I've wondered why you never ask me about your mother," Gloria says in a gentle tone. I have no answer for that. My father isn't fond of too many questions, and for far too long after her death, he hadn't allowed us to even mention her. I shrug, feeling guilty, like I should have asked questions and the fact that I didn't meant I don't care. The awful weight of my selfishness presses on my shoulders. I'm a horrid daughter.

"I've spent a long time deciding what I would say to you and how I would say it when you finally got around to asking me about your mother. But you never did, so consider this my gift to you, amore." She smiles at me with the saddest expression I've ever seen, sadder than even the one she wore at my mother's funeral. Tears pool in her eyes and slip down her cheeks.

"She was my best friend," she begins the story of my mother's life, telling me all about how they met in Sunday School one summer when she came up from Florida to spend the summer break with her grandparents, and eventually moved in with them full-time after her mother left her abusive father.

"Even then, she was a free spirit—wild, unrestrained, loud. Mean, too. She had so much fire, that one." The woman she describes doesn't sound like my mother. The Esmeralda I knew had been docile and quiet. She practically tip-toed around my father, and I only heard her raise her voice maybe once. But I don't dare interrupt Gloria's story, I find myself wholly fascinated.

RIDE

"The last time I saw your mother," she says, holding my hands in hers with a sad smile on her face. "She said two very important things to me. The first was that no matter what, I was to keep you and your brother safe, and you trust that I'm doing that now. Don't you?" I nod, not understanding where this is going, but I do trust her. She's all I have.

"The second thing she said to me was that her sister will take care of you." She opens the photo album up to the first page, which displays a photo of two baby girls lying next to each other in a crib. At the bottom of the page, written in choppy cursive, are two names: Esmeralda and Ruby.

"I didn't know my mother even had a sister," I admit, feeling even guiltier for not asking more about her. I've never met any of my mother's family before and haven't a clue how an aunt I've never known existed can care for me. I'm no longer a child, old enough to be married off, old enough to leave my father's home for my husband's bed. My mother is dead, my brother's been shot, my father's been arrested, and only now do I find out about an aunt I've never known. I want to be excited over this piece of history, to ask so many questions. But I don't. Gloria smiles brightly. How she has so much energy, I'll never know. I'm so tired, my eyelids are dropping. I reach for my Coca-Cola from the coffee table and take a large drink. The caffeine is supposed to wake me up, but it's done nothing but make me sleepy.

"Oh, she did. They were twins, just like you and Michael." She continues on through the album. As the girls age in the photos, their personalities become more apparent. One of the girls is always smiling politely, while the other usually has a cheesy grin on her face and stands in some grand pose. The girl with the polite smile, who seems to accept being in her sister's shadow, has slightly darker caramel brown hair than her sister, but other than that, they have the same brown eyes; same small, swooping nose; and same full lips. I touch my face, realizing how very much I look like my mother.

"Which one is my mother?" I ask, unsure. The way Gloria talks about my mother, it seems she was so very different in her youth than her adulthood—lively, joyful, rebellious. The Esmeralda Mancuso I knew was none of those things. Loving, gentle, kind—sure. But she most certainly was not rebellious. She lived by my father's word.

Gloria points to the photo before us—showing the girls in their late teens—and lands her finger on the girl with the lighter hair and her tongue sticking out. "This is Ruby," she says. Then she points at my mother. "This is Esmeralda." Esmeralda, in the photo, had been the shy one in the corner.

"Whatever happened to Ruby?" I ask, hoping for a direct answer.

"Last I spoke with her she was out in California." Gloria stands up and pulls me with her, marching us up the stairs and into my room. "Heaven knows how close she is to New York now."

"What do you mean?" I ask. Gloria is acting weird, even for her. She purses her lips and straightens her back in thought. I allow her to lead me to my bed and tuck me in as though I'm a small, incompetent child. Everything she's done since we left the hospital feels intentional. The entire situation leaves me reeling, my brain jumping from asking one question to another, ending with few answers and more questions than I can keep straight.

RIDE

"Just that I'm not sure where she is right now," she confirms. "It's a big country." She smiles and smoothes my hair away from my face.

"You trust me, Alex?" she asks. I blanch at the question, my nerves on high alert.

"Why do you keep asking me that?" I demand more forcefully than I intend, surprising Gloria with the volume of it. My body is so worn out and feels heavy with sleep already. I just want to drift off.

"Because, I need you to know that everything I've done is for you," she says and goes into another speech about how I need to trust her. I try to pay attention, really I do, but I can't keep my eyes open anymore as I fall into a deep, dreamless sleep.

Chapter 5

Trust your instinct to the end, though you can render no reason.
- Ralph Waldo Emerson

I SLEEP WELL for the better part of the night. My mind is groggy, confused. I try to keep myself alert and aware, but can't get my brain to function. Something's wrong with me. My limbs are heavy and slow to respond. I can still breathe and function despite the haze, but something definitely feels wrong about all of this.

Light shines in through my window, much to my dismay. It isn't quite morning yet, but it's now moved into that place between darkness and light. It's too early to be so awake, too early to be dealing with—well, anything. I hear my bedroom door crack open and try to move my head, but it's too much effort. I give up and wait. Gloria comes into view with a nervous smile on her face. She's carrying a short stack of clothes.

"We need to get you up and ready," she says. For what, I want to ask. The words stall on my tongue. She sets the clothes down on the night table beside me and peels back my covers.

Gloria helps me with everything from brushing my hair and putting it in a long braid down to tying the shoe laces to my Chucks. She's dressed me in fitted jeans and a baseball tee—one of my favorite outfits. It's plain and comfortable and it doesn't tell the world who I am, unlike most of the clothing my father prefers I wear. "We have an image, Alex" he says. It's his image, not mine.

"Why am I so tired?" I ask her as I search through my closet for my favorite hoodie. It's old and worn and so very comfortable.

"I'm sorry, Alex," Gloria says as she stands next to me. "I didn't want you to flip out so I..." And then I remember something—years ago right after my mother died, I'd been inconsolable. Aside from wearing her dirty nightgown day and night, I'd also been plagued with insomnia. It was awful. After a week or so, I became a zombie. That was when my father took me to the doctor, who had prescribed me some pills that would calm me down. I turn and look at Gloria, eyes bugged out and jaw slack.

"You drugged me," I accuse. In my head it's a fierce yell of betrayal and anger. Out loud it sounds more like a child's bedtime plea. My voice is hoarse, and the words come out slow. No wonder I had trouble moving in the night and have been in a haze since Gloria pulled me out of bed. I'm angry, though in this moment, I can't feel it. This is why I stopped taking the anti-anxiety medication. I really hate how it makes me feel—compliant and unable to argue.

Gloria finds my hoodie and helps me get it on. The sun isn't quite up yet, though it isn't far off, from what I can tell. We walk out of the closet and Gloria hands me the small bag she put together yesterday. A loud rumbling sound comes from the street, growing louder with every moment. It's so noisy and so overpowering that I can't help but feel it in my bones. It sounds like a motorcycle engine, but not just one—many. I've heard this many motorcycles before—it hadn't been good. The motorcycle club from Queens made a visit here a few years back, making demands on my father's business. I don't know what came of it, but that the club left in a good mood and my father was grouchy for a good week. I haven't so much as seen or heard more than one stray bike drive past the house since. My stomach sinks.

"Ruby is here to help you, baby," Gloria says, and she clamps her hands on my shoulders, keeping me in place. I stand there, unable to even think about what's happening. Ruby, as in my mother's sister? My head spins.

Suddenly, the noise stops and what sounds like a thousand men on the pavement below race up to the front door. With three loud bangs, they're inside the house. Did they break down the door? Gloria whispers reassuring things in my ear as though it's supposed to help. It doesn't. I'm panicking, but know well enough that I can't get away. Heavy feet sound, climbing the stairs and walking down the hallway, closer and closer to be my bedroom. I want to scream or cry, or do something. But Gloria said it's going to be okay, that Ruby is here to help me, and since I don't have anything else to cling to, I have to hold onto that with the ferocity of a thousand suns.

My bedroom door flies open and there stands a man with black hair that is closely cropped on the sides and longer on top, a hard-set jaw, and sun-tanned skin—and he has a gun pointed at us. I grab for Gloria as tears fill my eyes. For the second time in a short period I'm on the losing end of a gun. But the man doesn't shoot, and Gloria doesn't seem fazed.

"They're in here!" he yells and lowers the gun. He isn't one of my father's men or anyone my father has done business with, that's for sure. He wears black jeans with black boots and a black short-sleeve tee shirt underneath a leather vest that's been adorned with various patches. Over his heart is a patch that reads FORSAKEN, and below that, one that says FORT BRAGG, CA. On the other side of the vest at the same height are two more patches. The top one reads ROAD CAPTAIN, and the one below it reads ANGEL OF DEATH. I don't know what the patches mean to him, but I know what they mean to me. He's a dangerous man. Just then, two more men walk in; one close in age to him, while the other is much older. They're all tall and wearing similar vests.

"Jim," Gloria says and lets go of my shoulders. She walks over to the older man and smiles at him. He smiles back, and they greet one another with a quick hug.

"Sorry we're late. Should have been here last night," Jim says.

"Move over, Jim," a strong feminine voice says from behind the men. Gloria's face gets impossibly bright, and she pushes Jim off. The woman comes into view and I know instantly that this has to be Ruby. If Gloria is friendly with these people, then I shouldn't be too afraid. Ruby embraces Gloria like they're family. I suppose, in a way, they were at one time. I keep myself in the back and hopefully out of notice, though I gave up thinking they weren't here for me some time ago. Ruby pulls back and looks over at me. Her face drops and she freezes. I try to give her a smile.

"Alexandra," she whispers, her voice catching in her throat. All three men stand silent behind Ruby. She takes one step forward in her tall leather boots and black jeans. She wears a dark waffle shirt with a leather jacket over. Her jacket has no patches. I guess she isn't a member of their club. I want to nod my head and acknowledge her, but I can't stop staring. She looks so much like my mother—so much like me.

"Alexandra," she says again with such reverence in her voice it takes me aback. Her eyes fill with tears and she nods. "Hi," she says and takes another step forward. Did she really miss my mother so much that she's this touched by meeting her niece? I feel guilty for not having the same reaction to meeting her—after all, I've only found out she exists last night. Her hand clamps down over her mouth as she holds back a painful scream, and she rushes for me, wrapping me in her arms. I return the hug nervously. I don't really know what to do.

"Gloria," Ruby says, "she's gorgeous." I look over Ruby's shoulder to find that the men are all looking away like Ruby's show of emotion makes them uncomfortable. Gloria steps forward and puts her hand on Ruby's back.

"You guys better hurry," Gloria says. Ruby pulls back and gives me a sad smile then looks to Gloria and nods. Gloria reaches over and gives me a tight hug. "I love you, Alex. I'm so sorry that this has to happen, but it's not safe here for you anymore." Gloria's given me every clue that this was happening—that I was being sent away. I was just in shock. I guess I didn't wanted to believe the truth of it.

I want to rewind the last few days and go back to before. I want to refuse to go for gelato with Leo. I want to stay home and hear about the awful things that happened by listening through my father's office door. But then where would we be? Tony would be dead—that guy who had the gun on him wasn't playing. He'd been shot once, and I think the only thing that saved Tony's life had been my interference. But Michael would have still been shot. And Leo, who Gloria says is in critical condition—I don't even know what would have happened to him. Maybe he could have diffused the situation safely. And where would I be? I would be on my way down the aisle, marrying a guy who thinks of me as a status symbol rather than a partner. In the back of my head I wonder if perhaps this isn't the better option.

I clutch my small bag to my chest as Gloria leads me downstairs with Ruby beside her and the men in vests behind me. At the foot of the stairs, Gloria turns and gives me a quick hug then pulls away and holds me at arm's length.

"The club and Ruby will protect you and keep you safe. You understand why you're not safe here, don't you?" Gloria asks. I want to play dumb and say that, no, I don't understand. I really can't stand to hear my transgression aloud though. It's best to just agree with her. Deep in my heart, I know what happens to people who talk. I had just been lying to myself that the *principessa* was somehow exempt from the same code of conduct that led to Sal's death.

"Yes," I say and leave it at that. I don't know what to do or how to act, and I'm still battling the haze thanks to the anti-anxiety mediation.

"Goodbye, Miele," Gloria says, calling me honey one more time. She smiles. "Do not be afraid, no matter what. Promise me," she says.

"I promise," I say as I watch Gloria stand back and walk a few feet away. Ruby follows her. They stand facing one another, both smiling and laughing.

"Avoid my nose, please," Gloria says, sending Ruby into a fit of laughter.

"Got it done, did ya?" she asks. Gloria nods. Ruby laughs and turns her body around before spinning back and punching Gloria square in the eye. I scream and run for Gloria without thought. A strong arm holds me back. I scream again as Ruby throws three more punches—one more to the eye and two to the mouth. Blood pools in Gloria's mouth and drips down her chin. Gloria holds her arms in the air, taking the abuse, and Ruby throws a few punches to her gut. I fight against the arm holding me back, but it's no use. I look over to see it's the younger man with the wavy black hair who's holding me back.

"Your aunt isn't fighting back," he says. "If she needed your help, she wouldn't be taking the hits." He makes a good point, but that doesn't stop me from trying to stop Ruby from throwing her punches. I feel sick to my stomach at the thought of leaving with these people—not that I have another option. A few more blows and Ruby is done. She and Gloria laugh and smile at each other. God, these people are sick.

The next few moments happen so fast. Gloria tells me to go with Ruby, and I do. We run out of the house and into a black van with tinted windows. Outside the house stand ten more men clad in leather vests, standing in front of a sea of motorcycles. I don't get a good look at any of them. Inside the van, another man sits across from us and closes the door. I peer out through the tinted windows. There's a loud ruckus coming from inside the house, then screams, and finally—gunshots. I jump from my seat and try to fend off Ruby's attempts to restrain me. The man across from us pulls out a black gun and points it at me.

"Sit," he orders. I do.

"Put that fucking thing away," Ruby yells at him and he complies. "And don't you ever pull a gun on her again," she says. I sit; shocked at the way she speaks to him. No woman I've ever known is allowed to speak to a man of power the way she has and not be punished for it. He nods and claps his hands together and looks away. "Gloria isn't hurt, Alex." I look at Ruby like she must be out of her mind. Then again, looking at the crowd she runs with, I have to say my guess is likely spot on.

"You know what your father is?" Ruby asks. I nod my head. "Then you know that I can't very well walk into that house and take you with me without making it look like a fight. What do you think your father would do to Gloria if he thought she sent you away?" Oh God. And there it is—the reason for all of this. When Gloria was trying to get me to understand, what she was doing, this is what she was talking about. If my father thinks that Gloria has undermined him, he could have her killed. It doesn't matter that she's his underboss's wife—and his sister. Nothing matters but the family he's sworn himself into.

"I didn't enjoy hitting her," Ruby says. "She was my best friend once. But would you rather I be the one to bang up on her or one of those guys?" she asks, pointing out at the men who are walking out of the house. The older man with the black-gray hair has his hand gripped around Gloria's neck. She looks frightened and in pain. Ruby assures me that Jim isn't hurting her; he just has to make it look like he is.

Jim walks with Gloria to the sidewalk near the van and the men—the ones who had been inside the house and the ones waiting outside, form two lines. One line faces the street and the other faces the house with their backs to one another. They draw their guns, and the men facing the house begin firing. They shoot out windows and fire at the wooden siding. I cry as I watch the only

RIDE

home I've ever known be turned into Swiss cheese. One by one, when the job is apparently done, men put their guns away and walk to their motorcycles. The van door opens, and in climb two more men. Both the front passenger and driver's doors open, and a man climbs in each. The van starts up and we pull away, flanked by several men on bikes in front of us and more behind us.

Chapter 6

*When we are no longer able to change a situation -
we are challenged to change ourselves.*
                                    - Viktor E. Frankl

I SIT IN the van, unable to move, unable to speak. We drive for what feels like hours before the images of my Aunt Gloria being hit and my home being shot up finally cease. The sun rises fully and brightens the world around the van. Inside, it still feels so dark. I let myself cry when I feel like it, which is most of the trip. I'm run down and unable to think about where we're going or what will happen next. At one point, I catch a glimpse of the man who sits across from me. He has short blond hair and a baby face with nearly a week's worth of stubble. He wears patches like the guy with the black hair, but on the right breast of his vest are the patches DEVIL OF DEATH and SECRETARY. What the distinction is between an ANGEL OF DEATH and a DEVIL OF DEATH in this community, I don't want to know.

When I eventually calm down and the scary guy across from me falls asleep, I take a good look around. Ruby sits beside me, poking through her phone. Outside of the van all I can see are stretches of road and, every few miles or so, a farmhouse far away from the highway. Eventually we pull off of the highway and onto a deserted stretch of road with absolutely nothing visible for miles, save for the small gas station we pull into. The van doors open and the "Angel of Death" smiles at me. Not so much in a welcome way, more mischievous if I had to guess. For a second, I allow myself to consider how attractive I think he is. He's just a few years older than me, not enough for my attraction to him to be wrong or creepy, but enough that I notice he's all man. There is not a trace of boy left in him-- not in his body, not in the way he carries his large frame, and definitely not in the way he speaks.

"Anyone who has to piss, come with me," he says and turns around. I fly out of the van and rush up to him. I haven't thought of my bladder in hours, but once he mentions possible relief, the need is overwhelming. Ruby and the scary guy climb out of the van and walk behind us.

"Hey, Trigger," a rough, masculine voice calls from behind us. The dark-haired "Angel of Death" comes to a stop and turns around. I follow his lead and assume by his response that he is called Trigger. What a curious name.

"Yeah?" he says.

"Where are you going with the kid?" the man asks. He's tall and lanky with shaggy light brown hair and a scar that runs from his left eyebrow down to the tip of his ear. His face is set in a hard line, and annoyance radiates off of him. It takes me a moment to realize when he says "the kid" he means me. He doesn't look like he can be so much older than me. Jerk.

"Around back," Trigger smirks, but his buddy sees no humor in his comment. I flush in embarrassment. My father and his men made crude remarks often, but never in the presence of me or my aunt. I've haven't been in a situation like this since high school, when the neighborhood boys had half a mind to hit on me.

"You're not funny," the guy says. Ruby scoffs and pushes Trigger then wheels around and shoots a look at the shaggy brunette.

"You," she says to the man whose name I still don't know, "fill up the tank." Then she turns back to Trigger and slaps his arm. "I ought to rip your ear off for that comment, Ryan," she says. So Trigger's real name is Ryan. He's still a mystery, but at least I have one other person's name. I'm not about to call him a stupid name like Trigger if I can help it. Ruby sidles up to me as we reach the bathroom.

"Ignore them." She smiles and ushers me in. "You'll get used to the club, I promise." I nod, but my curiosity piques.

"Who is that guy?" I ask. Ruby's brow crinkles.

"Which one? We're surrounded by a lot of guys, baby," she says looking around at the men who have formed small groups, talking amongst themselves while they fill up more gas cans than I can count.

"The guy with the light brown hair."

"That young punk is my kid," she says and looks around again, her eyes landing on Ryan. She beckons him over. "His name is Ian. And this punk is Ryan, my step-son." Ryan smiles at her and kisses her cheek.

"Don't let her tell you nothing," Ryan says, giving me a half smile. "She lies." My mouth pops open and Ruby laughs loudly.

"See? A punk," she says and jerks her thumb at him. "No respect." I laugh at their easy relationship and shake my head. These people have a real bond. It doesn't feel forced or manipulative like it sometimes does in the Mancuso household. And, for the first time since all of this began, I feel like maybe I'll be okay—as long as I get to the bathroom, stat.

I rush into the bathroom, avoiding touching as much as possible. I'm not a germaophobe, but the filth level in

RIDE

here is off the charts. After I've emptied my bladder, I wash my hands. There is no soap, but I make do with what I have available to me. I can't help but look at my face as I slosh the water over my hands. The image looking back at me is one step short of awful.

Normally, I consider myself a pretty enough young woman. I take pride in my appearance and put work into maintaining it. Gloria may be all about pushing the rules as far as she can, but still, both she and my mother always pushed me to look my best. "Men respond to pretty things," my mother would say. "You want a good husband; you have to show you can be a good wife. And that includes putting your face on every day," was another of my mother's sayings. I can't remember ever seeing her without makeup. Even when she was sick, she had Gloria apply her makeup for her every morning. Even on her deathbed she didn't want to disappoint my father.

But right now I can't bring myself to really care what I look like. My face is void of makeup, which isn't so awful. But I feel like I've been put through the ringer, and that makes the not looking good twice as bad. No wonder I look like a kid to Ian. I'm half his size, covered in a baggy hoodie, and without makeup.

I leave the bathroom and walk toward Ruby, who is curled into the older blond-haired man's side. Jim, I think his name is. If I have it straight, Jim is Ruby's husband and Ryan's father. Ian is Ruby's son, and that makes him my cousin. So then Ryan is my step-cousin. I stop where I am and watch as a big guy with a few extra pounds and a jovial smile on his face elbows Ryan in the middle of his back. Ryan moves forward a foot before turning around quickly, his fist flying through the air at the man who's elbowed him. Ryan's fist connects with his jaw and an all-out fight begins. I take a few more steps back. In my father's world these kinds of fights are rare. Men don't engage in physical contact unless they're going to make a point. Violence is never fun, my father says. It is sometimes necessary, but never fun.

Ruby eyes me and carefully sidesteps the brawl. Nobody has moved to break it up yet, and now both men are in the dirt, the man laughing while he has Ryan in a headlock. "It's okay, Alex. They do this shit all the time," Ruby says. I nod in understanding, but I don't really understand, so it's a lie.

"But why?" I say. In the background I can hear Jim telling them to knock it off. We have to get back on the road.

"They're men," she says with a shrug. She walks past me, giving my shoulder a pat, and then steps into the restroom. The firm thud of the closing door and the click of the lock sets me on edge. I slowly turn around and eye the scene before me.

The men, at least twenty in number, stand around in a loose circle. Jim is speaking. His shoulder-length hair is tucked behind his ears. In the early morning light it looks grayer than I previously thought. His face shows his age, lined with years of sun exposure from long rides, I'm willing to guess. He has his arms crossed over his chest.

"Straight through to Nevada, boys," he says. I glance around the crowd. They're all watching Jim intently. Some of the men look pissed off, like they've heard this before. Others, though smoking or chewing, have their eyes on him. Everyone is looking at Jim—with one exception.

Ryan's eyes are on me.

I flinch under the intensity of his gaze. His hands are on his hips, head tilted slightly to the side, feet shoulder-width apart, his face carefully blank. But his eyes bore into mine. I search his face for a sign of—well, anything. But nothing comes to me. I can't figure out what he's doing. Then I realize that he's sizing me up. This whole thing is for me. Aunt Ruby promised Aunt Gloria that she'd keep me safe, and this is her keeping me safe. I can feel my eyes grow wide as I consider the twenty or so men before me. Leather-clad, dirty, and tired...

They've been riding for days, I think. California is an awfully long way from New York. They didn't fly, which would take but a few hours. No. They *rode* on their bikes and some even in the van. For days, I'd venture to guess. I suddenly feel compelled to express my appreciation. No matter how awful this is for me, that's the thing—*this is for me.* Ryan doesn't need to be here, saving my big mouth. Jim doesn't need to be here. Maybe Ruby does by way of some familial obligation, but the rest of them don't. But they're here.

Before I can think better of it, I mouth, "Thank you," to Ryan. He blinks, but keeps the mask on his face. No polite "you're welcome" and no acknowledgement, blinking aside, that I've extended this olive branch. Why I want to extend it to him of all people, I'm not entirely sure. I just know that I'm going to try to make this work. And he just keeps watching me.

Hearing shuffling behind me, I turn as Ruby's elbow lands softly on my shoulder, letting me feel her weight. "He's handsome, isn't he?"

I feel the heat on my cheeks, and I break eye contact with Ryan. I can feel his eyes for only a moment more before he turns his attention elsewhere. The ground beneath my feet is nothing but dirt interspersed with bits of mud here and there. I try to imagine drowning in the small pool of mud.

"I know you were watching him, Alexandra," she says. I spin and look her, going for my best innocent look. It's the one even my father falls for. She rights herself, hands on her hips.

"Who?" I say. She chuckles lightly and shakes her head, then her face grows serious.

"These *men* are off limits to you. You're a pretty, young woman—don't think they haven't noticed. And I love those men. They're family. But you're far too young. You got that?" I nod, unable to do anything else. The crowd breaks up, and only two of the men don't move. Ryan's eyes are once again on me, but behind him, Ian's eyes are on Ryan and he looks none too pleased.

The men climb back onto their bikes with the exception of the ones who are riding in the van with us. They stand around kicking the dirt beneath their feet. As Ruby takes off toward the van, I dutifully follow her. Climbing into the van, my nose is assaulted with the smell of gas. I try to cover my cough with the sleeve of my hoodie, but it's no use. Even Ruby puts her hand over her mouth as she climbs into her seat. The Devil of Death climbs into his seat opposite me and gags on the odor that's permeating our surroundings. In the front seats, the men roll their windows down, and crank up the A/C. The forceful winds that slap at my face as we take off back toward the highway is too much and I turn toward the back of the van, where I see the culprit of the smell. Peeking out beneath a cover of old, torn carpet is a collection of gas cans. It appears the entire back of the van is full.

RIDE

Very quietly I ask, "What's with the gas cans?"

The man in front of me smiles predatorily and says, "How far do you think a Harley can go without gas?" Ruby chuckles lightly, but shoots him a warning glance despite her amusement. All I can offer in response is a faint, "Oh." My question just goes to show exactly how much knowledge I have of motorcycles.

Chapter 7

We fear violence less than our own feelings.
Personal, private, solitary pain is more terrifying
than what anyone else can inflict.
— Jim Morrison

ONCE WE START back on the road, the man in the
front passenger seat and the one across from me fall
asleep immediately. My eyelids are heavy, but every time
I close them, a string of images assault my mind. From
Tony bleeding out to him in the hospital, then to Gloria
and me at the house, and eventually Ryan. I don't know
why Ryan makes his way into my subconscious, but he
does. The way his eyes bore into mine like he was trying
to figure me out. There were questions there that I don't
understand and I doubt I'll ever have answered.

As the hours pass and Pennsylvania bleeds into Ohio,
Indiana, and then Illinois, I allow myself to zone out. The
stark countryside is beautiful in a neglected, desolate sort
of way. Spring is in full effect, and summer waits just
around the corner. The heartland is gorgeous with its corn
fields and rows of vegetables and even the occasional
dairy farm spotting the landscape. But after a few
hundred miles, even the pastoral charm of the Midwest
wears off and I'm left with the choice between attempting
to sleep despite the haunting images that barrage my
mind, and the landscape. Neither is appealing, and
eventually the mind-numbing dullness of the situation
takes over, engulfing actual thought in favor of autopilot.

We stop three times for gas, mainly to fill up the
bikes and to give the riders a rest. The Devil of Death and
the other two men in the van switch seats at the first stop

and don't switch back until the last. I study their patches and their demeanor all the while studiously avoiding Ruby's occasional forays into consciousness. Though she is quite kind, she is mostly quiet. I find her attention on me more often than I'm comfortable with. I feel the urge to promise her that I'm real and I'm not going to suddenly turn into a ghost, but that would be rude, so I just pretend I don't see her staring at me. It's not easy.

Along the highway I see the signs for Chicago and hear grouchy muttering from the front seat about having to "get the fuck as far away from Chicago as possible." The driver answers a cell phone, says a few words, and pulls it away from his ear, sliding it back into his jeans pocket. As we pass the signs for Chicago, some of the bikes pull off the highway.

"Rig's crew is going to make sure Chicago stays in the Midwest," The Devil of Death says. I stare at him quizzically, and he lets out an annoyed sigh then, after a pause, he clarifies in an annoyingly condescending tone. "Your daddy's a mob boss, right? Yeah, so he's got buddies in Chicago. You're the mob's property, and we've got you. Now, how happy do you think they are about that?"

Despite knowing nothing about these people and what they're capable of, I feel an annoyed tick in my jaw. I bite back my sarcasm as much as possible and say, "Thank you for the clarification."

"What's a matter? Did I annoy you, Princess?" he asks in a mocking tone. I fold my arms over my chest and turn away from him, focusing intently on Ruby's sleeping form.

"Thank you," I say again, because I was raised to be, if anything, polite. "For coming to get me."

"It was a club vote and I lost. You ain't my kid, and this ain't my baggage."

"Still," I say, a bit quieter. Thanking someone who is so hell bent on pissing me off is challenging at best. Having had enough small talk for the time being, I settle into my seat and lean my head against the blackened window, hoping sleep will claim me.

When I wake, the sun has already set, and night time is upon us. The high-pitched squeal of the van's brakes as we stop rouse even my new friend across from me. As his eyes flutter open, I smile at him as happily as I can muster. His eyes land on me immediately and a grimace appears. If he can't bring himself to be kind, or even tolerant of me, perhaps I can kill him with kindness. Literally.

To my left side, Ruby stretches out, having slept most of the way since we left Brooklyn. "Where are we?" she asks, looking at the men in front.

"Some hick town in Iowa," the passenger says. The driver puts the van in park and cuts the engine. It isn't until the guys who have kept time with us turn off their engines that I realize how loud they really are. In their wake is a glorious silence that immediately makes me feel infinitely more at ease.

We climb out of the van and step onto the cracked pavement of the Williamsburg Motel, whose florescent neon sign flashes, sporadically cutting out. For the first time since we locked eyes at that gas station, I see Ryan in the crowd. He's standing, hands on his hips, surveying the men around him. Ruby takes my arm and gently leads me past him and into the motel lobby, following Jim, who manages to score an impressively low group rate. Upon inspection, there's ten riders with us, half the number that

RIDE

there were to begin with. As we emerge from the office, Jim tosses out four room keys, then he hands one to Ryan. He hands one of the remaining two keys to Ruby, and finally, one to me.

"Duke, Diesel, and Bear are going to keep watch for the night since they got to sleep in the van. You'll be safe, but I figured you'd want a little privacy." I nod, grateful for the consideration.

"Yes, thank you," I say, and it is perhaps the most genuine thing I've ever said.

I rest up, trying to make this situation a little more bearable with a hot bath and lots of sleep. Not knowing when I'll have a chance to shower again, I load up my bag with the extra soaps and a few washcloths. Though the men never bother me, I hear when they change shifts. Jim told me one would be at the door to my room and the other would be around back beneath the high bathroom window. Not only are the window and the door the only points of entrance in my dusty, rundown room, they're also the only points of escape. Not that I had been thinking of an escape. I'm not stupid enough to believe that I'd fare better on my own in the wilds of the Midwest than I will with Ruby and Co. Still, I've spent a lifetime under Carlo Mancuso's thumb, and I know better than to assume that the only thing the leather-clad, gun-wielding men are attempting to stop is a break-in.

By morning, I already feel a hundred times better, having rested and cleared my head. I'm still feeling the lingering effects of the anti-anxiety medication Gloria slipped into my milk, but at least now I feel like I have my wits about me again. Today, our trip feels very much like yesterday's did—long with a series of short stops along the way for beer and snacks, but more often than not we break for bathrooms and to fill up the tank. Today, I'm more aware of my surroundings. I've noticed the motorcycles stop more frequently than the van, but before they do there's always a call in to one of the guys. The conversations are never lengthy, saying only what absolutely needs to be said, and when the bikes pull off the highway to refuel, the van keeps going, but at a slower pace. The bikes always keep up and the remaining riders adjust their formation to fill in the gaps left by the departing riders. Seeing all of this, the way the riders work together, keeping the van surrounded, is fascinating. In all of my years of watching and listening to my father's business, I've never seen such fluid teamwork from such a large group.

When the van stops for gas, all of the riders stop, whether they fill up or not. Ryan stays close to Jim's side, and Ian stays close to Ryan's. The three men cast me the occasional sideways glance. For Jim and Ian, it's almost like they've just remembered I'm riding in the van. But for Ryan, the way his gaze tracks me, it's like he's making sure I'm still there. Like he's never forgotten me. I don't allow myself to forget Ruby's warning from yesterday, so I don't engage. I do, however, watch. Despite being among such a large group, I feel so very alone. And Ruby isn't much of a talker, though she's trying here and there. There's so much I want to say to her and so very little I can bring myself to.

The day winds down in another rundown motel, this time in Wyoming. I hear stilted talks of Nevada and something about territory. The general idea is, I think, that we're getting closer to home, which is, as far as I know, somewhere in California. Aside from that, I know nothing—because I've asked nothing.

On the third day of our journey, we're nearing the end, which is unfortunate. Though I'm worn down and out of clean clothes, I'm settling into life on the road. I find myself in that space between expectations of normalcy and chaos. I'm learning the ticks of the men around me. Duke, the Devil of Death, is at his best in the late evenings. Anything too early and he's an asshole. I don't know if I'll see him much once we get 'home,' but I'm working on figuring out his sweet spot with whiskey. Too much or too little and I find my foot itching to kick him.

Since yesterday, I've learned the names of the other two men who have accompanied Ruby and me in the van. Neither man is chatty enough on his own, so I had to ask Duke for their names. The man who does most of the driving tends to keep himself scarce, and has a shaved head. He goes by the name Diesel. His long-sleeping companion goes by the name Bear. After watching him sleep for days on end, I can see that the name was aptly applied.

As for Ruby, I'm doing the best I can to open up to her, but it's not easy when she is so hot and cold all of the time. Any time I've tried to ask her about my mother, it's been a disaster. Her entire body goes rigid, and she just shuts down. The guys even notice it and tense up. One of Duke's few redeeming qualities is that he's protective over her. I can't stave off the petty jealousy that flares when he gives me a look, warning me to back off when I've stumbled upon a sensitive topic. I don't even *like* Duke, but the loneliness is getting to me, and I've found myself wanting to talk to him. I'm out of my element, essentially alone, and a guest among a gathering of family. So I vow not to bring my mother up again, not until I can form some kind of relationship with Ruby. I want to get to know her, especially if she's going to help me get on my feet, but that's going to be quite difficult if I continue to upset her.

Quietly, I clear my throat, catching Ruby's attention, and I say, "Thank you." Since I've spent the past day or so mulling over how to get on her good side, it's suddenly occurred to me that I don't think I've thanked her until now. I don't understand much of what's going on here and why she would go through all of this trouble for me, but I do understand that she did. And regardless of whatever rift they had, despite my mother's death, Ruby's helping me. I don't know where I would be without her right now.

"Not a problem," she says with a tired, but friendly smile. I shake my head.

"But it is," I protest. "It's kind of a big deal to drag these guys across the country for me."

She nods. "Yeah, that kinda is a pain in the ass." The men chuckle—the first sound I've heard from them in hours. It's not even noon yet, but we've been on the road since early this morning, long before the sun ever rose. And just like that, the men are talking, and Ruby is laughing. She's telling them I'm such a pain that I'll fit right in. For the first time in days, I feel like maybe one day I could belong to something or somebody again.

Just as I join the conversation, a loud boom sounds outside, and the van crashes off to the side of the road. The driver swerves, cursing along the way. The passenger gets on his cell as the sound of angry shouts and motorcycle blast into my ears. I look out the window to see the bikes, checking that everyone is okay. Ruby does the same. The bikes swerve out of the way as we come to a screeching halt, but not before plowing into the edge of a corn field. I'm tossed forward, landing with a bang, my knees hitting the floorboard. Instinctively, I cover my head and fight back the tears that are coming. My lungs strain for enough oxygen, but it feels impossible. There just isn't enough air. Sucking up enough air as I can, my lungs struggle to find a steady rhythm. It's no use.

Chapter 8

Is freedom anything else than the right to live as we wish? Nothing else.

- Epictetus

VOICES CLAW AT the corner of my consciousness, fighting for attention. I hear "It's okay" again and again until I begin to believe it's all in my head. But as I slowly pull myself together, steady my breathing, and shut down the tears, I realize the voice isn't mine. It's Ruby. She's hunched over me, her torso pressed into my back, and arms draped over mine. She rests her head on the back of mine and continues to soothe me. Little by little, I force down the acid rising in my throat and shake off the feeling of impending doom.

"It's just the tire," she says. "It blew."

As she pulls away slowly, I feel the insufferable need to be held once again. My father isn't one for coddling and, though he didn't fight my mother's way of caring for us, it was obvious that it displeased him. I learned early on that she was two different people—one when he was around, and one when he wasn't. She was so good at hiding things from him that I sometimes wonder if I really knew her at all or if she was another way when I wasn't around, too.

But I can't think of that now, or the desperation chewing at my stomach to have Ruby's comfort again. I raise my head and firmly plant my hands on the floor of the van. My humiliation over my reaction to a flat tire only worsens when I realize the side door of the van is open and Ryan and Jim are standing shoulder to shoulder,

RIDE

watching me. Ruby rubs my back and says, "Ignore them."

"Go on, it's not like none of you've ever seen a girl cry before," Ruby says. Ryan's eyes leave me, focusing on Ruby. A smirk finds its way to his lips. Jim guffaws loudly.

"With you around? Come on, Ma, when's the last time you cried?" With Ryan's words, the men focus on him and Ruby, leaving me to my embarrassment. It takes her a moment as her face pales. It's a sore subject, it seems. Her eyes dart to mine and then back to Ryan. His smile drops some, and she clears her throat.

Then she composes herself, the smart shell back on, saying, "The day I realized I was stuck with you." They smile at one another broadly. Jim shakes his head and turns around, his dark hair whipping at his jaw.

"Ignore her," Ryan says. "I kick ass." His eyes are back on mine, a smile crinkling the corners of his eyes. I let out an embarrassed laugh, trying to stave off the irritation I feel at my own reaction. Of course it was a blown tire and not a mob hit. What a silly thing to consider. Here, in the never-ending farmland, with nobody and nothing within fifty miles of us. No, that's not how my father works. He's typically a little more orderly than that.

"Damn girl, don't be embarrassed over that," Duke says with a dramatic roll of the eyes. "You gotta learn to handle yourself better than that if you want to hang around here." He's teasing me, giving me an opening to make light of the situation—exactly, I'm guessing, what one of them would do.

"Sorry about that, I'm new to this being on-the-run thing. I could use some pointers. Got any?" The crowd—

which now consists of the entire group—breaks out into rowdy laughter. Duke gives me a smile, an actual, genuine smile. I smirk, knowing I've gained his approval for the time being. Ryan's eyes light up as he sticks out his hand in offering. I look down at his dry and cracked hand, palm up, and then back at him. He gives me a small nod and I reach out, happy to make contact with him.

Ryan's grip on my hand is tight, his skin warm. I never realize how cold my body runs until I touch another person. It's unfortunate how little physical contact I've had with others that even the smallest touch matters to me. With a slight tug, he has me crawling out of the van and stepping into the low grass on the side of the road. Once I'm steady on my feet, he releases me, but keeps his body close to mine. Feeling brave for just a moment, I let my hand graze his. He hooks his pinky around mine, then lets go. I shudder involuntarily. He gives no reaction, leaving me to wonder how much another's touch means to him. Is it inconsequential, even innocent as it was, or is it routine for him? I allow that thought to take precedence over the sight of the blown front tire of the van, the damaged cornstalks, and the disgruntled bikers. Because in that moment the only thing that matters is Ryan and the way his pinky felt wrapped around mine. As stupid as it sounds, it matters to me.

A strong elbow nudges my upper arm, bringing my attention back to reality. Looking up, I see it's Ryan. "Huh?" I ask.

"I asked if you've ever ridden on a motorcycle."

I think back, realizing I have. "My brother got a BMW for his birthday last year."

Ryan chortles. "How far did you go?"

"Um, around the parking lot," I say. "My father wouldn't let him take me anywhere on it. He said it was too dangerous for me." Ryan shakes his head, looking at the men around him.

"Well, today's your lucky day. You're a sitting duck here with the van. You get to ride with me."

"I get to ride on your—" I sputter off then stop. Already, I have more freedom here with these people than I ever had with my father.

He leans in close and whispers, "Careful, little girl. You don't want to go there."

Ryan's answering wink is enough to do me under, but it's the words that spill out of his mouth that send shivers down my spine. Maybe I don't want to be careful. And maybe I do want to go *there*.

Before I can embarrass myself further, Ruby comes around to my side, giving me a reassuring smile. "I'll be riding with Jim, right beside you."

I nod and give her a small smile, praying that she can't see how excited I really am. Having lived my entire life in what amounts to, essentially, a glass bubble, the prospect of getting out and doing something wild is exhilarating.

As the bikers talk amongst themselves, Ruby leads me away with Ryan and Jim hot on our heels. I focus on putting one foot in front of the other. We come around the van to the bikes haphazardly parked, set-up on their kickstands, in a large cluster. I can't make out which one is Ryan's. They all look the same—black and chrome with worn leather seats and cargo bags strapped to the sides. They each appear to have something unique about them. One has a second seat, another has a backrest, and a third has red flames painted into the black. Despite some of the wear and tear, each bike is obviously loved and cared for.

A heavy arm rests on my shoulders. Instinctively, I know it's Ryan. He has this particular scent of leather and his own personal musk. Looking up at him, I catch the half-smirk on his face and allow myself to gift him a small smirk of my own.

"Trying to figure out which one's mine?"

I shake my head, fighting the impending laugh, "They're very similar looking." He bends his arm at the elbow, closing in on my head until he has me in a full-on head-grip. Swatting at his chest, I giggle uncontrollably. Urged on by my reaction, he reaches up with his other hand and rubs his knuckles across the top of my head until I have no doubt that my hair's a mess.

"My bike is nothing like the rest of them," he grinds out. He firms up his grip on my head, turning my body in toward his. My eyes are closed, letting the rest of my senses take over. I breathe him in, enjoying every bit of who he is that I can. There's something in the way that he's strong and playful at the same time. He keeps me close to him, tucked snugly into his chest. For just a brief moment, as I'm inhaling his scent and his warmth, the rest of the world melts away. There is no danger, no fear, and no rough and rowdy bikers around us. There's just me and Ryan.

When Ryan finally lets go of my head, I pull back, smack his chest one final time, and attempt to smooth down my hair. I keep my scowl in place, almost daring him to do it again.

"You messed up my hair," I accuse. He gives me a flat look and steps back, leaning on one of the bikes. Nobody moves to protest, so I assume the bike is his.

Ryan's bike is a Harley-Davidson—I think they're all Harleys—but his does look different from the others. While all of the other bikes are chrome with shiny black paint, Ryan's paint job is a black matte finish. The word FORSAKEN is painted over the matte in a shiny black finish. Without taking his eyes off mine, he reaches for his helmet and hands it to me. Clumsily, I grapple with the thing, surprised by its weight. It looks rather dinky, unlike the one my brother has. Where Michael's helmet has a window for him to see and covers his entire head, Ryan's merely covers the top of his head, leaving his face exposed to the elements.

"Careful, you drop that and it's no good," he says. Immediately, I tighten my grip on the helmet and hold it to my chest. I don't really know what he means, but he's asked me to be careful. I don't want to ruin his things.

"You're going to need to put it on your head," Ruby says. She comes up beside me and takes the helmet from my sweaty palms. Placing it on my head, she brushes errant hairs from my face. She's so close, her eyes are fixed on mine. Her large brown eyes and heart-shaped face contort painfully in a rush of emotion. She brings her hands to my cheeks as her eyes pool with unshed tears. She gives a small smile and whispers, "You're beautiful."

She looks so much like my mother, it's almost unbearable.

Jim comes up behind Ruby and places a helmet on her head. It looks exactly like Ryan's. As he snaps hers into place almost blindly, she pulls herself together and snaps mine into place as well. It's feels a little loose, but I decide not to make it an issue. There's too much going on in my brain right now to worry about it.

Turning back to Ryan, I see he hasn't moved. His expression is a cross between indifference and sorrow, I just can't decide which. I wait a moment until he snaps out of it and moves to sit in riding position. With his hands gripping the handlebars he gives me a quick nod and a mischievous smile. I walk awkwardly to the bike, trying to calm my nerves. Having watched these men ride for the past few days, I've been both curious and nervous about the prospect of getting on a bike. Up until now, only in my fantasies have I been able to passenger with Ryan.

Don't be a baby.

Smiling at him, I place my right hand on his leather-bound right shoulder, using it for support as I awkwardly swing my left leg over the bike. I find myself on wobbly footing, but Ryan's right hand grips mine as I dig my nails into his leather vest, and his left arm snakes behind him, pulling me closer to him. With his guidance, I land properly on the back of his leather seat.

"Not used to having something this big between your legs?"

"I bet you'd like the answer to that, wouldn't you?" I say before I can catch myself. Ryan turns just enough so that I can see the lascivious smile that's spread across his face. His tongue darts out and licks his lips, sending a shiver up my spine. My father would have had a holy fit had he caught me being mouthy in front of his men. Carlo Mancuso likes his women compliant. But the way Ryan's looking at me, with his eyes practically glazed over, I'm guessing he likes his women mouthy.

"How long till Nevada, Cap?" A deep voice asks from somewhere behind me. I fumble with getting my feet situated on the small foot rests that stick out from the rest of the bike.

Surprising me, Ryan clears his throat and says, "A few hours." The surrounding bikers mount their Harleys and start up their engines. Ryan follows suit and the bike come to life with a deafening roar. The bike's intimidating rumble vibrates every inch of my person. I take advantage of my position and wrap my arms around Ryan's midsection, pulling myself as close to him as possible. He leans back minutely. I let my cheek rest on his shoulder blade.

Slowly, the bikers spread out along the side of the highway, facing the road. Ryan steers the bike through the crowd and, like a shot, we're the first on the highway. We kick into another gear and speed up, the rush of the wind and the sudden speed jostling. I let my fingers dig into his taut abdomen as we sail down the concrete stretch, surrounded by nothing at all discernible beyond the neatly laid rows of green that stretch for as far as my eyes can see.

A little too late, I realize I've left my bag in the van. My Aunt Gloria gave me that bag, and it has the few worldly possessions I now own. Fear claws at my heart. If I lose that bag, that money, then I have nothing.

"Ryan?" I ask, but he doesn't react. I say it a little louder this time, and still nothing. I give myself a moment before screaming his name as close to his ear as I can. He jumps in place, but somehow keeps the bike steady.

"What?" He asks loudly, though not nearly as loud as I was.

Leaning toward his ear I say, "My bag! I left it in the van." I think he's not going to answer me, given how long it takes him. But when he does, there's a noticeable smile in his voice.

"It's safe," he says. I know better than to ask how. Men of power, who have power because they've taken it, not because it's been granted, they aren't to be questioned. So I let myself trust him, even though I don't know him yet.

The highway stretches out before us, but nothing changes. No matter how many miles we clock or how long we ride, it all just stays the same.

"How do you like it?" Ryan shouts over the cacophony of engines. I snuggle into him, not knowing if I'll ever get another opportunity to be this close with him.

"It's incredible," I say. A smile breaks out on my face and I laugh. The rush of the wind and the power of the bike overtake me and, for just a moment, everything feels right.

"You're smiling," he says.

"You can feel that?" I ask, surprised by the attention he's paying to my movements.

"Oh, I can feel a lot more than that." He revs the bike and speeds us up, leaving the others in our wake. They catch up in a minute; a few of the men flip Ryan the bird and shout curse words at him. We're going so fast, my entire body goes rigid. My hands clamp down tightly onto his hard abdomen, feeling his flexing muscles beneath the leather. My thighs tighten around his hips, searching for confirmation that I won't fly off the back of the bike. Beneath my touch, he shivers. Whether it be the wind or my touch that's affecting him, I imagine it's my touch. Testing the theory, I run my thumb in small circles on his abdomen. Straightening his position, his breathing changes. It picks up at first, and then catches before evening out. And I know, without a doubt, that it's me that he's reacting to, a thought that both excites and terrifies me.

My hair whips up, slapping me in my face, and tickling my neck. The wind breezes past us with such force I worry if I let go for even a moment that I'll take flight and be tossed into the green beyond. I close my eyes and let the feeling overtake me. Wind slicing into my skin, leaving gooseflesh in its wake. The bright afternoon sun, beating down on me, its warmth washed away by the brush of the wind. Everything is more intense out here. With every pull of my lungs and every beat of my heart, I actually feel the world moving around me. Everything feels alive, and active, not merely existing. From the birds flying overheard down to the occasional insect buzzing past. But it's the bikes that make my skin taut with excitement. Ryan's hips between my legs and his bike underneath me keeps my body in a constant vibration. But the bikes around us create a cacophony of noise, all rumbles and echoes of roaring engines, unlike anything I've ever heard before.

My father always said that I was far too precious to engage in anything dangerous. What he really meant was that I was too important an investment, a pawn, to do anything fun. Here, in the wind, it comes to me that I may just hate him a little.

Chapter 9

I take things like honor and loyalty seriously. It's more important to me than any materialistic thing or any fame I could have.
- Llyod Banks

WE RIDE FOR what feels like days, maybe even a week. Though I know that's not possible. The afternoon sun moves little, and there is no telltale darkening of the sky. My backside cramps, and my legs long to stretch out. Even in my discomfort, the thrill of the ride hasn't waned any. Being huddled into Ryan makes me think I could stay here forever.

I take the time to watch the men, who are mostly silent, but occasionally crack jokes and tease one another over the growling engines. The flat expanse of highway allows the bikers to spread out as they ride. Though they sometimes swerve and loop around one another, likely to keep things interesting, they all return to their original formation.

Ryan slows the bike, and the rest of the men in the club follow suit. I peer around his shoulder and tense up at the sight. Before us by perhaps a few hundred feet, there's a collection of men on motorcycles, all wearing black vests, lining the highway just after the "Welcome to Nevada" sign. I work very hard, but nearly fail at stopping the impending tears from falling. Ryan's muscles haven't tensed under my touch, and the men that surround us haven't given any indication that this is a problem. But until I know for sure that we're safe, I'm not going to relax. As the motorcycles slow to a crawl and eventually stop just before the sign, I squeeze my eyes shut and bury my face in between Ryan's shoulder blades. If this is an ambush, I'd rather not see it coming.

But just then a raucous chorus of laughter sounds and even Ryan's body is shaking with the effort. The bike begins to move again, and with the sounds of excited laughter surrounding me, I open my eyes. The men at the border largely appear to be pleased with our presence. One by one they start their engines and tear off in front of us. When they're all on the highway in front of us, we pick up our pace to keep up with the pack.

After riding along for no more than five or ten minutes, we pull off the barren highway and onto a dirt road the feels like it stretches for miles. Eventually, we pull up to a collection of decrepit old wooden cabins, sprawled out from one another, that make up the West Wendover Rustic Motel. Somehow, when they named the place, I don't think this is what they had in mind.

A cabin identifying itself as the office sits in the center of the cluster. Its sign hangs precariously by the one remaining, intact chain. Its neon letters are busted with their remnants scattered on the wooden porch beneath it. The windows haven't fared much better, nor has its neglected porch, which houses three rocking chairs, two of which are occupied by old bikers who look like they've got one foot in the grave already.

Just as Ryan cuts the engine, the men of the Forsaken Motorcycle Club collectively cut theirs and dismount their bikes. Our new friends watch me with curious eyes. I even have the attention of the old bikers in the rocking chairs. Nervously, I dismount as gracefully as I can. Despite some minor shaking, I make it off the bike and on my feet without incident. Ryan dismounts quickly and comes to stand behind me. He's so close I can feel the edges of his vest brushing against my back. I catch Jim's gaze. His brows are drawn together, and his lips forms a flat line. His eyes look so cold I can barely reconcile this man with the one who first wrapped Gloria in his arms just a few days ago.

"Who are these people?" I whisper so that only Ryan can hear me. His chin brushes my temple; the rough drag of his days' worth of stubble scrapes at my skin.

"Family." His breath washes over my face. I relax, surveying the scene around me. The new faces all wear vests with the same Viking warrior and the word FORSAKEN on the back. The only difference is theirs say NEVADA on the bottom, whereas the men I'm traveling with vests say CALIFORNIA. Ryan leaves me and strides across the dirt lot to mingle with his men. Once he's gone, I feel intimidated by the gathering. The Nevada Forsaken must amount to thirty in number. I'm barely getting the hang of communicating with the men I already know, much less this crowd, which ranges in age from mid-thirties to late seventies, if I'm guessing correctly.

"What are you doing over here?" I jump at the company, not having noticed anyone approach. To my ride side stands Ian. He's expressionless as always, but he seems to have relaxed since the last time I caught his attention.

"Am I not supposed to be here?" I ask. His jaw ticks before he shakes his head. There's some kind of struggle going on within him that I don't understand.

"You're supposed to be here," he finally says, his voice a little lighter than a moment ago. "Ruby, she uh," he begins, but doesn't finish. I turn and face him fully, practically begging for answers. There's so much I don't understand about what's going on and why. I'm willing to take anything he's willing to give. I can't squander this opportunity.

But he's all tight-lipped and silent now. I take a deep breath and push it out quickly. "Please," I say so softly that it brings back unwanted memories of every time I've asked my father for lenience and he refused to grant it. The memory is anything but welcome.

Finally, Ian turns so that we're face to face. He's average height for a man, which means he still comes close to a foot taller than me. Searching his eyes for answers I can't decipher, I'm struck by how much he reminds me of my brother. Though his coloring is much lighter than Michael's, they have the same eyes. My mother's eyes. Ruby's eyes. My eyes.

"Just give her time, okay?" he says. I tilt my head to the side as I focus on my breathing. *In and out. In and out.* The creeping kick of sorrow begins to engulf me. All I have left of my brother and my life before are my memories. A life I can never have again. But she's not here, nor is anybody I have ever loved. I don't understand these people or their ways.

"For what?" I finally choke out, hoping it doesn't sound too much like I'm on the verge of tears, even though I am. For the first time since meeting him days ago, Ian gives me a moment of vulnerability. His face softens, and he tugs his lower lip into his mouth.

"She's not good at this shit," he says then walks away, leaving me disappointed. I could chase after him and beg for answers, but he's shut down. I have no hope he's going to give me any more than he already has.

I spend the next few minutes observing the people around me. I catch the attention of most of the men who pass me; a few nod their heads, a few just stare, but nobody stops. It isn't until I grow restless enough to contemplate seeking out Ruby that I see her. She heads toward me, an apologetic smile on her face. Urging me toward the center cabin, she tells me there are people I need to meet. She introduces me to men who I won't remember with nicknames I'd blush if I said aloud. They all become a blur after a while. Thankfully, bikers aren't the most talkative of folks, so the introductions are quick. Finally, we reach the old men in the rockers.

"This her?" the one on the left asks. He's so wrinkly and hairy I can barely make out the tattoos that cover most of his flesh. He has a full-length beard that mostly covers his leather vest. Beneath the distractions, his blue eyes sparkle with a rare kind of interest. It's both a curiosity and an appreciation that, surprisingly, doesn't feel creepy.

"Alexandra Mancuso," I say, without waiting to be introduced. I offer my hand and give him my most respectful smile. Slowly, he lifts his hand and places it in mine.

"Rage," he says. Though life and age have gotten the better of him, I have no doubt he earned his name, just like they all have. And with a name like Rage, I choose not to discount him, despite his friendly demeanor. His grip tightens on my hand, though the effort appears to tire him out as his hand shakes. "I'd change my name if I were you."

"You think I need a nickname?" I ask, trying to keep the mood light.

"Mancuso isn't a friend," he mutters. My stomach sinks in fear. I want to trust that Ruby, my mother's sister, wouldn't go through all of the trouble to save my ass just to bring me here to a group of men who hate my father enough to take revenge on him through me. Still, what do I really know about Ruby?

"You can't have loyalty to Forsaken and Mancuso. I don't care if he is your father."

Gathering all the courage I have, I say, "I have no loyalty to his family." As awful as it sounds, it's the truth. Carlo has always put his family before mine. Never once have I felt he loves and appreciates me for who I am, but rather what I can do for him. I want to believe he loves me, in his own way.

"Don't make us regret this."

And just like that, our conversation is finished. Ruby takes me by my arm and leads me away from the crowd, around the corner of the cabin. Night is falling now, and the sheer darkness of the desert is intimidating.

"The van will be here soon, but we won't be leaving until morning," she says gently. I nod and open my mouth, but nothing comes out. She catches the movement and raises an eyebrow. "There something you want to say?"

"I don't know," I admit. I'm not sure what I should say, if anything. Staying in this place overnight strikes a chord of panic within me, but I can't really say that aloud. I'm so anxious to get to wherever home is and to see it with my own eyes, that I can barely contain the frustration at this delay.

"It's Jim. He and Rage have some shit to work out. If it were up to me, we'd go straight through."

"It's okay," I say, but she shakes her head.

"Who is Rage?" I ask. He seems to carry himself with a certain amount of authority, but I can't place where he fits into all of this. I know Jim is the president, but I don't know if that means he's the president of all Forsaken members or just the ones in his group.

"He's Jim's father. Old bastard retired out here some years ago," Ruby says, clearing her throat. She shakes her head and gives me a forced smile. "Ryan's going to keep an eye on you until Duke and the others get here. Since you two are getting along, I thought you'd prefer that to one of the other guys."

"Thank you," I say, trying to control the nervous excitement that pulsates through my body. Unlike the other night when the men stayed outside of my room, I'm hoping Ryan comes inside. So far, he's the only person who's really talked with me. Ruby's made some sort of effort and Ian is getting there, but other than that, it's been a lonely journey.

In the distance, I see Ryan approaching. Despite the encroaching darkness, I can see the pleasant smile on his face as he nears. In his left hand is my bag, and in his right is a similar-sized leather bag. He comes to stand beside me, shifting both bags to his left hand. He places his right hand on my lower back, guiding me toward the surrounding cabins. From behind me, I hear Ruby shout, "Remember what I said!"

Those men are off limits to you.

I tell myself I'll respect her wishes, even if the thought of being alone in a cabin with Ryan gives me other ideas.

Chapter 10

Love begins with an image; lust with a sensation.
- Mason Cooley

RYAN LEADS US to one of the most isolated cabins. It's set back a few hundred feet from the rest. There is no porch light to guide our path and no walkway for us to follow. But he seems to know the way. I think back on what Ruby said, that Rage is Ryan's grandfather. I imagine that Ryan's familiarity with the land has something to do with that connection.

On the rickety front porch of the cabin, I'm suddenly nervous at the prospect of being alone with him. Even though I want this time with him more than anything right now, my stomach is alight with an intense fluttering of nerves. Ryan is all man. He's tall, and muscled, and tan. He wears his black jeans (the same he wore the day I met him), black leather, and his tattoos with an arrogance that is as much a part of him as his bike is. I've spent more than my fair share of time around arrogant men— men who think the world owes them something, and they owe the rest of us nothing—but not a single one of them has anything on Ryan. Aunt Gloria says I'm a good judge of character. If I were to judge Ryan, I'd say that all he's really missing in his life is a good woman on the back of his bike.

But I'm also nineteen and hopeful as all hell.

"You comin' in?" he asks, breaking me from my thoughts. He's already inside with the light on. I let out a shallow breath and cross the threshold, shutting the door behind me. Inside, the room is barely furnished, but Ryan's presence is so overwhelming it fills up the space.

There's no cheesy artwork on the walls, no phone from what I can see, and certainly no Bible in the bedside table. There is, however, a twin bed and a recliner. Like the rest of the cabin, they've seen better days. The walls are covered in signatures and phrases that would send my mother running to church.

"You take the bed," he says, plopping into the recliner, letting the bags drop at his feet. Now that he's sitting, he leans his head back, takes a deep breath, and closes his eyes. The long ride must have worn him out. Even though he's used to riding, I can't imagine going for so long doesn't take its toll.

"I'm going to take a shower." I lean down beside him, letting my arm brush against the side of his leg, and retrieve my small bag. When I go to stand up, his eyes are open, fixated on my every move. Whatever confidence I had about being in such close quarters with Ryan have disappeared. The butterflies are back. I'm so out of my element here, it's not even funny.

I shuffle backward and dart into the open bathroom. It's empty, not even a bar of soap or a towel. Thankfully, I have the soaps and washcloths I shoved in my bag. I turn on the water and fiddle with the knobs until I figure which is hot and which is cold. Even after figuring it out, the water is room temperature at best. The soap is harsh on my dry skin, but it's all I have. It's funny how we take the little things in life for granted. Growing up, I never wanted for anything material. Not really, anyway. My father was the reigning boss before I was born, and his position afforded us a very comfortable lifestyle. Whenever we traveled, we never used the hotel soap. When I was a child, my mother would say it wasn't good for my skin and so she would always pack my soap from home. After she died, it just stuck with me, I guess.

Dragging the white bar across my body, I feel anything but clean. A film forms on my skin that is uncomfortable and binding. My hair is stringy and feels like straw. It seems so stupid and materialistic as I stand here, trying to clean myself in this rundown log cabin, but I really miss my bath products.

Thinking about my absentee bath products is a dangerous road. Before I know it, I'm thinking about my bedspread and my pillows. Neither were particularly sentimental or expensive, but they were mine. I knew exactly where the lumps had formed in my pillows and how many blankets to use in the winter when snow would fall outside my bedroom window. My father's house was one of the nicest on the block, but it was also old and drafty in the cold winter months.

Tears well in my eyes, and I'm unable to stop them from falling down my cheeks, only to be washed away by the spray of the water. Once the first tear has fallen, I'm a goner. The rest hurry to catch up. They seem to fall faster the more I think of everything I'll never have again. My mother's nightgown—the one she died in—is gone. And that thought is my undoing. I let out an agonized scream at the top of my lungs. Placing my hands on the plastic walls of the enclosure, I slap at the plastic in a half-hearted attempt at releasing some frustration. That nightgown was the only thing that ever made me feel connected to her. She never was one to keep material things, and she was so reserved there were times I felt like I never really knew who she was. But once she passed and I dragged myself into that nightgown, it felt like a missing piece had been put into place. I could smell her, and see her in a way.

Every time I wore that thing I remembered her laugh and her smile. I remembered every bruised knee she bandaged up and how she so perfectly fit herself into my father's side. She loved that man with everything she was, and even though I often wondered why, I respected it. I think one of the only reasons I'll miss my father is because my mother loved him. And if she loved him, there must be something in there worth loving and missing.

The bathroom door flies open and, before I can react, Ryan's flung the shower curtain back and he has a gun pointed at the wall beside my head. His eyes are everywhere but on me. He's not even meeting my eyes. Through the tears and sorrow, I can feel a breakdown creeping up on me. He only has the curtain open for a moment before he's closed it again.

"Why were you screaming?"

I have no real response I can bring myself to give him. Telling him about the soap and shampoo just makes me sound like a spoiled brat who's found her circumstances to be beneath her. Trying to express the loss of the life I once had to a guy who's been wearing the same clothes for days now seems fruitless. So I say nothing. I stand beneath the cooling spray.

God took my mother from me. My father took my brother from me. Officer Davis took my father and uncle away. Ruby took Aunt Gloria away, and her crew of bikers have taken my privacy away. My grief is the only thing I have left that is solely mine, and I'll be damned if I have to lose that, too.

"Fine. You don't have to talk," he says. "But get this, you scream, I'm gonna have a .38 out and ready to shoot. Unless you want any accidents, keep quiet."

The pain in my chest has morphed into frustration, and I want nothing more than to scream, but I don't dare. Ryan's voice is already teetering on the edge of angry. I try to remind myself that he's in here, trying to protect me. He could have ignored my screams, not knowing what was going on. He could have taken the opportunity to eye my naked form. He could have done a lot of things that he didn't.

"Thank you," I whisper as loudly as I can bring myself to, but he's already gone. The last thing I want to do is to be polite. I want to be the rude one for once, the one everyone else has to dance around because you never know what she's going to do. But I don't, because despite everything I wish I was—strong, independent, brave— I'm none of those things. I'm barely sassy. Mostly, I'm as my mother raised me to be—agreeable, polite, and docile. And as much as I love her, I despise what she's turned me into. Girls like me get to be the good little housewife. They don't get to be the girls on the back of a man's bike.

After I've rinsed the measly little bit of conditioner I had out of my hair, I cut off the water and step out carefully. There's no bathmat to keep me steady. As I pat my wet skin down with the washcloth, I decide that alone time is the last thing I need. Every time I'm alone, I start to think about everything and it makes me resentful and angry, not to mention really, really sad. Because as much as I hated being treated like a porcelain doll, at least it was something I was used to. There were no surprises.

I dress quickly back in my dirty clothes. One thing Aunt Gloria didn't pack for me was clothes. I've been over this time and time again in my head, why she packed the things for me the she did. Apart from the money, most of the small items in my bag have little to no true use. Surely, there was room for a pair of underwear and a spare bra. When I'm clothed, I walk back into the room to find it empty. Backing into the wall behind me, panic hits me square in my gut. Aside from the fact that I'm not comfortable being alone with my thoughts, I'm just plain uncomfortable being alone. Then I see him, outside on the porch. He's huddled in some kind of conversation with another man. Instead of standing around, spying on their conversation, I drop my bag at the foot of the bed and sit down on the corner.

I'm not certain when the last time was that they changed the sheets or replaced the pillows, but it's better than sleeping in that stupid van, something I wish never to repeat. Summoning the courage, I inch up toward the pillow and lay my head down atop it. It's dusty and there are cigarette burns in the corner, and the odor is just awful. This place isn't a motel. It must be some kind of club thing. I can't imagine anyone ever paying to stay in a place like this. It's beyond filthy.

Lying on the bed, I let my gaze travel the walls. Barely an inch of the painted wooden beams has been spared. Words are written in a sporadic fashion, overlapping each other, making half of them unreadable. In what looks like black paint, the word FORSAKEN is painted in letters nearly two feet high. Beneath that, it says, WHERE SOULS SPOIL AND HEARTS ROT. On the opposite wall in equally large lettering is NEVADA.

I shove my wet hair out of the way, letting it soak the pillow. I'm so far away from home it almost feels like some sort of bad movie. Even having been raised by a mob boss, I'm not prepared for this stuff. It's just crazy.

Outside, Ryan's voice booms. He's yelling now and seemingly unafraid of who can hear him. I want to stay right where I am and not try to listen in, but old habits are hard to break. Crawling off the bed and tiptoeing toward the door, I try to keep out of the line of sight from the sheer curtains covering the window.

"I see what you're doing, son." The voice is familiar. Jim's, I think. It's the logical choice, so I go with it.

"Don't," Ryan says.

"Ruby won't like it," Jim warns. The moment he says her name, I know for sure that it's Jim. With his warning, I know he's talking about me. I'm not a stupid child, nor am I as innocent as Ruby seems to think I am. What is so bad about being interested in Ryan?

"I don't give a fuck, and I'm not doing a fucking thing. Get off my back."

"I'm just trying to help you out," Jim says, then the sounds of heavy footfalls disappear into the distance.

"Fucking Christ," Ryan says from the other side of the door. I move away quickly and stand beside the bed, separating my hair in preparation for braiding it. He storms in and slams the door behind him. I give him a casual sideways glance and then go back to focusing on braiding my hair. His mood wafts off of him and is covering the entire room with a layer of anger and frustration.

Plopping down in the recliner, he pulls out a bottle of whiskey from between the arm and the cushion. I try to keep my eyes on my damp hair, but it's difficult to pay attention to anything but him. He's like a vortex, sucking me in.

"Like something you see?" Ryan says.

I look over my shoulder. Without removing his gaze, he takes another drink from the bottle of whiskey. He swallows heartedly, and a few drops remain on his lips. My tongue sneaks out and licks my lips before I realize what I've done, the invitation I've given. He mimics my motion with his own tongue. A warm blush rises on my cheeks, and I look down at my feet as my hands resume working at the braid.

"You really are just a little girl, aren't you?"

As I loop a loose strand around the end of my braid and secure my work in place, a new kind of heat rises to my cheeks. A mixture of frustration and exhaustion overtake me as I shoot him one of my best angry looks.

"You don't know anything about me," I snap. Now that my hair is secure, I have nothing else to distract me from his presence. I toss my braid over my shoulder and turn to face him. I'm really over being called a little girl and being treated like I'm going to break at any moment.

"I know more about you than you know." He takes another gulp and rests the half-empty bottle on his knee. I move my arms across my chest before correcting my position and place them on my hips. I refuse to wither under his criticism.

"Do enlighten me," I say, trying for my best smirk. I have absolutely no practice at being snarky, so I'm sure the effect isn't what I intend. He raises his brows.

"You're sheltered. You know nothing about the way the world really works. You've never actually done anything worth mentioning, even though you think you have." His words hit me straight in the gut. It doesn't matter that he's hit the nail on the head. It still feels like a dull butter knife is being shoved in between my ribs. I don't want to be that girl anymore. I just don't know how not to be.

With my fingers digging into my sides, I eye the whiskey bottle. It only takes a second for me to make my decision. Dropping my hands to my sides, I walk toward him slowly. He remains silent as I sit on the edge of the bed before him, our knees touching, and take the bottle from his grasp. I bring the bottle to my lips, close my eyes, and take a small sip. The burning tang of the alcohol is brutal going down. But I force it down anyway. Opening my eyes, I shake my head free of the buzzing that's already begun.

"Again," Ryan says. His voice is hard and commanding. I'm trying so hard to prove to him that I'm not a baby and that I can hold my own—maybe even that I can make it here with this leather-clad bunch of roughians. I close my eyes and toss back some more whiskey, barely keeping it from coming back up.

"Again." And once more I follow his orders, but it's the last time. I set the bottle down on my lap, barely keeping it in hand and use my other hand to keep myself from falling backward. It's not my first time trying whiskey; it's just the first time with cheap whiskey. I force myself to breathe steadily in order to control the impending nausea.

When I dare open my eyes, Ryan's cold expression looks foreign. It's like there's a part of him that's actively working on killing the part of him that can actually feel things.

"I may be a spoiled mob brat who's never had the chance to do anything worth noting, but what the hell have you done?" As the words leave my lips, I start shaking with fear. I've never spoken to anyone but my brother like that before.

I'm rewarded for my boldness with a glimmer of amusement in his eyes. Leaning forward in the chair, he places his left elbow on his knee and grabs the bottle of whiskey with the other hand. He's so close now, he has to angle the bottle to the side to avoid hitting my face. My breathing becomes ragged as I imagine what it would be like to have those lips on mine. He lowers the bottle, but says nothing. I won't be getting an answer, so I try another question.

"What's with the nickname?"

"Everybody's got 'em," he says without elaborating.

"And they have meaning, right? So why Trigger?"

"I was fourteen the first time I shot a gun," he begins. Both of his elbows now rest on his knees with the bottle hanging from his right hand. Feeling a little more stabilized and brave from the liquor, I take the bottle back and down some more. The more I drink this crap the less it stings going down, so I try for another two gulps before I decide that drinking myself stupid is probably not the best idea.

"Okay," I say, encouraging him to keep talking.

"I accidentally shot Rage in the foot."

Unable to control myself, I bark out laugh that dissolves into a fit of giggles.

"He said I shot before I was supposed to."

I peek up at him through my lashes, still shaking with laughter. "Is that a problem for you, shooting early?"

The surprise on his face urges me on, and I give him a flirtatious wink. But I've forgotten the world I'm in and who I'm talking to. Ryan is no school boy, nor is he impressed with my ability to banter. The amusement is gone, and so is the shock. In their wake is an intensity I can't process. Swiftly, he takes the bottle from my hand and drops it on the wooden floor. The farther he leans over me, the farther back I have to lean in order to avoid bumping heads.

He places his right hand on the bed beside me, his left knee coming up beside my outer thigh. As he hovers over me, I do everything in my power to keep my heart from straight-up beating out of my chest and to stop myself from losing consciousness. With his free hand, he grabs the back of my neck, squeezing so hard I worry he'll leave a bruise. *Maybe that's what he wants.* Pulling me in, our noses collide and a rush of pain shoots up between my eyes. My ears heat from the stinging sensation. With labored breaths, my lips part. My chest rises and falls and suddenly, I can feel my beating heart everywhere. From my wrists to my neck to my lower belly.

"What are you doing," I whisper. His warm breath wafts over my face, coating me in the sickly sweet scent.

"I'm going to fuck you. That's what you want, isn't it?"

I pull away and push on his chest, but it does me no good. The more I push him away, the closer he gets, bringing his body directly on top of mine, his pelvis resting between my legs. Unable to meet his eyes, I focus my attention on the marked wall over his shoulder.

"Please, no," I whimper. He angles my neck, forcing me to look at him.

"Don't worry, I don't fuck little girls," he sneers. Releasing me, he crawls off the bed and storms out of the cabin, leaving me to my thoughts. I scramble to the center of the bed and curl into myself. He's not who I thought he was. No matter what impression I got of him, clearly, it's just what I wanted to see. He's not lonely; he's just a bastard.

Chapter 11

There are far, far better things ahead than any we leave behind.

- C.S. Lewis

WE LEAVE SO early the next day that the sun isn't quite out yet. After Ryan left last night, I lay in that bed, staring at those words on the wall for what felt like hours. I fell asleep eventually. It was sometime after I heard Duke's voice at the door.

WHERE SOULS SPOIL AND HEARTS ROT.

There's so much I've wondered about in my lifetime as far as my father's family goes. Like, how can these men go out and do these horrible things, then come home to their families? It always happens, you see. A wise guy goes to work and things happen on the job. Maybe it's a slow day and all he's got to do is threaten somebody. Maybe it's a busy day and he's got to teach somebody a lesson. Maybe that lesson has the guy ending up like Sal, with a bullet hole in his throat. But when these guys get home, they're all hugs and kisses to their wives and children. They talk about ballet recital and hockey practice. They dispense words of wisdom about how important respect and earning a quality education is. But they don't talk about life the way it really is—bloody and painful. They don't talk about where the money comes from to pay the mortgage or what truck their wife's fur coat fell off of. We all know, but they never talk about it.

It wasn't until I had been staring at those words on the wall for so long that I was worried I'd slipped into some kind of coma that I finally understood how people do such awful things and then manage to play the part of the loving husband and father. They just let a piece of themselves die and when they've done enough screwed up stuff, I think they just stop caring. Because it only matters—all the death and pain—if you let it. So in that bed, I made a vow to myself and to God that I would stop letting it matter. If Ryan, and my father, and all of my father's men can shut off the guilt, then surely I can shut off the pain.

We've been in the van for hours and hours on end now. Morning passed and bled into afternoon. That was around the time we crossed the state line into California, which was, apparently, a big deal as horns sounded from all around us and echoed in the silence inside the van. Duke said once, a while back, that we had about an hour or so left. The excited buzz from the men is starting to rub off on Ruby, who has been particularly silent today.

The highways have gone from wide and expansive to narrow and winding a few times since we made it into California, but this has got to be the worst yet. Driving on the side of a mountain—which Duke insists is a *small* mountain—that twists and turns and has a small shoulder is making my stomach a little flighty. My knuckles are white as my hands clamp down on the torn fabric seat beneath me. About ten minutes back, I decided to stop looking out the window. The highway is, mostly, one lane going in each direction, with the occasional rest stop carved into the dark brown rock of the mountain. Trees, taller than I can see, line the highway, their trunks dug deep into the ground at least a hundred feet below the concrete.

"Just a few more minutes," Ruby says, leaning toward me. Her shoulder bumps mine, and I take the opportunity to peek at her.

"Isn't that what you said like a half an hour ago?" We speed around another curve, and then we begin our descent. I glance over her shoulder out the windshield, seeing nothing past the bikers but a flat concrete strip nestled between scattered redwood trees and the occasional house or barn. I let out a deep breath and thank God about a hundred times.

"So sue me. I was trying to be comforting," she says with a wistful smile. The closer we get to Fort Bragg, the more she relaxes. Her jaw has loosened up, her brows have finally become two distinct units, and her mouth turns up slightly at the corners. Catching my look, she gives me a real smile and says, "What?"

"You're relaxed," I say. Having been caught staring is a little uncomfortable, but trying to lie about it or cover it up would only prolong the conversation.

"I just wanted to get you home is all. You're much safer here." I nod my head, letting the conversation end there. The bikes start up on their horns again, and Duke, Diesel, and even Bear break out into an excited laughter. Just as I'm looking around trying to figure out what all the fuss is about, I see it. A wooden sign with the words WELCOME TO FORT BRAGG, CALIFORNIA is up ahead. Beneath that, carved into the wood, it says POPULATION 7,723. My eyes nearly bug out of my head at the prospect of living in a place with such a small population. I've spent my entire life in Brooklyn, New York City's most densely-populated borough.

Intuitive in only the way a mother can be, Ruby picks up on my change in mood. She pats my knee and offers me a smile, accompanied by a soft laugh. "It's small, and not very cosmopolitan, but it's safe. It's home now."

"I don't know what I was expecting," I admit. "But I'm sure it's going to be cool."

For the first time in hours, Duke addresses me. "Fuck yeah, it's going to be cool. Ain't no place like it."

I meet his eyes and shake my head, trying to fight off the smile that's threatening to overtake me.

"See, you like me," he says. I tighten my jaw, but it's no use.

With a smile, I say, "I've gotten used to your particular style of conversation."

We come to a dead end that intersects at the left and right. Far off in the distance, beyond the low-level houses, beyond the road before me, beyond several hundred feet of land, is an expanse of blue sky as far as the eye can see. Diesel rolls down his window and the fresh, salty ocean air wafts in through the open window, leaving a heavy dampness to settle on my skin. I've never smelled anything this pure and unfiltered before. Even at the beaches on the New Jersey shore and Long Island, which have always been favorite spots of mine, the natural scent of the ocean is covered by the smell of sunscreen and sweat, and the rhythmic sound of crashing waves is diluted by the volume of the people. I'm excited to explore my new home.

"Is that," I ask, but I'm cut off before I can finish my thought.

"Pacific Ocean," Ruby says, a smile covering her entire face. I've never seen the Pacific Ocean before.

We hang a right at the light, turning onto South Main Street. We pass a few blocks of strip malls that house everything from local relators to attorneys' offices right beside buffets and fast food restaurants. I can still smell the salt of the ocean to our left. We drive over the Noyo

River on the right, which spills into the bay on the left. The bay is a large alcove that spills into the Pacific. It's absolutely gorgeous the way the rocks jut out against the tide and curve inward, creating a definitive line between the bay and the ocean.

Beyond the river, the strip malls give way to local businesses and street signs that proudly hold banners on either side that welcome us to downtown. Here, the streets are formed in tight grid patterns off of Main Street to the right. From what I can see beyond the commercial buildings, small, older homes make up the local area. To the left, the coastline shrinks the closer we get to the heart of town, providing a better view of the water and the pure blue sky.

Ruby takes the time to tell me as much about what I'm seeing as possible, and even though our first few days were rough with her being so hot and cold all the time, I'm so grateful I have her. Even if I didn't know she existed a week ago, I can't imagine not having her in my life now.

Just as the van makes a right down Oak Street, the bikes both in front of us and behind continue forward. My heart sinks in confusion. Until this moment I hadn't realized how safe I felt with the rumble of the bikes embracing our journey westward. Now, as we make our way through a residential part of town, the cacophony of Harleys fades into the distance. I look at Ruby, searching for answers.

"They went to the club house," she says.

"Oh."

"We're safe. I promise."

"It's just quiet now, without the bikes," I admit.

Duke smiles and shoots Ruby a mischievous smile. His entire face lights up, creating dimples in his cheeks.

"Like mother, like daughter," he says. Her face falls as she eyes the pair of us and then levels her gaze on Duke.

Oak Street morphs from densely-packed single family homes with little land to homes of the same size with larger yards that sit farther back from the road, eventually sprawling out to residential properties that sit on at least half of an acre each. The farther we get from Main Street, it seems, the closer we get to the country. The straight shot of Oak Street winds and bends as it becomes Sherwood Road. Minutes pass before we slow and turn down an unmarked gravel drive.

Up ahead is a dark-brown one-story ranch house that sits parallel to the curving drive, then bends at the mid-point in a forty-five degree angle that features a large sun room with a furnished deck jutting out into the tall, wild grass. The house is nothing fancy, but it looks cared for, if not updated. The van pulls up around the side, revealing an attached three-car garage, and another deck that leads up to the front door. Behind the house, nestled in a wide-open field, is a large red barn. Diesel stops the van in view of the front door, which opens and out step two men, both wearing leather vests. One is tall and slender, the other is rather squat in comparison. They rush toward the van eagerly and slide open the side door.

"All right, princess. Get the fuck out. You're home," Duke says with a smile on his face. I try to smile, but the arrival of new people puts me on edge. I crawl out of the van first and Ruby follows. One of the men shuts the door behind us, and the van speeds off.

"Ma'am, it's good to have you home," the tall one says, addressing Ruby. She nods her head and lets out a deep breath. He looks to me and gives me a polite smile. I try to smile back, but all I really want to do is to find a bed and sleep it in for the next year, maybe two.

"Welcome home, Alexandra," the shorter one says. I notice neither of them have any patches on the front of their vests. The tall one turns around, followed by his buddy. The only patch on the back is at the bottom, curving up at the ends. CALIFORNIA.

"Where are their patches," I whisper-shout to Ruby. She walks toward the house and steps onto the deck.

"Prospects," she says, turning back to the house. Well, that makes sense. They're not full club members yet, which is why they're here with us rather than with the rest of the club. It's what my brother calls "bitch duty". They look after the stuff the club members don't want to be, or can't be, bothered with. A bitter thought hits me. Ryan must be relieved to be off "bitch duty" now that he has prospects who can deal with me.

Two dogs race out of the front door and excitedly leap at Ruby. With a short laugh, she bends down and gives each of them a pet. One appears to be a German shepherd while the other is, I think, a pit bull. I try to keep my distance, but it's no use. Gloria has a dog, but he's a small little thing. My best friend back in Brooklyn, Adriana, has a few dogs. I never interacted much with them, though. First the pit bull rushes at me. I tense up, tears springing to my eyes, and keep my arms at my sides, afraid to move. It jumps and claws at me. A moment later, the shepherd joins in. Through the fear, I realize they're not biting or growling. They're just panting and whimpering, but their nails dig into my skin and dirty clothes. I peek down at them, still unable to bring myself to move.

"PJ! Tegan!" Ruby shouts, and the dogs stop jumping. They stand beside me with wagging tails. "They wouldn't hurt a fly. They just get excited around new people."

"I'm okay," I say, trying to shrug it off. I give Ruby my best smile and wonder if this hollowness in my gut will ever go away. We walk up the deck; as I step across the threshold, I know I'm home. I just don't feel it yet.

JULY

Chapter 12

Family means no one gets left behind or forgotten.
- David Ogden Stiers

"THAT'S IT," RUBY says, barging into my room as she so often does. Quickly, I shut my laptop and smile. I've been curled up on my full-sized bed for the last hour checking out the local college's upcoming fall course schedule. I haven't said anything to Ruby or Jim about it yet, but if I want the chance to go, I'm going to have to do it soon.

"What's wrong?" I shove the computer off my lap and stand up, adjusting my tank top and jean shorts. Jim swears the house has air conditioning, but in this early-July, record-setting heat wave, I'm calling bullshit.

Inviting herself in, Ruby puts her hands on her hips and surveys the space. It's a little barren, I'll admit. When I got here two months ago, all the room had was a tall, wooden dresser, and a used full-size mattress set that sat on the floor. Ruby immediately apologized for not getting me a new one, saying she hadn't had time to go find one. I was close to taking her up on the offer of buying me a new bed until she mentioned it was Ryan's old mattress from before he moved out. That's when I decided to keep it and just get a good frame for it.

The room says little about me. I haven't accumulated much since arriving in Fort Bragg. The walls are empty, and I'm using Ryan's old bed set. My closet has enough clothes and shoes in it, and I have quality beauty products now. But as far as putting my stamp on the place, I just haven't felt like I should, even though Ruby's been mentioning that we need to fix it up for weeks now. I think she's finally reached her breaking point with me avoiding the topic.

"This room," she says, pursing her lips. "We have a ton of shit to get for the party tonight. But before that, we're fixing up this room."

"Okay," I say quietly as I fiddle with my belt loop. Her expression softens as she points at my bed and nods. She moves to sit on the edge of the bed and I follow. Taking my hand she looks into my eyes and lets out a heavy sigh.

"Why don't you want to fix up your room?"

I squirm under the attention. I've been avoiding this conversation the past few weeks. Knowing it was coming, I did what I could to prepare an explanation that would make sense.

"What's going to happen to me?" I whisper. I've been holding that question in for two months now. Ever since I woke up that morning in a haze to Gloria ushering me off into my new life. So loaded with the potential to break me, I don't want the answer. Not really, anyway. But Ruby needs to know why I'm so hesitant to settle in and make my mark on this place.

"You're going to live happily ever after," she quips. But I shake it off, unimpressed with her response.

"What's going to happen when my father's family finds me? What's going to happen when he has his men shoot up your house just like Jim and the guys did his?"

"Mike knows exactly where you are. We weren't quiet about our presence, if you remember." She always refers to my father as Mike for some reason. Even my mother called him Carlo, which is my father's middle and preferred name. She takes my face in her hands and, with teary eyes, says, "There are four roads in and out of this town. We're isolated. The club has friends in all of the surrounding precincts. When I tell you that you're safe, I mean that bastard is going to have to go through me and the entire fucking club, across three thousand miles, and through a bullet to his chest to get to you."

With that declaration, I burst into tears. Nobody, not even Gloria, has ever promised to protect me like Ruby just did. My body sinks into hers as she wraps her arms around me while I cry. Eventually, I pull myself together and wipe away my tears.

"I don't know what I did to deserve this."

"You were born, baby," she says, placing a kiss on my forehead.

AN HOUR LATER and we're heading into town. Our first stop is the club house/garage so Ruby can get money from Jim for the party supplies. I've only been by the clubhouse twice and inside once. It smelled awful, and every surface I touched was sticky. I choose to pretend I sat and put my hands in spilled beer, rather than what Ian alluded to, which is just nasty. At exactly the moment I reacted to Ian's comment, Ryan stepped out of a back room, zipping up his fly. He barely looked my way as he steered down a hallway and out of sight. It was the only time I've seen him since I arrived in Fort Bragg.

Ruby steers her red Chevy Suburban onto Main Street from Oak and quickly maneuvers into the left lane, where she turns into the Forsaken Custom Cycle parking lot. The shop is on the corner of Main and Alder. Behind the Forsaken property line is a few hundred feet of dirt and rock before the ground drops down into the ocean. I've never gotten close enough to see for sure, but it has to be at least a twenty foot drop down into the water. The dirt lot between the water and the club's land is property of the federal government, as it once served as a military post.

The lot is deep, with the shop set back from the road. Behind the ample lot is the fenced-off clubhouse. There doesn't seem to be much business on a daily basis, but according to Ruby, it's a hobby business anyway. Whatever that means.

She parks the SUV and we both climb out. She shoots me a questioning smile. I just shrug. After putting my hand in the questionable substance and then seeing Ryan's cold indifference toward me, I basically vowed never to return. But after our talk, I figure I ought to make an attempt to get to know these people a little better. I'm going to be around for a long time, and it's probably a good idea to try to make this place my home.

The office to the shop is locked up, and a sign hanging on the inside of the glass door reads GONE DRINKING. BE BACK WHEN SOBER. I snort while pointing at the sign. "So they're closing up for good, then?"

Ruby snickers and leads us past the closed garage bays. The very last bay, just before the gate to the clubhouse, is open; sure enough, the guys are sitting around drinking. Not a single one of them has a useful tool in hand. Jim leans over a red tool chest on wheels, his elbows resting on top as he takes a pull from his beer bottle. Duke is parked in a black metal folding chair with a cigarette in one hand and a beer in the other. Sitting on the cement, Ian picks away at his nails. Not a single one of them notice us until Ruby clears her throat.

Jim looks up immediately, a smile spreading across his entire face. I stand aside awkwardly as he stalks toward Ruby and wraps her in his arms. Choosing to skip

out on the front-row action of seeing them make out like
a pair of teenagers, I walk up to Duke and give the leg of
his chair a kick.

"How goes it, Princess?"

"It goes," I say. Duke and I have formed a strange
relationship over the last two months. He is—in his own
words—kind of a dick. But he's also not that bad when
the mood strikes him. We've moved past our rocky first
meeting into what I would almost call a camaraderie.
Mostly, I strike up conversations with Duke because he's
easy to talk to. There's no awkward avoidance like there
is with Ian. And aside from the prospects, who rarely ever
talk but to repeat orders and ask for direction, Duke is
kind of my only friend around this place. Now that I think
about it, that's really depressing.

"What brings you to town?"

"Sherwood Road," I say, unable to stop myself from
smiling. Duke raises his head and grins like a maniac.

"You're turning into such a smart ass."

"You give good lessons."

"That's not the only thing I give good," he says, his
smile turning lascivious. My eyes are wide, my jaw slack,
and I think I'm brighter than a cherry tomato. My heart
thrums in my gut as my eyes fall on the one person I
hadn't expected to see here—Ryan. He's been so absent,
I could swear it was on purpose. I have had to remind
myself that I don't know his routine and if this is normal
for him. I could be making a mountain out of a molehill,
except that Ruby's asked Jim where he's been a few
times.

Ryan watches me from the shadows. His presence
both infuriates and flusters me. We've spent, essentially,
no time together. I've clocked more hours hanging out

with Duke. And yet I can't seem to let this thing go. A few weeks back, after I'd caught myself moving around in bed, trying to figure out which side Ryan slept on, I tried to diagnose myself. Recalling all of my conversations with my former therapist, I'm pretty sure the only reason I'm obsessing over him is to avoid what's really been going on. Being in a new town, especially one that's so different from Brooklyn, and having no life, is weighing on me. I thought I was bored in my father's house. At least there I had responsibilities. Jim's big request from me is that I lighten up, and Ruby's is that I let her in emotionally. Neither of them wants the kitchen cleaned, which would be a heck of a lot easier than dealing with this emotional crap.

"Is that so?" I ask Duke, seeing Ryan's expression darken as my suggestive comment is realized. Duke is in the middle of taking a sip of his beer when he realizes the opening I've given him and he nearly spits it out in response. From behind me, Ruby and Jim laugh quietly. Ian, as per usual, doesn't react. The rest may be amused, but this is for Ryan's benefit.

I place my hand on Duke's shoulder and ask, "Anything special you want tonight?" Tension grows as Ryan's eyes bore into mine. Duke sits up a little straighter and more interested than he was before. I can't see Ruby and Jim from where I stand, but maybe that's a good thing.

"Whiskey," Duke says. "The good kind." I pat his shoulder and lift my hand, letting the tips of my fingers drag across the leather of his vest.

"I hate cheap whiskey," I remark, knowing full well Ryan is catching the subvert message. "It always disappoints." With that, I turn around, and Ruby and I leave to run our errands. She hasn't told me where we're going next, just that she's going to buy me a few things for my room. I protest, telling her I'd rather she not spend her money on me. I offer to pay for my own stuff, but she won't hear of it.

We spend the afternoon avoiding the Fourth of July festivities, but it's not easy. She drags me in and out of at least a dozen stores. We pick up mineral makeup from a local makeup artist/chemist who started his own line in town, then we head over and find some throw pillows and a desk for my room. Ruby shoots off a text to Jim, who promises one of the prospects—Tall or Squat—will pick the desk up for us. I still can't remember either of their names since Ian thought it would be funny to tell them they can't tell me their names, so now I'm left to my own devices to identify them.

"Can we just stop for a coffee?" I ask, eyeing the sign for the coffee shop up ahead. My arms ache under the weight of the shopping bags we've accumulated in the last two hours. It's been years since I've been out shopping for this long, in so many stores, all in one trip.

"I think that's a good idea," she agrees. We walk the fifty or so feet to Universal Ground. The door chimes when I open it. Immediately, the scent of brewing coffee wafts across my face, promising an afternoon pick-me-up. The coffee shop is narrow, but deep. The walls are lined with photographs of bikers and their friends at various town events and celebrations; most of them wear black leather vests. I may not get out much, but I know enough to know that the club is special to the town, even if some residents won't admit it. My father made our neighborhood in Brooklyn, but the club makes this entire town. Its impact is evident in the way the locals regard the men as they pass through on their bikes.

Behind the counter, a young woman scribbles in a notebook, her long blonde hair resting on the wooden surface. Ruby catches sight of her and stops in her tracks. Looking from the woman to Ruby, I stay silent, unsure what to say. She wears a spaghetti-strap tank top that's practically skin tight, showing off her numerous tattoos. The woman looks up, revealing black-painted eyes and bright red lips. Her makeup is heavier than I normally find attractive, but she wears it well.

"Can I get you something?" she asks, her tone laced with irritation. I take a step forward to order, but Ruby stays still. It takes her another moment, but then she composes herself and steps up to the counter.

"I didn't know you worked here," Ruby says, clearing her throat. She leans over the counter, back to being the confident woman I've grown to love. Whatever startled her about this woman's presence has since evaporated. The woman doesn't respond.

"Okay, if that's how you want to play it, Nic." Ruby squares her shoulders and looks over the menu hanging above the espresso machine against the back wall and orders. I follow suit with an iced vanilla latte. Ruby pays for our drinks, and we grab a table in the back corner while waiting for our order to be called up.

"Who is that?" I ask, careful to control my volume.

"That's Nic. She's what the club calls a lost girl." I tilt my head sideways, not understanding. "She doesn't have an old man."

"Okay," I say, trying to string the clues together, to no avail. She blows out a breath and levels me with a flat stare. "She seems pissed."

"Her dad hung around the club before he went to prison. Her mom hooked up with some of the guys before she split, leaving Nic with her younger brother. She's pissed all right."

"Wow. That sucks," I say. "But why is she called a lost girl?"

"When a woman hooks up with a member, but isn't his Old Lady, she's a lost girl." Nic nods her head at me, supplying our coffees at the pick-up station. I quickly grab the drinks, giving Nic a grateful smile, and plop back down in my seat, now totally engaged in this conversation.

"So, who did she hook up with? Was it Ian?" My mood has taken a turn for the better, much to Ruby's enjoyment. She smiles back at me, clearly amused by my interest in this subject.

"Why Ian?" she asks.

"Because he's all brooding, and she's all grouchy. They just seem like they'd fit together." She shakes her head, laughing. I try to think, and then it comes to me. "Duke," I say with a nod. Her answering smirk tells me I've hit the nail on the head.

"And how did you come up with that?"

"Because he's such a whore," I blurt out, then cover my mouth in regret. Duke has made a habit these last two months of stopping by and catching me up on his dalliances, not that I want to hear them. Ruby's jaw is slack, and a moment later she throws her head back in laughter. My cheeks are hot with embarrassment. Shaking my head, I find myself mortified by what I've said.

"I didn't mean that," I protest, but it does me no good. Ruby's enjoying my honesty a little more than I'm used to.

"Oh, yes you did. I'm glad you feel comfortable enough with me to be honest like that."

"I'm not," I say, taking a sip of my iced coffee. "What if he overhead me say something like that?"

"So what if he did? It's not like you insulted him," she says. I shake my head and pull in more of my refreshment. A giggle escapes me. Even imagining calling Duke a whore to his face makes me nervous, much less actually doing it. Though, if I'm being honest with myself, in the back of my head, I'm contemplating doing it the next time he calls me Princess.

"So, when are you going to ask me about school?" My head shoots up at the implication. She's on target, of course. But still. *How does she know?* My shock registers on her face, and she leans in close.

"I saw the search history on the desktop."

"I was going to ask. I was just putting it off."

"Why?" she asks. I let out a heavy sigh, unsure how to explain this to her. Despite the fact that my father had put me in the most exclusive private school in Brooklyn, one that promises its parents a ninety-nine percent graduation rate and a ninety-six percent college acceptance guarantee, he never intended for me to go to college. He's old-school Italian like that. Before my mother even gave birth to me, I was expected to grow up into the perfect Principessa, marry the family man my father most approved of, and to provide my husband with as many male children as I could. Not that I ever asked, but he never mentioned it, either.

"I'm afraid you'll say no."

"Alex, you make your own choices. Jim and I don't get to decide that for you."

"I also want to get a job," I say, before I can stop myself. Getting a job is something I've been thinking about for the past month or so. The money Gloria gave me will last me for a good, long time, but I want to be productive. I can't just sit around the house all the time. It's driving me nuts.

"I'm sure Jim can find something for you to do around the shop."

"I'd like that." And I would. So far, this day has been a serious rollercoaster of emotions. So much that I had been holding in these past two months came to the surface today. I have a home, a family, I might even have a friend in Duke, I'm actually getting to go to college, and I might be getting a job. And finally, this feels like my life is taking a turn for the better.

Chapter 13

You were once wild here. Don't let them tame you.
- Isadora Duncan

MY ARMS ARE like jelly after shopping for the party. When Ruby told me we were going to be picking up party supplies, I expected a few bottles of each kind of alcohol and even a few cases of beer. What I hadn't known was that we'd be filling up the Suburban with enough food and liquor to supply the entire town. It took us visiting two grocery stores and three liquor stores to find everything we needed. Thankfully, when we got back to the house, the prospects took over grilling and setting everything up. I have never been so grateful for Tall and Squat before.

The noise outside of my bedroom door is at an all-time high. Even PJ and Tegan, who are normally in everyone's business, have taken to hiding out in here with me. The house has never been this noisy before, but then, Jim and Ruby haven't had people over like this in the time I've been here. Not that I would really know what's going on out there. The moment Ruby turned away to find Jim, I snuck off into my room to hide and check out the fall schedule for Redwoods College. But that was over an hour ago, and the school isn't very big, a few hundred students at the coastal campus at the most. There's a selection to choose from—art, history, science, and even automotive technology courses available. But some of them require other courses be taken first, and I don't know where to start. It isn't helping any that I grabbed a bottle of vodka before sneaking off. It's not like I've been sitting here chugging it out of the bottle or anything. I'm classy. I grabbed a glass to pour it in.

Frustrated, I close my laptop and set it on top of my dresser, swaying a little when I stand. I look around, suddenly annoyed that I don't even have a desk in here. I'm so unprepared to start classes, it's not even funny. But I'll worry about that later. Right now, I just want to loosen up a little. I've had exactly enough alcohol to lower my inhibitions, but not so much I'm not aware of what I'm doing. Before the last couple of sips of alcohol, I had been convinced that all I needed for a proper party was in my room with my laptop and the vodka. Now though, my curiosity has been piqued. I've seen how mobsters party; now I want to see how bikers party. I give the dogs one quick look and find that they're curled up together beside my bed. It's crazy to think I was once scared of them.

A crash sounds outside my bedroom door and then loud screams followed by a chorus of laughter. Before I can think better of it, I swing the door open and peer down the hallway. A suffocating strain is put on my chest at the sight before me. Ryan is pressed up against the other side of my bedroom wall. His head is tilted back against the wood paneling, his eyes closed. A woman, curvy with jet black hair, drapes herself over him. Her lips are attached to his neck, her pelvis rubs against his, and her hands travel up his abs. Words fly through my head at such high speed they threaten to fly out of my mouth.

Whore.
Bitch.
Skank.

Something primal strikes me. I have to grip the doorframe to keep myself in place. It's stupid, this jealousy. Wanting Ryan when I've barely seen him for two months. Wanting him after he was such a bastard. There's just always been something about the things I can't have. I want them more than anything.

"Princess!" Duke's deep voice sounding behind me makes me jump. Ryan shifts his head, staring me down with angry, bloodshot eyes. A quick look at Duke, and I see he's leaning up against the wall with a grin on his face. The sickly sweet scent of pot wafts off of him. His normally rigid posture is slack and his eyes are unfocused. In his left hand is a bottle of whiskey, and in his right is a lit cigarette that's nearly burned right down to the filter.

With my eyes back on Ryan, I back up until I'm next to Duke. Taking the bottle of whiskey from his hand, I bring it to my lips and suck in as much of the vile stuff as I can without breaking eye contact with Ryan. Lowering the bottle, I lick my lips. His body vibrates in irritation, his jaw ticking as he fights to keep himself still. Duke fumbles behind me, throwing a heavy arm over my shoulders.

"Again," Ryan says huskily, giving the woman on him a gentle push. Oh, he wants to do *this* again. She pauses for a moment then continues her ministrations on his neck, her right hand reaching down to cup his dick through his jeans. His lips part. I've seen enough, but I can't help myself. I bring the bottle to my lips and suck down twice as much as the last time, never letting my eyes leave his.

"Again." And just like last time, I take another draw from the bottle. Duke watches us, his eyes slowly moving between Ryan and me.

"Something going on here?" he asks. Ryan's eyes cut to Duke and then narrow when they fall on me. I don't know what his problem is, but he's pushing me in ways I can't handle. I shake my head and turn to Duke. My belly is a flutter with a mass of nerves. I think I'm either going to be sick or pass out, perhaps both. My head is swishy, and my knees feel a little weak. Perhaps I imbibed a little more in the comfort of my room than I realized. I can't chicken out, though. I want to prove that I can handle it here, and that means not running away to my room every time something happens that's even remotely uncomfortable.

"I want to have fun," I say. Duke tightens his grip around my neck and gives Ryan the cockiest smirk I've ever seen.

"Princess wants to have fun," he says, leading me toward the kitchen, past Ryan and that stupid bitch who still hasn't let go of his neck. With every step that brings me closer to Ryan, my heart rate speeds up little by little. Brushing past them, a calloused finger reaches out, wrapping itself around my pinky. His touch sends waves of heat and bolts of anger through my entire body. I don't want him touching me, but my body craves it. The more distance I put between us, the farther our arms must stretch to keep the contact. And we do for as long as possible. A quick look back, and I find Ryan's arm reaching out, his index finger slipping from its grip on my pinky. We lose contact, and suddenly I'm not nearly drunk enough for this shit. Turning my attention toward the kitchen, I bring the bottle of whiskey to my lips, intent on making everything so blurry I won't be able to remember what Ryan's touch feels like.

"What are you up for?" Duke's breath washes over my face, an olfactory reminder of how high he is. I check my nerves in the hallway and bring my face to his.

"Anything," I whisper, letting the word drawl out in a husky breath. Really, I could fall over right now with how terrified I am of my own actions. If I thought I was in over my head with Ryan, I'm not sure what I'm thinking as I lead Duke on. The smile on his face is blinding. He leads us through the kitchen, where men I've never met play poker. Women who are nearly naked flank their sides. One conspicuously has her hands beneath the table, and the man beside her looks like he's having trouble focusing. I turn away quickly. It's not much different through the rest of the house, where people have crowded into smaller groups and talk amongst themselves. Out of the corner of my eye, I catch a few couples making out up against walls, or in the corner of furniture. Through the open windows in the living room, Ruby and Jim, she in his lap, entertain another group in the sun porch beyond.

We round the corner to the foyer and exit through the front door, making our way down the deck. We pass men in vests who smoke cigarettes, grope the women who stand beside them, drink straight from the bottle, and even what looks like a coordinated fight between two of the prospects, but I can't make out who it might be.

We make it to the barn before it quiets down enough to really hear anything of substance. The closer we get to the cracked barn door, the more it smells like they're burning sage in the barn, only wetter and sweeter. I know better than to assume they've lit incense to help soothe their nerves. The smoke coming from the barn is thick and stings my eyes more with every approaching step. I take another drink from the whiskey bottle and shake off the shiver that runs up my spine. Now that we're out here, I'm less nervous than I was in Ryan's presence.

"This is why I like you, Princess. Underneath that little girl act, you're wild."

Tears spring to my eyes as a flurry of emotion bursts inside of me. I barely contain the scream that wants to escape. My chest rises and falls with labored breaths. I push my body up against the front of his and whisper, "I'm no little girl."

His arm falls from around my shoulders and cups my hip, his fingers splayed on my ass cheek. He lowers his face, his eyes darting to my lips. The energy's changed between us, and suddenly Duke, my friend, is Duke with the piercing blue eyes and the firm grip on my ass. His fingers kneed my pliant flesh, and I press into him.

"No, you're not," he whispers and lowers his lips to mine. His kiss is rough and persuasive, like he's trying to convince me of something. But I don't need to be convinced of anything in the state I'm in. I want it all. No matter the disaster I'm going to face tomorrow, I want to enjoy the trip down the rabbit hole tonight. I open my mouth, inviting his tongue inside. I keep my eyes closed tight, trying to block out the feel of his goatee against my skin. Ryan doesn't have a goatee, but if I focus on the way his tongue slides against mine enough, maybe I can block the differences out. I let myself drown in the idea that it's Ryan who's wrapped himself around me, whose dick is pressing up against my stomach, and I become greedy, needing more than he's giving me.

He speeds the kiss up hungrily and then slows it down, withdrawing his tongue until he's merely placing chaste kisses on my corner of my mouth.

"You taste good, Princess." His voice is a painful reminder that it's not Ryan here with me, that I'm self-medicating. But it's not enough because Ryan's in the house with that stupid bitch. His neck must look like a victim of domestic violence by now with how hard she was sucking on the skin. I wonder what else she sucks on that hard.

"Shut up," I snap against his lips. Duke's eyes focus for a moment as shock registers on his face. Then he's descended on me again. I take my frustration out on his mouth as I nip and suck at his soft lips. Slowly, we slide to the damp grass and tangle in one another's limbs. Every time he grunts or moans, I find myself irrationally ticked off. I try to limit how often I hear his voice by keeping his mouth busy.

His body covers mine, his right hand trails up the outside of my bare thigh. Fingers drag over my jean shorts. My body responds to the attention immediately as I dampen my underwear. I let my head fall back into the grass, arching my back in anticipation. Clenching and unclenching the muscles in my lower stomach, my breath hitches as Duke unbuttons the top of my shorts and then tugs down the zipper in one smooth movement. His thumb circles the top of my pants and then dips below, brushing against my soft curls. My body tenses as his thumb makes contact. Moving in a clockwise motion, he keeps his speed steady. My core pounds with a wanton need, pushing me to the edge. As he slips a single finger inside, I think back to Ryan wrapping his cracked pinky around mine when the tire blew in the van, the ride into

Nevada, and even his angry rant. As I dissolve into a thousand little pieces, the only face I can see is the same one that's been haunting me for the last two months. I bite down on my bottom lip to control the scream as my muscles tighten and I spasm around Duke's finger.

Barely coming down from my release, Duke moves off of me. His middle finger is pointed up, covered in my juices. He dips it into his mouth and sucks it clean. Looking more sober than he has all night, he adjusts himself in his jeans. I prop myself up on my elbows and stare up at him in confusion. A mixture of shame, embarrassment, and fear overtake me as he gives me a cold look and turns to walk away. The more distance he puts between us, the more painful the rip becomes in my chest. *What have I done?*

I want to ask him where he's going, if I did something wrong, and even beg him to come back. I fight the urge to zip up my shorts and chase after him. I have such little experience. I've dated, sure. And I've fooled around. I've had sex. But never have I let some dirt bag finger me in a damp field before. Never have I just been left like this before. And never have I wanted to just disappear this much before. So I don't chase after him, I don't even zip up my shorts. I just lay there, in that field, for as long as I can take the encroaching cold. Silent tears stream down the sides of my face as I stay perfectly still, in the same exact position he left me in, feeling like the most pathetic person to ever live.

I drag my zipper up, catching my index finger in the process. It throbs, but I force myself to ignore it as best I can. Just then, the night sky lights up in an explosion color so vibrant it makes me blink away the spots that dot my vision. Fireworks shoot high in the sky, like missiles they wheeze through the air and then burst with pops. I watch them, mesmerized by how lovely bolts of fire and light can be in the near total darkness surrounding me. Lying here, alone with the fireworks, I whisper to myself, "Happy Independence Day."

Chapter 14

Whatever is begun in anger ends in shame.
- Benjamin Franklin

TELLING RUBY I wanted to get a job wasn't the best of ideas, in retrospect. True to her word, she talked to Jim about me helping down at the shop, and he agreed that he could use the help. After what happened with Duke at the party, I thought better of working with them, but it's not like I can say anything. I should be grateful for the work, but really, I'm too nervous to feel much of anything else right now.

"How should I answer the phone?" I ask, standing behind my new desk, surveying the space. I raise my eyes to meet Jim's. He's got his hands on his jean-clad hips as he smiles at me.

"I don't care," he says with a shrug. I tilt my head to the side and fold my arms over my chest. This has become a thing between him and me.

"I need specifics, Jim," I plead. We've been over this. My father always had a specific way of doing things. There was nothing in my world he didn't have an opinion on, and he was never shy about letting me know how he preferred things. Jim, on the other hand, is so laid back it's frustrating. The only thing he ever cares about is club business. Everything else, he defers to Ruby.

"Okay, how about 'Forsaken'?"

I twist my mouth up, thinking on that one, and finally decide, "I'll ask Ruby."

"She knows more about running this business than I do."

"I'm not surprised," I say with a smile. Jim stretches out his arms with a smile and waves me off as he leaves through the front door to the office. As is typical with him, he hasn't given me any instruction. I have a mountain of paperwork on my desk that I think needs to be sorted. Or filed. It might be a stack of invoices that need to be paid. I don't even know.

I flip on my work computer and wait for it to boot up as I eye the stack in front of me. The sheet of paper on top is a photocopy of a receipt for a turkey sandwich from two years ago. I can't understand why Jim would have kept this, much less photocopied it, but it's not really my call. I set it aside and scribble RECEIPTS on a sticky note, for later reference.

The old desktop computer is up. I spend a good half an hour poking around to see what kind of software Jim has installed on this thing. He has small business accounting software, a spreadsheet program, and some kind of part-ordering program. The first thing I do is find the operation manuals for the programs online and save copies to the hard drive just in case I need them in the future. The rest of my morning is spent sorting through the paperwork. I find more receipts for luncheon items and even a few for beer runs. There are, maybe, five receipts that relate directly to the business in here.

My head pounds in confusion. Surely there *must* be a good reason Jim has all of these food receipts that date back some more than three years. I mean, how else do you explain stacks and stacks of photocopied receipts for everything from fast food to condoms? After finding *that* one, I'm just glad I didn't find one for an escort service. Not that the guys have to pay for it—they might—I just have no idea what to expect anymore. Giving up for the time being, I rest my head on my desk and let the world slip away.

THERE'S DROOL POOLING in the corner of my mouth, and my heart's beating a million miles an hour. It takes me a moment to figure out what's going on. Last I remember, I was laying my head down to try to clear my thoughts. A chorus of laughter sounds from around me. Picking my head up quickly, I try to wipe the drool away as inconspicuously as possible, but I've been caught.

Duke and Ian laugh heartedly from across my desk. It's the first time I've seen Duke since the fourth of July. That lingering residue of shame is suddenly thick on my skin once again. Unable to meet his eyes, I focus on Ian.

"What do you guys want?" I pull myself up straight in my chair and wait for a response.

"Just saying 'hi' is all," Duke says. Out of habit, I look at the person who's speaking to me. Duke's blue eyes betray his smiling face and relaxed demeanor with their intensity. I don't want to notice this, but I can't help it. No matter how difficult the answer, but I can't stop myself from wondering why. Why did he take me to that field, and why did he use me, and then just leave me there?

"You've said it. Now I've got work to do." I look away from both of them to re-straighten the stacks on my desk. Ian leaves without a single word, but Duke remains. Now that we're without an audience, I feel on slightly better footing.

"What do you want?" I snap. Duke's blue eyes bore into mine. He takes long strides to reach me, and, when he does, I'm cornered. Standing up from my seat, I pull back into the wall behind me. Invading my personal space, he places his hand on my hip, fingers splayed across my backside, just like the other night.

"Don't touch me," I whisper. He doesn't retreat. Instead, he moves in closer, blocking everything else from my line of sight. All I can see and smell is him. But everything about him reminds me of Ryan, and that's painful. Because while Duke may be a dirt bag, Ryan's a bastard, but the bastard doesn't want me. Neither is any better than the other, but at least I don't feel as inconsequential with Duke as I do with Ryan. He may have left me in that field, but at least he saved the degradation for afterward, which is more than I can say for Ryan.

"You like it when I touch you, Princess," he breathes into my ear. Pulling back to meet my eyes, he licks his lips. With all my might—which isn't much—I shove back on his chest. At that exact moment, the office door opens and there stands Ryan. He's got a few days' worth stubble on his chin, a dirty, wrinkled white shirt on under his leather best, and once again, black jeans with black boots.

"Give us a minute," he grinds out. For a split second, I pray he's talking to me. I'd gladly leave right now if only I had the option. But it's Duke who removes his hand from my hip and steps away, leaving me in an even less comfortable situation than I was in when Ian left me alone with him.

"Are you fucking him?" Ryan asks. He's in a mood where he apparently can't be bothered with pleasantries, not that he and I have anything pleasant to say to one another. All I really want to tell him is to go choke on a sock, but since I know I don't have the courage to do that, I lift my chin, refusing to answer.

"I said," he repeats, moving closer. "Are you fucking him?" He stops at my desk and, instead of coming around, cornering me like Duke did, he places his hands atop the Formica surface and leans in. "Well?"

I blow out a breath and clench my eyes shut for just a moment before all of my battling emotions get the better of me. I was safe once, back in Brooklyn with my father. I may not have been happy, but I was safe. I could have lived that life, ya know. I could have married Leo. I could have dealt with the hand I had been dealt. Instead, I'm here, in this small town where the closest Macy's is almost two hours away.

"We grew up together," he says. His arm muscles tense under the weight of his upper body, his hands turning red. "He's the closest thing I have to a best friend. But I don't want him fucking you."

"You don't want me, remember?" I snip. His eyes flash something fierce and angry before he shuts it down.

"I never said that," he responds.

"*I don't fuck little girls.*" I spew his words back at him. His eyes search mine; the earnestness that shows through them makes me squirm.

"You gonna hold that over my head forever?" The tiniest of smiles breaks free through the angst of his features.

"You'd deserve it if I did," I whisper, suddenly breathless. He pushes off the desk and stands up straight.

"I mean it. I'm not going to be happy if I find out you let him fuck you."

"Oh, shut up," I say. It's the first thing that comes to mind and then bolts out of my mouth without permission. Back in Brooklyn, had I told any of my father's men to shut up, he would have likely let them slap me around for being so disrespectful. But Ryan, he doesn't even blink.

"Don't let him fuck you," he grits out. His jaw barely moves, and his eyes are so still, so intent on scaring me into submission, that he begins to looks statuesque in his anger. His heightened emotions sets something off within me. From every gentle touch to every cold word he's said, I can't keep up with the flurry of emotions this man can run through in a single minute. And I'm done acting like an idiot just because I thought he was a good guy. He's not. Lesson learned, and it's time to move on. Part of moving on is refusing to let him intimidate me.

"Go to hell," I say, stomping my way toward the door to the outside world. I barely make it past him before he's turned, and is brushing my arm. I stop immediately. His touch is so gentle, almost reverent in the way the back of his dry hand glides over my exposed forearm.

Bending his head down, the tip of his hair brushes against the top of my head. He smells faintly of stale beer and peanuts and another scent I can't make out. Something fruity, but still somehow human.

"Thinking of him touching you, having his fingers inside of you—I'm already in hell." I blanche at his admission, my face heating, and I run so fast out of the office I barely make it outside and to the sidewalk before my vision blurs with unshed tears.

Chapter 15

What loneliness is more lonely than distrust?
                                        - George Eliot

SHAKING OFF HIS admission—what he knows—I head up Main Street, looking for someplace, anyplace to go. I'll head back to work. Eventually. But right now, I just need some space. Main Street is a long, mostly straight stretch of road that acts as a main thoroughfare through town.

Two blocks north of the shop, I find myself in familiar territory. I recognize the shops and restaurants from mine and Ruby's shopping trip the other day. Even though the prices were a little more expensive than I would have liked, Ruby insisted that it's good business to patronize the local establishments, even if we can get a lower price in another town. I filed that lesson under "Things about Small Town Life" and stowed it away for future reference.

I cross Main Street and head up Laurel Street, relieved to have remembered where Universal Ground is located. Patting my face down for any stray tears that may have escaped, I take a few deep breaths and head up the half-block to the front door. A slice of wind picks up, reminding me that I'm not in Brooklyn anymore, and even in the middle of summer here, it's perfectly acceptable to wear a long-sleeved tee-shirt.

The doorbell chimes as I walk in. The girl from the other day, Nic, is behind the counter again. This time, she's covered her body art up with a three-quarter sleeve blue plaid button-up, and her long, pin-straight blonde hair is pulled back in a low ponytail. Approaching the counter, I give her a quick wave. I cringe inwardly, afraid it was too friendly. The way she moves behind the counter, at least last time I was here, reminds me of a skittish woodland creature. Like she's going to run off at any moment. And I really don't want her to run off. She's about the closest person to my age I've met since I got here. Even if we never become friends, I'd like to remain friendly. Universal Ground is in a good location, just close enough to the shop, and not too far away from Redwoods College. Back in Brooklyn, I had a 'place.' It was in a nearby café. I'm hoping to replicate that here.

"Hey," she says, meeting my eyes. Her head bobs, looking around me. "You're alone today?"

"Yeah," I respond flatly. After the disaster in the office, I'm feeling a little braver than usual. So I ask, "You're not a fan of my aunt?"

"You just dive right in, don't you?"

I shrug with a smile.

"Ruby's cool, I guess. It's the rest of them I don't care for." Agreeing with her makes me feel like I'm betraying my family, so I opt for a subject change.

"This might sound desperate, but what on earth does a girl do in this town? I mean, I think you're the only girl my age I've met." Her shoulders shake with silent laughter. "Stop laughing at me," I protest. "I'm surrounded by dirty, skeezy men. All.Day.Long. I need a friend who can keep his hands off his crotch for like five minutes."

And now she's dissolved into hysterics so loud that the other patrons are turning and staring.

"You seem pretty cool," she says, sizing me up. "But I don't hang with the MC or their chicks. Sorry." I'm taken aback by her response. I'm trying so hard to put myself out there and to create some semblance of normalcy in my life. But between Bastard and Dirt Bag, and now this, I'm about to give up. But before I do, I'm going to try one more thing.

"One," I say, arching my eyebrow and setting my hands on the counter. "I'm nobody's chick. Two, I'm not a part of the club. And three, I *am* cool. And I need a friend. So—please—don't make me be that desperate girl who begs strangers to be friends with her, because that's just pathetic."

"Fine," she smiles, and I think it might be genuine.

"Wait." I put my hand up in mock seriousness and say, "You're not agreeing to hang out with me just because you feel sorry for me, are you?" She puckers her lips to avoid bursting into laughter again.

"Does it matter?"

I don't even need to think about it. I need a friend and she's accepting.

"No, not really," I say. A customer walks in behind me and waits patiently while we wrap up the chit chat and I order my coffee. On the back of my receipt she writes her number and her name. As I wait for my coffee, I pat down my jeans pockets, realizing I don't have a mobile phone anymore. I haven't needed one since I don't go anywhere without Ruby—or at least, I didn't. I mentally add a mobile phone to my list of things I'd like to get. It's been easy to forget all I left behind, but now that I'm out on my own, I find myself wanting for the things I no longer have. Still, I will forever hold the few things I still own very close to my heart.

I have the money to buy and pay for a phone—I just don't want to be wasteful with that money. It's plenty to last me for a while if I spend little, but not so much that it could pay for rent, a car, and all of life's other necessities for very long. Then where will I be? So I try to check myself and to stop wishing for all of the things I don't have.

Nic lets me know when my order is ready. She tells me to text her, something the landline at home can't do. I say, "No phone." Her eyes nearly bug out at my confession.

"That's kind of fucked up," she says in a whisper. Covering my mouth to suppress the laughter at her expression, I head out of the shop with my steaming cup of coffee. The embarrassment of not having a mobile phone eats away at me as I make my way down the sidewalk back toward Main Street. I've probably been gone for a good half an hour now, at least. Jim is bound to notice I've run out, and, no matter how casual he is with everything, I can't imagine bolting on my first shift would sit well with him.

Lost in my thoughts, I hold the cup of coffee close to my face and take a sip of the yummy goodness. Just as I reach Main Street, I hear the familiar rumble of a motorcycle. One of the few things I've learned in my short time in town is that, just like Mafioso have territories, so do motorcycle clubs. I've seen all but two or three independent riders breeze through town. Every other motorcycle—and there are plenty—belongs to a member of Forsaken. Hearing a motorcycle's deep rumble through the streets sends my senses into overdrive. I stop in place and peer down the street.

My eyes nearly bulge out at the sight of Ryan on his bike, his black hair blowing in his face as he steers into the right lane. Looking around, I realize I have nowhere to hide, and the doors to the closest shops are too far away to sneak into. I opt for standing there, waiting to be seen.

The second his eyes travel to my side of the street, he grimaces and darts around the corner, bringing the Harley to a stop halfway up the handicapped ramp for the sidewalk. A nearby woman shrieks in surprise. My heart is racing, but I give no other response. I don't want to encourage this kind of behavior. Not that I think anything I do will convince him to change his ways.

After cutting the bike off and pushing down the kickstand, he strides over to me, all muscles and anger in such a pretty package.

"Where did you go?" he asks sharply and without regard to volume. I simply wave the cup of coffee while giving him a flat look. I mean, hello. "Come on," he says, reaching out for me.

Even though I'd love nothing more than to climb on the back of his bike again and to drift off into that exhilarating freedom, I can't do this. Ryan is like a game of Russian roulette. It doesn't matter how it ends, it's not going to end well. I shake my head from side to side in protest. He takes a step forward, puts his hands on his hips, and squares his shoulders.

"I'm not fucking around. Get on the bike." The way he growls when he says bike lights a fire in my belly. I don't know what his deal is, but I really want to find out. And if I don't get on the bike, I might never figure him out. But I'm not about to just give up and act like the little girl he's so keen on accusing me of being. I take a deep breath, gathering what little courage I have, and I purse my lips, then shake my head. Bringing the cup of coffee to my mouth, I take a sip. Before I can even lower the cup, he's on me, breathing down on my face. With his knees bent, his eyes search mine, cold and demanding. Inwardly, I shrink, but do my best not to let that show in my body language. Looking up at him, I move my occupied arm out of the way and lean into him.

"You must be joking." But he's not. He rips the cup of coffee out of my hand, letting it fall to the pavement. I want to pick it up and throw it away properly, but I have no doubt that's a bad move. He takes my hand and drags me toward the resting Harley. Without letting go of me, he swings himself onto his seat and then gives my arm a tug. I climb on after him, just as unsure of what I'm doing as the first time I attempted this. Wrapping my arms around his midsection, I settle in.

He starts up the Harley and navigates it around the wary people, then out onto Laurel Street. We breeze through narrow residential streets, eventually finding our way back to Main Street. Neither of us attempt to say anything as he guides us through a part of town I've never been in. The north side of Fort Bragg is separated by a river inlet from the rest of town. Only a few businesses and some higher-end townhomes reside on this end. We travel right on through the north end of town and keep going. I curl into his back and rest my cheek against his leather vest.

We ride for a good half an hour until the tension in Ryan's back dissipates and he turns the bike around and we head back to Fort Bragg. We're close to town when he veers off to the right on a quiet road that hugs the last bit of land before you hit water. A new housing development is going up on both sides of the road, which will effectively cut off the view of the ocean from Main Street. I've barely been here two months and already I find myself attached to the mostly untarnished view. I scowl at the construction crews as they outline the lots and move their equipment around on the dirt.

Slowing down, we hang a right onto a dirt road that doesn't look drivable. Not that it matters, since Ryan clearly knows what he's doing and where he's going. Heading directly toward the water now, we come to a stop just as my nerves start to frazzle by how close we are to the shoreline. Cutting the engine, Ryan waits patiently as I stumble off the bike and cling to him for support. Now that I'm on my feet, I take a step back from him. He's brought me to a beautiful place, and so far he's stopped being an asshole, but that doesn't mean he isn't capable of dropping me off the cliff. Not that I think he'd really do that or anything.

Off of his Harley and onto his feet now, Ryan stares at me with a blank expression on his face. He reaches his hand out, palm up, and gives me a short nod. I don't even think about it. I place my hand in his instantly and slide up beside him. We walk hand-in-hand down the rest of the trail, following it as the dirt path narrows and dips until we're standing at the end, with the ocean directly in front of us.

"It's beautiful," I say, appreciating the gesture.

"Did you fuck him?" He asks quietly. And just like that, just like everything with him, all of the beauty surrounding us is shattered, leaving behind splinters that I know I'm going to be stepping on for weeks. Because just like that, I'm reminded who he is, but more importantly, I'm reminded who he isn't. He isn't romantic; he isn't gentle. He's pragmatic. I have nowhere to run out here. I yank my hand away and fold my arms over my chest.

"Why do you care?" I ask, folding in on myself. I'm such an idiot, getting on the bike with him, letting him order me around. Old habits die hard, I guess.

"Because I do."

"What kind of answer is that?" I wait for a response that never comes. There's something he's not telling me—I can feel it. Even though it eats me alive, I save my breath and choose not to ask what it is. He's not a child who can be coaxed into giving up information he doesn't want to. Well, neither am I.

In the following silence, I look around. This is my first trip to the Pacific Ocean, though it is a little lackluster considering the tension between the two of us. Underneath my feet is wet, compacted sand. But up ahead, sharp blue and greens, and even the occasional burst of red, glisten from the rising shore. I'm so mesmerized by the colors in the sand as I approach the water line that I don't even hear him come up behind me.

His fingers lightly drag along my spine from the bottom up, and then back down again. He moves achingly slow, never breaking contact. My breath hitches, my heart picks up speed, and I curse myself for enjoying his touch. His sudden tenderness settles in my chest, striking a blow. Allowing him to be hot and then cold and back and forth can't be good for my self-esteem. I don't move, but I emotionally detach myself from the situation in an effort to think clearly. So I ask the question that's been on the tip of my tongue since he stormed into the office. Expecting him to deny it, I gear myself up for a fight.

"Did you fuck her?" I ask.

"Who?"

"That woman from the party."

"Yes," he says. There's no awkward pause or uncomfortable groan. It's like a slap to my face, but that's not something I can deal with right now.

"Where?"

He moves in, the front of his body flush with the back of mine. Bending his head down, his breath heats the side of my face. "Against the barn. I followed you out there. I saw him. With his hands on you, touching you. You laid down in that field for him. You let him shove his finger in your pussy. You let him taste you." The way he says the words, detailing my transgressions, it makes me sick to my stomach. I move to step away, but his arm snakes around and holds me in place. Tears spring to my eyes, my gut twists in knots, and everything apart from him melts away. I can't feel the chilly breeze on my skin, nor can I smell the salt and seaweed of the ocean. All I have left is his indignation.

"I fucked her. I don't even know her name. I had to fuck her, or I would have killed him. Right there, in front of everybody, I would have slit his fucking throat to teach you both a lesson. So instead, I fucked her. So hard she asked me to be careful. But I couldn't be careful, because you let that fucker in your pussy."

I close my eyes, letting the tears fall on my cheeks. The picture he paints is so vivid I can practically see it happening.

"I don't want to hear anymore."

"Does it bother you, knowing I fucked her?"

"Yes," I admit, having no fight left in me.

"Good."

Chapter 16

*Walking with a friend in the dark is better than
walking alone in the light.*
                                        - Helen Keller

IT'S BEEN A few days since Ryan pulled that stunt in
town and took me to the beach. I've been trying not to
think about everything he said, because that just brings up
the shame of what I did with Duke in that field. It
reminds me that I couldn't even stand to hear Duke's
voice when he was inside me because I'd wanted it to be
Ryan. But Ryan is a whole new kind of screwed-up that
I'm not used to.

I need to walk away. I just don't want to. Just a few
short months ago, my entire life had been planned out
before me, and nobody had asked if it's what I even
wanted. It was what was expected of me. And I hated
every single second of it. The moment I got in the van,
everything changed. Nobody around here gives a shit
about manners or projecting an image. They just are who
they are. And as much as I hate the bullshit, I love the
insanity. I didn't realize it then, but during that first ride
on the back of Ryan's bike, I picked him. He was the first
thing I chose in what might be forever. And for whatever
reason, in his own fucked-up way, he's kind of picked
me, too. Now I just have to figure out a way to keep him.

Instead of spending any more time thinking about
Ryan, I've been focusing on moving forward. I have an
appointment with an admissions counselor at Redwood
College in the coming days, and just yesterday, I got my
new mobile phone. When Jim and I were at the shop the
other day I asked him where I could get a phone, and,

much to my surprise, he had several burner phones. It's nothing fancy, but it does the job, and Jim says the club's covering the cost.

My phone chimes, letting me know I've received a text. It's from Nic, telling me she's outside. I roll my shoulders and stretch my sore muscles. I've been working at fixing up my room for most of the day. It's almost looks like someone lives in here now. Shoving my phone in my back pocket and grabbing my hoodie, I rush out of my room. My room has a sliding glass door that opens onto the front deck, and there's a sliding glass door in the rec room next to my bedroom. I could leave the house out of either, and they'd both be closer to Nic's car than the front door, but I can hear Ruby's voice in the kitchen. I don't want to run out without telling her where I'm going.

Approaching the kitchen, I realize only too late that this was a bad idea. Ruby's seated at the breakfast table, laughing with Ryan, whose back is to me. Picking her beer up, she meets my eyes and waves me over. Entering the kitchen, I see Jim and Ian in the other two chairs. A long, glass pipe lays on the table, remnants of burnt weed scattered about. Two silver lighters sit in front of Ian. The air is heady with the sickly sweet scent.

I'm standing behind Ryan when he leans back in his chair and gifts me a devastating smile. His gray eyes wrinkle in the corners. Caught off guard by his demeanor, I don't see it coming. He reaches his right arm behind him and around my waist, pulling me in and down on his lap before I can even make sense of the movement. I knew he had long arms, but that was like some sort of octopus move or something.

Shocked, and unable to control my reaction, I twist in his lap and glare at him. His bloodshot eyes and exaggerated pupils make my chest feel like it's on fire. Of course he's being playful, he's high. Every emotion I've tried so hard to keep at bay boils to the surface in one swift motion. Barreling back with my left arm, I swing around and make contact with his right bicep. He laughs.

"Stop it!" I scream, leaning into his face. The volume makes him jerk backward and drop his hands from around my waist. I just need him to stop touching me. This on/off switch he has where he can so easily be attentive and present and then a moment later be so cold and callous is making me crazy. I can feel it in my bones. I think it might actually be making me insane.

Taking advantage of his surprise, I move off of his lap and stand just as my phone chimes. *Nic.* She's still out in the car waiting for me. I don't have time for Ryan's shit. I move away from him and look up to leave. I'd forgotten about Ian, and Jim, and Ruby. They clearly haven't forgotten about me. Each has a different look about them, and yet every arched brow and pursed set of lips tells me that none of them approve. Whether they disapprove of the way I spoke to Ryan or his attention toward me, I don't know.

I look down for just a moment before forcing myself to raise my head. Looking Ruby in the eye, I softly say, "I'm sorry". Her eyes widen, her lips thin out, and just when I think she's going to scold me, she throws her head back and her body shakes with silent laughter. Soon Jim and Ian follow. I don't have any earthly idea why they're laughing until they taunt Ryan for getting yelled at.

"Nic's here. Can I still go?" I ask.

RIDE

Ruby composes herself as much as she can and says through her laughter, "I keep telling you, you don't have to ask permission. Just be safe, and call any of us if you need anything. And keep an eye out, okay?"

"Where are you going?" Ryan asks. Setting a switchblade knife on the table, he leans over and grabs the pipe. He flicks open the blade and scrapes the debris from the bowl of the pipe and blows on it. He doesn't meet my eyes.

"Out with Nic," I say, reluctant to give him too much. I want him, but not like this. I want him to just be better. I've seen the better side of him, and I have to believe there's more of that underneath the surface.

"And where exactly is *out with Nic*?" He pulls a plastic baggy from his jeans pocket, sets it on the table, and pulls off a chunk of weed. Putting his elbows on the table, he rests his cheek against one of his hands and looks at me. This is the way I like him, even if I'm not crazy about the question. More freedom or no, I still have men ordering me around and keeping tabs on me. I guess some things never change.

"I don't know." I shrug. "This town is like three miles wide. How far *out* can we really go?" I raise my arms, palms up, and lift my shoulders.

"When will you be back?" His voice lowers, but not in a peaceful, calming manner. With every word, he sounds more detached than before. It's unnerving how his stare penetrates everything within me. Every lesson I've been taught about manners and kindness, even the ones I've learned by the back of my father's hand, fall away when Ryan's around. Frustrated, I look to Ruby. She's watching Ryan carefully.

"Let it go, son," Jim says, breaking the silence. His deep baritone reminds me who's in charge around here. He and I have developed a rapport over the last couple of weeks, but that doesn't mean he doesn't intimidate the hell out of me.

"Bad move, Pop." Slowly, Ryan turns his head, facing the opposite direction. Dropping his elbows from the table, he leans back in his chair. "You drag two charters across the country, shoot up fucking *Carlo Mancuso*'s house, take his kid, and after all of that fucking effort, you're letting her walk out of this house without having a man on her?" I tense the moment his words register. I try to fight off the panic flaring in my chest, but it's no use. I lock my jaw, taking deep breaths in order to keep my irrational stupidity from being too obvious. Of course it's about *that*. For a brief, ignorant moment, I thought he might possibly be worried about *me*.

"This sounds like club business," Ruby says, pushing away from the table. Ian watches guardedly, eyes moving between Ryan and Jim.

"Stay," Jim orders, pointing his finger at her, then down at her chair. I've heard him snap at the guys before, and I've heard him cop an attitude with a parts rep over the phone. I've never heard him sound as mean as he does in this moment. He sounds so much like Ryan, it's unnerving. Probably wisely, Ruby sits back in her seat, pushing her hair over her shoulder and folding her arms.

My phone chimes from my back pocket again. I silence it as quickly as I can, fumbling over the buttons in the process. Leaning back in his chair, Jim stretches his arms out and slinks down in his seat. "This isn't club business, it's family business."

"Whatever's going on between you two," he says, pointing at me and then Ryan. I find myself unlucky as his eyes travel to mine and stay put. "It ends now. I don't want you thinking you're going to be on the back of his bike, or in his bed. You're not one of them whores like your friend, and you're not Old Lady material." Tears well in my eyes, not so much from the order he's laying down as much as from the humiliation of him saying this in front of everyone else.

Though Jim's speech feels like it's gone on forever, it's really only a few seconds. Just enough time for Ryan to push off from the table.

"Where do you think you're going? We're not done here." Jim stands, his voice echoing off every nook and cranny in the house.

"You can consider this family meeting over," Ryan says. As he stands from his seat, he jabs his index finger into the wooden table. "I fuck who I want, when I want, and how I want. Don't get going on some power trip, Old Man, and start thinking you own me. I ain't Ma."

Disappearing from the kitchen, Ryan leaves the absolute most uncomfortable silence in his wake. I stand awkwardly for a moment before heading toward the front door. Just as I reach out and pull on the knob, Jim walks up behind me. He's spitting mad from the look on his face, and the set of his shoulders. I turn around to give him my full attention, like I was raised to do for a man in a position of power. In a faux-friendly move, Jim leans against the front door, effectively shutting it.

"I don't know what you're doing to him, but that little tantrum he just threw is the kind of shit that's going to get him killed. You reign in that pussy of yours, or it's going to end up costing him his patch."

"I don't," I begin, but he cuts me off.

"I don't want you to think I'm the villain here. I'm just a guy, trying to do what's best for my family and my club. He's third generation Forsaken. I'm not going to let a piece of ass fuck that up for him."

"I'm sorry," I whisper, trying desperately to keep the tears in my eyes from falling down my cheek. The words *I'm sorry* are so played out, I can't even stand it. My body feels like it's being covered with slime and dirt as they spill out of my mouth. I feel like it's all I ever say anymore. I'm sorry for trying to save my brother. I'm sorry for betraying my brother's trust. I'm sorry for not being pretty enough, or sexy enough, for Ryan. I'm sorry for being too young, or I'm sorry for being too naïve. I'm always sorry, and I'm sick of it.

"Why are you saying this to me?" I ask, knowing better, but I do it anyway. He loosens his stance, and brings his hand up to my face. Gently cupping my chin in his palm, he raises my eyes to meet his. I fight back the urge to turn away, knowing he'll just get his way in the end anyway.

"Because you talked," he says and lets go of my chin. Rounding the corner, toward the other side of the house, he disappears down the hallway that leads to his and Ruby's bedroom. Everything slowly comes into focus. The conversation outside of the motel cabin and Ryan's sudden change in mood that night suddenly makes sense. Before that, he freely looped my pinky in his, joked with me, and smiled at me. He drew me in with every touch, with every word, and with every unspoken hope that I let build in my heart. I thought we could work through all of his mean, and his angry. But this, I don't know if this is something I can fight my way through. Or if I should. For all the club's talk of freedom, these men are no freer than my father's men are. They're all just soldiers in another man's army.

I rush out of the house and down the drive just in time to see Nic backing up her old sedan. I wave her down, and she stops the car, as I close the distance between us. Now that I'm close enough, I can see the firm line of her brow and the pout of her lips. She is really displeased with me, and I can't have that.

Getting in the car and plopping in the seat, I throw my hands up in the air and grovel my ass off. "I am *so* sorry."

She purses her lips, narrows her eyes, and swings the Corolla out of the drive and onto our desolate dirt road, before gaining speed and flying around the corner onto Sherwood. Neither road is very wide, and she's going a little faster than I'd like, but I remain silent. I had to beg her to come pick me up tonight then kept her waiting. She's obviously not happy with me.

"I hate that house," she grumbles, but doesn't offer up anything else. I try, unsuccessfully, not to take her comment personally. But that's my home—for now. The things Jim said to me were positively unnerving, but there wasn't really anything I could argue with. He didn't threaten me or hurt me. He just laid it out for me. I've no doubt that he'll do what he thinks he has to in order to keep things the way he likes, but for now, as long as I avoid Ryan, I think I can stay on Jim's good side. I do have, after all, a lifetime of practice at toeing the line for a powerful man. I know this part all too well. It may make me sick to my stomach to think of going back to being that person, but it looks like I don't have a choice. Ryan is off-limits. And not in that "he's no good for you" kind of way, either. Jim said I would end up costing Ryan his patch or his life. I can't let either happen.

Chapter 17

*Men seldom, or rather never for a length of time and
deliberately,
rebel against anything that does not deserve
rebelling against.*

\- Thomas Carlyle

"DO YOU REALLY want to head back to the house and
watch a movie?" she asks. She's calming down some,
which is good. I rest my head on the headrest and close
my eyes.

"Not really," I say. I try to keep Jim's harsh words
from infiltrating my mind, but it's tough. I want to be
shocked, and maybe even appalled, at the way he
approached the situation. But I'm not. My father may
have said everything with thinly-veiled code words and
under the guise of concern, but that doesn't mean he
wasn't ever mean. Because he was. And Jim's mean, too.
Ryan isn't any better. And I guess all women like me,
stuck in their world, can do about it is to learn how to
play along.

"Do you ever get sick of it?" I ask, allowing myself
to vent for the first time in months. The last time I really
let it out was with Adriana right before Sal's wake.

"Sick of what?" Nic asks, turning her head just
slightly. She drives into town and turns before she hits
Main Street. I've no idea where we're going, nor do I
care.

"Everything," I say a little louder than I intend to.
"People bossing you around, people being mean, people
being selfish. Just all of it. I kind of just want to forget."

"I'm pretty much always sick of people," she says flatly. She swings the car around the corner and parks on the side of the road. Everything is mostly quiet, with the exception of a well-lit, two-story house up ahead that has a large, loud crowd assembled in front of it. Turning off the car, she twists in her seat to look me in the eye.

"Listen, I don't want to piss you off, but I think you need to hear this whether you want to or not. The club seems cool and all, but it's not. The guys may be okay on their own, but the patch owns them. I know you're kind of here by default, but just don't forget this, okay? The club destroys people."

I fight the urge to tell her she's wrong and that they saved me from a life of misery—or worse, no life at all. Had Ruby and the club not shown up, I might be like Sal right now—with a bullet in the center of my throat, my dead body on display in the center of my father's front parlor. That would be good for business. Nobody would be stiffing him on their protection money.

"Is this about your dad?" I ask. Before I can say anything else, she turns and opens the driver's side door and gets out. I follow suit and fight to catch up to her as she hurries down the street toward the party up ahead.

"Sorry," I say. I feel like I can't get anything right lately—not with Jim, not with Ryan, not with Nic. The only ones who I don't seem to be pissing off are Ruby, PJ, and Tegan. Even then it's spotty with Tegan. She's kind of a grouch late at night.

"I'll be ready to talk about my shit when you're ready to talk about your shit. Until then, let's just get too fucked up to think about everything that's wrong with the universe, okay?"

The closer we get to the house, the more intimidated I become by the prospect of walking inside and being amongst all of these people. Michael's told me about every single party he's ever went to in varying degrees. He's always been most fond of regaling the debauchery that goes on—and he's often a part of. Why he thinks his sister would want to hear about him getting laid, I'll never know.

The heavy thumping bass rattles everything around me as we near the house. We pass by similar houses, all simple two-stories that show their age, sitting center on narrow lots fenced off in chain-link. People, mostly college-aged, stand around in the front yard drinking beers and talking in small groups. As the crowd thickens, Nic takes my hand and pulls me through the sea of people until we reach the front steps.

Stopping, she looks around, bites her bottom lip, and leans in. Her brows draw together as she says, "Go on in. I have to make a call." I just nod my head and make my way up the steps on shaky legs. Where in the hell is she going? She brings me to this house with no one I know, in a part of town I'm unfamiliar with, and she takes off less than a minute later?

At the top of the steps, I turn and survey the people around me. For the first time since I left New York, I'm in a crowd of people where not a single one of them seems to be wearing a leather vest, nor do I hear any Harleys in the distance. Despite being a little nervous about the fact that Nic left me here, a bubble of excitement starts in my chest and begins to spread. I've never been to a house party before, at least not outside of the fourth of July party that Ruby and Jim threw, but I don't count that. Everyone in attendance was affiliated with the club in one way or another. But here, it looks like I'm out from under the watchful eye of the club. A grin slowly creeps up on my face, and I can't control it.

"You look way too happy to be here," a masculine voice says from beside me. Slightly startled by the intrusion into my thoughts, I jerk away and shoot the perpetrator a dirty look. He's a young man, close to my age, if not a bit younger. He has broad shoulders and a firm jaw, both of which I'm sure he'll grow into. His brown eyes look almost black under the dull porch light. Giving me a sheepish smile, he shoves his dark hair off his forehead and blows out a breath.

"Sorry," I say, waving at the crowd before me. "I was just thinking."

"About," he prompts.

Without even considering it, I say, "This is the first time since I got to town that I'm not entirely surrounded by leather vests." I give him an encouraging smile, but it falls flat. His face drops, his lips forming a line.

"You're with the club." It's more of an accusation than anything. I bite back a snide remark and opt for remaining silent. I expect some kind of vindication of how awful the club is—something along the lines of what Nic said in the car—but instead, he just walks off, leaving me in my place. My first meeting having gone over so well, I decide it's best just to keep to myself while I wait for Nic to return, just a moment later.

"Okay, let's get this party started," she says, rushing up the stairs while shoving her cell phone into her back pocket. She leads the way through the front door and into the living room. Much like Ruby and Jim's party at the house, here people are sprawled out on furniture, making out, drinking beer, and someone in the corner is sucking on a large glass bong. It's not until we've walked through the living room and into the kitchen that the crowd thins out.

On the kitchen table, Nic finds a bottle of tequila, and while tequila and I have never been good friends, I don't argue. I just want to forget everything Jim said. All of his words hit me right in the heart. I try to remind myself that it's just the way these guys speak, but it's hard.

"Come on," Nic says. She crosses the house, clearly knowing exactly where we're going. We walk down a long hallway that dead-ends in a room that looks near identical to the living room. There are fewer people back here, but the ones that are appear to be close to passed out. Nic finds us a spot on one of the three couches randomly scattered in the room. Taking a swig of the tequila, she coughs, nearly choking on the vile liquid. She hands the bottle off to me. Tilting my head back, I take a hearty drink as fast as I can, trying not to breathe while doing so. As I suspected, it's horrible. My throat constricts, and my stomach churns at the taste, but I keep it down. I hand the bottle back to her and focus on regulating my breaths. If I don't keep myself calm, the tequila is going to come back up.

We sit here in silent as the minutes pass, and I begin to wonder if this is the typical college experience. Every time Adriana would talk about some "killer" party she'd been to, or a frat house, or a bar that she's too young to legally be in—I wonder if this is what it was like. If they're at all similar, I don't see the appeal. A woman stumbles into the room, her eyes glassy, and her makeup a total disaster. She grips the wall to keep herself upright. To the right of the room, there's a door that leads outside, into the backyard most likely. It takes her what feels like forever until she finally makes it there. Swinging the door open, she bends at her waist and expels her stomach's contents into the unknown. Immediately, I cover my mouth, close my eyes, and try to block out the sound of her heaving.

Nic hasn't slowed down any on the tequila, and I can tell just by looking at her that she's three sheets to the wind. Her elbows rest on her knees, and her left hand holds the bottle loosely, letting it dangle close to the floor. Her right arm is bent, propping her face up as she sits there, hunched over and swaying slightly. If she drinks any more, she's going to be like the woman across the room, and that's not a very pleasant thought. I reach over and grab the bottle from her hand and take a small sip. I didn't prepare myself for the strength of the liquor. It knocks me back, sending the room spinning for just a moment. When everything stops spinning, I realize that maybe Nic isn't the only one who shouldn't be drinking any more, and I set the bottle on the floor.

"You're drunk," I say, smiling at her. She gives me a goofy, carefree grin. It's the first time she's ever looked so relaxed. The other times I've seen her, she's been so pensive.

"I am, and I don't care." Her voice is lighter than normal. She continues to sway lightly while smacking her lips. Her eyelids close for a second before flying open and then fluttering closed. I give her a light shove to keep her coherent. She's definitely in that blissful place where nothing matters.

Pulling my cell phone out of my back pocket, I realize we've been here longer than I thought. No wonder she's wasted.

"Who did you call earlier?" I ask. Nic isn't much for sharing when she's sober, so I'm hoping she's a little chattier when she's been drinking.

"My brother," she says, letting out a sigh. "He's got to meet with the principal tomorrow morning. I was making sure he knew that." I try to remember what Ruby had said about Nic's family, but I'm drawing a blank. There was something in there about taking care of her brother.

"Where are your parents?"

"Dad's in San Quentin, and mom's probably out there somewhere sucking dick," she says, as casual as can be. I can feel the shock register on my face. The more information she gives up, the more I like Nic after she's had a bit too much to drink. She gives me a sideways glance and blows out a breath. "Well, she probably is."

Going back to her happy place, Nic lays back into the couch and curls in, trying to get comfortable. My muscles tense as I realize she's probably trying to take a nap. I really don't want to be stuck in this shithole all night, and neither of us is in any condition to drive anywhere. Looking at my phone in my hand, I bite the bullet and find Ryan's name in my contacts list. Thankfully I listened when Ruby insisted I program each of the guy's numbers into my phone.

HI, I text. It's lame, but I don't know what else to say. I just, kind of, want to talk to him. Before I can even focus my attention elsewhere, my phone chimes.

WHERE ARE YOU, the text reads.

HOUSE PARTY DOWNTOWN, I respond. Now that I've texted him, I'm not sure I should have. Sticking my phone back in my pocket, I pick up the bottle of tequila and take a few sips. My stomach rolls with each drink, but I don't stop. Everything in my life feels like a rollercoaster out of control. From the fact that I'm even here instead of back in Brooklyn to the thing with Ryan and whatever the fuck went down with Duke, I just don't know which end is up anymore.

ON MY WAY, he texts back. I don't even try to pretend I don't want Ryan here right now. I'm working my way to being buzzed enough to do as I'd like without concern over the consequences.

Looking around the room, I decide that I'm not much for house parties. At least not the non-Forsaken kind. This is lame. I could be sitting in my bedroom drinking to my heart's content, and that would be a lot more comfortable than this is. Beside me, Nic's soft snores fill the mostly empty space. In the time since we sat down to now, the crowd has thinned, leaving us alone on the couch. Giving Nic a shove, she wakes immediately.

"You're such a lightweight," I say. She nods and blinks away the sleep. Bringing her right hand up in front of her face, she distances her index finger half an inch from her thumb.

"Just a little," she says with a slight slur. "It's just been a hard life. I wanted to forget. Like you said, I just want to forget." Her voice is so small as she repeats my words from earlier. She looks so fragile, all curled up there on the couch. Her thin frame folded in on itself, her dark makeup somehow still intact, and her dyed blonde hair something the state of Texas could be proud of, she gives me a heartwarming smile.

In the distance, I can hear the rumble of a motorcycle, maybe two. Through the slightly muffled, but still loud, music, I listen to their approach. Nic doesn't seem to notice, or if she does, she thinks nothing of it. Now that I can hear Ryan coming, I'm not quite certain what Nic is going to think of it. She's been adamant about keeping the club at arm's length, and as much as I want to respect that, it's going to be hard to maintain a friendship with somebody who wants absolutely nothing to do with my family.

I can't hear the bikes anymore even though the music has been turned down. Conversation has largely stopped in the other rooms. Heavy footfalls sound from the hallway beyond us. I cast Nic a nervous glance, only to find her eyes are on mine. She slowly shakes her head and says, "What did you do?"

Before I can answer the question, Ryan and Duke round the corner, leaving a trail of silence in their wake. Neither wear particularly joyful expressions. If the guy on the porch's reaction to my association with the club is anything to go by, I'm guessing the people here aren't exactly fans of Forsaken. But none of that matters.

I look up at Ryan, and a smile overtakes my entire face. All of a sudden, I feel all warm and swishy inside. Maybe Nic isn't the only one who's a lightweight. He says nothing as he strides over and reaches out a hand to help me up. I take it graciously and, when I'm on two feet, I use the opportunity to slip my pinky around his. Once I've done it, there's a brief moment where I think I'm the biggest idiot on the planet. But then he grips his pinky around mine, and those familiar bolts of heat shoot through me. Being this close to him, our pinkies wrapped around one another, it feels intimate in a way I'm unable to describe.

Leading us through the house, never losing contact, Ryan moves slowly. Behind us are Nic and Duke. She's much more alert now than before, with her arms folded over her chest and her feet practically stomping into the carpet below. I check back on them to see Duke walks behind her, keeping his hands to himself. And despite the excitement coursing through my veins at being so close to Ryan, I can't help but be annoyed by Duke's presence. I still haven't forgiven him for leaving me alone in that field, and I don't know if I ever will.

Outside the house, and down the steps, we reach the sidewalk. The crowd is down by at least half now even though it's not even all that late as far as parties go. Duke and Ryan's Harleys are parked between two cars just off the sidewalk.

"We're heading out, Brother," Duke says, his giant hand now wrapped around Nic's tiny one. Her eyes are narrowed as she passes me, hissing words of revenge. I try to bring myself to feel bad, but I don't have it in me. Ryan's here, and I don't really give a shit. Duke backs his bike out and signals for Nic to climb on. She shakes her head twice before he points his finger at her, giving her a warning glare. She finally concedes, and in no time they're off and down the road on their way to God-only-knows where.

Ryan gives a slight tug on my pinky, bringing me up against his side. Leaning down, his breath brushes against my temple.

"Where do you want to go?" he whispers. My face heats from his nearness, and my stomach flips with possibilities. Emboldened by the situation, I look up at him, and say just as softly, "Your place." A wicked smile paints itself on his face, and a dark, mischievous glint dances in his gray eyes.

Chapter 18

Hearts will never be practical until they can be made unbreakable.

- L. Frank Baum

RYAN CLIMBS ONTO his bike, taking two helmets from the handlebars. He flashes me a smile and hands me a helmet. I strap it on and climb on behind him. Wrapping my arms around his midsection, I ask, "How did you know exactly where I was?"

He twists, looking at me over his shoulder, and says, "I didn't."

Starting the bike and pulling away from the curb, I'm left to ponder that comment. He was looking for me. I mean, Fort Bragg isn't that big, but still. It's the effort he's putting forth that makes me think maybe this isn't such an awful idea after all. The bike rumbles beneath me as we dart off down the road. All of my concerns over what we're doing here—despite Jim's demands—wash away, and it's just me and him and the bike blowing through the wind.

We ride for a few minutes before I finally recognize some landmarks. We pass the high school and then the community center. The school is in poor shape, but the community center is much newer. During one of my and Ruby's trips into town, she swung by here to show me some of the town's highlights. I doubt I'd be able to find my way home from here, but it's something. In the distance, the community hospital shines brightly. I remember this landmark because Ruby said after I've been around the club enough, I'll know all the back roads to get to the emergency room.

Ryan pulls up to an old cottage that's seen better days and into the narrow driveway on the right side of the property. Underneath the carport, he cuts off the bike and we climb off. My legs ache just slightly from the ride, though it's nothing like the previous times I've been on his bike. Ryan leads me inside the house. He's walks so fast, and I'm trying so hard to keep up with him that I barely notice how sparsely furnished the place is. We breeze through the kitchen and then a living room, both of which reek of stale beer and another odor I choose to ignore for the sake of my own sanity. At the end of the hall just off from the kitchen, he opens a door and stands aside, welcoming me in.

I find myself a mass of nerves and excitement as I peer into Ryan's bedroom. It isn't very big, only two-thirds the size of mine at Ruby's and Jim's, but he has even less furniture in here than I do in mine. Stepping inside, I find the room to be cooled by a rickety ceiling fan that's already on. It's one of those combination fans that has the small lights attached at the bottom. To my right is a tall and narrow window that's covered with a thin black fitted sheet that does almost nothing for privacy. On the same wall as the window is a full-sized bed and, beside that, a wooden crate that's being used as a nightstand. On top of it is an overflowing ashtray and a collection of open condom wrappers. On the floor beside the crate is a combination of empty beer bottles and even a whiskey bottle with the cap off.

Behind me, the door closes, shrouding the room in darkness. The already cool, dark walls look almost black. The faint sliding of metal against metal and the click of the lock send a shiver down my spine. He's locked the door, and I can hardly see anything. I take the few steps needed to stand beneath the ceiling fan. Reaching up with my right hand, I wrap the tips of my fingers around the bottom of the lower chain, but a rough, calloused hand comes out of nowhere and wraps itself around mine. His touch is gentle as he closes his grip around my curled fingers and lowers our hands. My arm bends at the elbow, Ryan guiding it down to my collarbone, with his right arm creating a cage. Though tender, his movements are carefully thought out and painfully slow. I can't escape the way we are now.

Stepping up behind me, his hips hit me at the bottom of my ribs, painting me a clear picture of what he has on his mind. Savoring the moment, I lean back against his chest and let my eyes flutter closed. My heart beats so frantically I worry it might jump right out of my chest, almost painful in its effort.

He moves so slowly, so intent on torturing me, as the cracked skin of the knuckles of his hand trace a line from the top of my head, down to my chin, swooping inward, and slipping down my neck. My breath hitches, my lungs straining to calm the nervous pant that Ryan's creating in his wake. Somewhere in the back of my mind, I'm not focused on his touch. This entire situation just feels wrong.

He's always so hot and cold with me, and I'm not supposed to even be here. It was only a few hours ago that Jim issued his warning, and yet here I am. Boredom and liquor have once again impaired my judgment enough that I'm making a poor decision. First, Duke in the field. Now, Ryan in this room that looks no better than what I assume could be compared to a motel that rents room by the hour. I try to pull away, but he tightens his grip on my hand, locking me in place, and brings his lips to my ear. "Relax, baby. I know you want this."

I do want this. I want all of it. If only he could just tell me he wants me, that I should fight to have whatever this is with him, I will. But I need him to tell me he wants me.

"Tell me you want me," I whisper. The words come out so quietly, I'm not certain he'll even hear me. But he does. He places his lips on the shell of my ear, his warm breath coating my cheek. His left hand slides down my chest and over my breast, brushing my nipple beneath the fabric of both my shirt and bra in the process. I bite back a gasp that threatens to escape.

"I want to fuck you," he says, pushing his pelvis into my back. Biting harder on my lip in surprise, I clamp my mouth shut to stop the yelp from escaping. His left hand slides down the front of my belly, over my tee-shirt, landing on the top of my jeans. His warm fingers slip under the thin fabric, rough skin against soft skin.

Flicking the button open on my jeans he whispers, "I want to fuck you. *Hard.*" It's not lost on me that he wants to fuck me, but I still don't know if he wants *me*. There's a world of difference between the two.

He takes a gentle bite of my ear and drags the zipper of my pants down. His fingers slide up my cotton panties and then dip inside, just hovering there at the top. A furious pounding escalates between my legs. The little *thud, thud, thud* builds to a furious roar as my muscles lock and my lungs stall. It's been so long since I've been touched like this—if I've ever been touched like this. He moves slowly as his fingers slide past my curls and press against me when they slide back up, one finger slipping between my lips. So pent up with frustration, my skin nearly breaks out in a sweat at the contact. Though brief, it's powerful, the way he touches me. And he knows it, too. I'm so awkward and ill at ease that he has complete command of me right now. If I had a lick of sense or self-respect in this moment, I'd run.

But I want this.

Turning around despite his firm grip on me, I place my hands on his hips just below his vest, and rub small circles on his jeans with my right thumb. I look up into his bloodshot eyes and blanch. Though his eyes bore into mine, they're unfocused. It's like there's nothing there beneath the surface. He licks his lips and brings his hand behind my head. Before I can stop him, he pulls me in and his lips are on mine. Plush, moist, and demanding, he takes ownership of my very soul.

All fear, and disgust with myself washes away at lust igniting in my body. Bringing my hands up around his neck, I try to pull him closer. As if I could consume him. As if he would let me. Our lips slide against one another, my nails clawing at his neck. Turning us and bringing my back up against the wall, he reaches out and places his hand over my beating heart. His eyes suddenly come alive, and his lips turn downward at the corners.

"Why did you do it?" he asks. Confused, I stare at him without an answer. "Why did you tell that cop where to go?" I blink back at his words. Though they're formed as a question, they sound more like an accusation. And this is a topic I've steadily avoided for two months now. I can't talk about this with him—or anyone, really—because the truth isn't pretty.

"You must have had a reason," he says in a pained voice. Tears pool in my eyes, and I slap away his hand on my chest. He pushes on my sternum in protest, keeping me against the wall. "Just tell me you had a reason."

"You wouldn't understand," I bite out in anger. Unable to look him in the eyes while we're talking about this, I focus on the patches on his vest. Nic said the patch owns them, and I guess it does. Like the oath Tony took to my father's family owns him, the patches Ryan wears on his vest own him even after he takes it off for the night.

"Try me," he says, shaking his head. I scrunch my eyes shut and let the tears fall down my cheeks. Not here. I can't do this here. But he isn't giving me much of a choice, so with trembling hands and lips, I try to explain. Beyond any sense of humility and reason, I want Ryan to want me. Not just to fuck me, but to want *me*. And I don't know if he ever will.

"I was property, not a person," I whisper. The truth of the *why* burns at my heart. Sniffling and calming myself down, I force myself to meet his eyes. Gaining my emotional strength back, I let the tears staining my cheeks dry where they are, and I bring my hands up to his wrist. With one swift motion, I yank his hand away from my chest. He's done protesting. Now he's just some fucked up mix of sad and angry, but the fight has gone out of him. For now. I don't know what to do with sad and defeated. It's not something I've seen often.

"No reason to be a rat," he spits, some of the fire returning. I like his fire, as much as it hurts. It's familiar, and even when it's painful, I appreciate a little familiarity. But that word... rat. It hurts in a way I don't want to admit. In both my father's and Ryan's worlds, the worst thing you can be is a rat. There are a few offenses that will automatically get you a bullet to your throat.

Killing a Made Man, raping a kid, and being a rat. I can't be a rat.

"Don't say that."

"It's the truth, isn't it? You've got a big fucking mouth, don't you?"

"No," I say more forcefully now. "I thought I was helping my brother. I just trusted the wrong person."

"Don't you see now? *That's* why *this* can't happen," he says. His shoulders vibrate with irritation as he seethes the words. And there it is—it doesn't matter if he wants me or not. The patch owns him. "I don't like being told what to do, baby. So here's what's going to happen—I'm going to fuck you out of my system."

He moves in, his lips back on mine, and every sense of reason flies out the window once again. He's a bastard, but maybe if I let this happen, he'll be out of my system, too. We can't keep going on like this.

Pulling at clothes, discarding shoes, and yanking off socks, we're a hurried mess of limbs as we strip one another down to our underwear. His hands wander over every inch of my skin he can touch. Pulling me away from the wall, he walks me backward to his bed. His left side is free of tattoos, but his right shoulder and chest, down nearly to his elbow on both his chest and his back, is a large piece of artwork. It looks like a mass of chains and painted steel—some sort of armor. Beneath the beautifully intricate piece is a falcon with its wings spread along his right side, spanning from beneath his pec down to his hip bone.

The back of my legs hit on the sharp edge of the frame, propelling me onto the mattress. He crawls on top of me, covering my body with his own. This could be good—us, together, despite it all. I bring his face down to mine, kissing him gently. But he won't have any of that, turning the kiss rough and forceful despite my silent pleas.

We're still in our underwear, but I'm so ready for him to take his off. Reaching down, I feel that they're boxers. I didn't catch sight of them in the hurried undressing. I slide my thumb in between the waistband and his skin and draw them downward, but a strong, masculine hand reaches up, stopping me.

Pulling his torso up, creating a gulf between us, he says, "Turn over, baby." So caught up in the moment, I don't ask any questions. I turn over and push my torso off the mattress and pull my hair over the front of my shoulder to give him access to my bra. Instead of unclasping my brand new black bra—that I bought especially for an occasion such as this—he places his hand on my back and pushes me down onto all fours. The linen sheets are rough on my skin and thinned out from age and abuse. They smell of cigarettes, weed, and body odor—none of which are especially pleasant—but it's the lingering smell of a fruity perfume that makes my stomach roll. From behind me, I can hear something rip and then a quiet rustling. Two calloused knuckles graze along the side of my butt cheek, bringing the fabric of my matching black boy shorts away from my body. They pull the fabric to the side.

Realization dawns on me what he's about to do, and I squeeze my eyes shut in anticipation. I've never had sex like this before. Not that I've had much sex, but it's never been like this. The nerves return, and my muscles tense. He places his knees between my legs, slowly spreading me farther apart. His left hand sneaks between my legs, dipping inside of my boy shorts and along my slit. I bite my lip, barely controlling the moan. His touches are so soft, and so few, that every little contact is like a compact little fire spreading across my skin. A strong hand comes down on my back, pushing my face sideways into the mattress—forcing me to breathe in the stale perfume from the last slut he's taken in here—as he guides himself to my entrance.

There's no gentle stroking, no loving preparation. Once he finds my center, he pushes himself inside, unbothered by how very unprepared I am for him. A loud groan escapes from his lips as his nails dig into the skin of my back. He brings himself back out and then slams inside. My muscles tense, my eyes fill with tears, and a tightening sensation claws at my chest. I feel raw and battered by the time he slows his pace. His fingers never find their way to my core again, instead, he holds onto my hip with one hand and my back with the other. He wasn't being coy when he said he wanted to fuck me hard. In and out, one razor sharp pounding after another, and I'm so tense, so frustrated, so not enjoying this, I'm close to crying again. If I didn't feel like a whore in that field with Duke, I certainly feel like one now.

"Do you want me to stop?" he asks through a grunt. He slows down just a little, and I open my eyes, relieved for a break from the battering he's doling out.

"No," I lie. Because I want to give him this, and I *need* to give myself this. He's treating me with, maybe, an ounce of kindness, and not much else. My eyes catch sight of the varied mess of open condom wrappers. I'm nothing more than another cum dumpster right now. This is what it means to be a Lost Girl—at the club's disposal, fucking without emotion, fucking because Forsaken wants to fuck. Not because I want to make love.

RIDE

These men are off-limits to you, Ruby had said that day at the rest stop. She said it before I even really understood why. Now I do, only it's too late to avoid getting hurt.

He picks up speed again, and it isn't long before he's grunting and jerking behind me, still providing no relief for me. When he stills, I hear him sniffle and mutter, "Fuck."

Once he pulls out and backs up, I quickly turn over and fold into myself, looking up at him. Blood is streaming from both of his nostrils. He tries, and fails, to wipe it away. Once he gets it under control, he grabs my arms and pulls me out of bed. I don't fight him. His jaw ticks; his gray eyes stare me down intently. I could convince myself he's hurting in some way, from the sad look in his eyes, but I'm done trying to convince myself he gives a shit about me. Bringing me to stand before him at arm's length, he says, "It's you or my patch. Your pussy's good, but it ain't that good."

He pulls the condom off, tosses it in a nearby overflowing wastebasket, and adjusts his boxers. His eyes dart around the room, looking everywhere but directly at me. Before I can stop myself, insults come flying out of my mouth in Italian at rapid speed. Still, he doesn't meet my eyes. He just ignores me and, after a beat, walks to the door, unlocks it, and leaves the room, slamming the door behind him. The last thing I see as he goes is a large tattoo of a Nordic warrior that spans his back from shoulder to shoulder and down to the line of his boxers.

I rush to get dressed, trying to ignore the uncomfortable burn between my legs. Pulling on my pants and then my shirt and jacket, I can't help but wonder what's become of me. I've lost all control, all sense of morals—everything. Once I have everything as it was when I entered this room, I wait until I have the courage to walk out. I have no idea what's going to await me. Eventually though, I tell myself that whatever it is can't be as bad as being stuck in here waiting for Ryan to come back. He doesn't want me here. He's made that abundantly clear. I can't bring myself to cry anymore. I just want to scream and let out some of my anguish and humiliation. I've been trying so hard to fit in here, but everything I do just makes me feel even more used and dirty. I hate it. *I hate this.*

Gathering my courage, I pull on the knob and walk into the hall. Directly to my right is a full living room. Ryan sits—still in just his boxers, in a Lay-Z Boy. Duke is across the room, sitting in a kitchen chair. His emotionless face turns murderous as he looks between me and Ryan. The attention makes me cringe, and want to retreat back the bedroom. But there's no way out through there. So I soldier on and walk the rest of the way into the room. Forsaken, at least seven in number, sit on couches, and the floor. A few stand. The one on the floor is rolling a joint and lighting it. Ryan leans over, snagging the first hit, completely ignoring my presence. If he's trying to make me hate him, he's fucking succeeding.

"Duke's going to take you home," he says, not even turning to face me. Duke's attention snaps to Ryan, his eyes narrowed with anger. Ryan pulls in on the joint, holds it, and then releases the content of his lungs. "Just fucking do it, or she's going to have to take a cab."

Duke shoots up from his seat, points a finger at Ryan and says, "We're going to fucking deal with this later." Walking over to me, Duke places a hand on my back and leads me out of the house. "Come on, Princess."

RIDE

Chapter 19

The truth is, everyone is going to hurt you. You just got to find the ones worth suffering for.
- Bob Marley

EVERYTHING ABOUT THIS moment makes me feel weak and exposed. The men in the living room watch as we leave. From the corner of my eye, I see Diesel lean in toward Ryan, who's bent forward, his full back tattoo proudly on display. Diesel takes a moment just staring at Ryan before shaking his head and saying, "No good, brother. This is no fucking good."

Diesel shoots up and darts past us and out the front door. I pause, but find myself pushed forward by Duke's hand on my lower back. The reminder that he's touching me makes my skin crawl. I can practically feel the layer of humiliation on my flesh. The last thing I need right now is to be reminded of sins not so long forgotten.

"Fucking idiot," Duke mutters, his eyes on Ryan's back, as we walk out into the cool night air. Walking down the driveway and onto the street, I see the bikes parked along the sidewalk in front of the house. How did I not hear so many bikes approaching? They definitely weren't here before.

He swings onto a basic black Harley and grabs the helmet from the handlebars, passing it off to me. I strap it on my head and move to climb onto the back of the bike, but he stops me. With his hand on my wrist, he looks me in the eyes, and just stares. His expression is cold, merciless.

"This isn't you, Princess. Letting him fuck you and toss you out like that? It ain't right."

His words sting me. The hypocrisy alone makes me want to call Ruby and beg for a ride back to the house.

"And what about what you did?" I ask in a snapping tone, unwilling to let him get away with that comment.

"I'm an asshole."

"Don't do it again," I warn, narrowing my eyes at him. A warm smile spreads across his face.

"You're so much like her, and you don't even know it yet."

"Who?" I ask, still throwing sass.

"Your moth—" he says, cutting himself off, and then finishing with, "Ruby." He turns away, looking at the road ahead, and mumbling to himself. My heart stops with what I think he's said, but then I think better of it. For a brief, pathetic moment I allow myself to think that just maybe he knew my mother. I open my mouth to ask, but think better of it. I'm really not up for anymore surprises tonight. Though I file this away for later. I've avoided mentioning my family in Brooklyn since I've been out here. It hurts too bad to think of them, let alone to ask any questions. So I just pretend like they're all gone, figments of my imagination. And as much as I love my brother, and my aunt, and even in my own twisted way my father—it's just easier to pretend they don't exist. At least, not unless I have to. The one person I've wanted to talk about is the one who's more of a mystery now than ever—my mother. It's time I asked Ruby about her.

I climb into the back of the bike and hold onto his waist, careful to keep as much distance from us as I safely can. Even though he's just giving me a ride home, it makes me feel even filthier having another man between my legs less than an hour after Ryan was there.

RIDE

He starts the bike and we pull away, darting down the street faster than I'm used to. The wind whips around, chilling me to the bone. It's an exhilarating feeling—being this exposed and unarmed from the elements. The slicing wind gives me something to focus on that's not Ryan or Duke, or any of the other bullshit. We breeze through town, making it to the house quickly.

The second Duke brings the bike to a stop in front of the house, I go to climb off. He turns the bike off and climbs off after me. I remove the helmet from my head and hand it over, but he doesn't take it. Instead, he reaches out, grabs my upper arm, and pulls me toward him. Instinctively, I drop the helmet and push on his chest.

"Don't touch me!" I scream. He flinches slightly, but doesn't loosen his grip.

"Shut up, Princess." Duke's deep voice resonates in the stark silence of our surroundings. "You need to listen to me. Trigger's fucking up. He's always been wild, but lately, he's fucking losing it." He lets that settle before continuing. "He hasn't taken orders like this from Jim in years, and he's not handling it well. Just leave him alone."

"Fine," I snap. A knot twists in my stomach. "After what he did, you have nothing to worry about." Duke sticks his chin out, releases my arm, and steps away. Picking up the helmet, he gives it a good look, then shakes his head.

"This thing is done for," he mutters and gives me a flat look. Inwardly, I cringe. I know better than to drop a helmet. The moment you drop them, they're useless.

"Then buy a new one," I say, and stalk off to the house.

"You're welcome for the ride," he yells.

"Bite me!" His laugh only irks me further, and I respond in a rare fashion by flipping him the bird. Reaching out, I go for the door knob. Before I can reach it, the door opens and before me stands Ruby. Her face is turned down, and her brows are drawn together. Whatever it is, I don't have the energy for it tonight.

"Didn't you leave the house with Nicole?" she asks. I squeeze in past her and turn around, crossing my arms over my chest. She closes the door as Duke starts up his bike and flies down the drive. She turns and leans against the door, her face still contemplative.

"Yeah, I did. She got wasted and couldn't drive." I blow out a frustrated breath. I really just want to get in the shower, but Ruby's obviously got something to say; so I wait.

"Alex, um, some things are happening. We're going to tighten security up a bit." Fidgeting, she pushes off the door and strides to the kitchen table, where she picks up a beer and takes a long pull before looking me in the eyes.

"What's going on?" I ask, following her into the kitchen.

"Nothing," she says way too quickly, her voice lifting at the end.

Ian strides into the room behind me and plops into a chair. He keeps his eyes on Ruby as he says, "The truth, Ma."

Her face scrunches up and she takes another drink of her beer. Setting it down on the table, she fixes me with a look of sorrow. "Gloria called. Your cousin Tony's figured it out. Gloria's said nothing, but Tony had her visit your father and uncle, who are being temporarily held at Rikers. Tony wanted her to talk to Carlo and

Emilio about what he knows. She hasn't, but she's running out of time."

My gut twists in knots and my mouth goes dry. I knew the calm had to end sometime and that the storm would roll in. I'm just not ready for it yet. I might never be ready for it. "Is she okay?"

"Yes, baby. She's okay. We're just going to up security because we don't know when and how they're going to get here."

"They're coming here?" I shriek. Loud footfalls sound behind me and a heavy hand rests on my shoulder. I look over to find Jim's gray eyes, wrinkling at the corners, staring back at me.

"Don't worry," he says.

"Don't worry?" I ask, raising at eyebrow at him. "How in the hell am I supposed to not worry?"

"We'll talk over the details in the morning. Just get some sleep for now," Jim says, walking to the fridge across the room and pulling out a cold beer. Using the bottle opener on his keychain, he pops the top and sucks in a long pull.

"You people expect me to sleep after this?" I let my jaw go slack as my gaze travels from Jim, whose amusement shows on his face. The corners of his mouth are turned up, showing a rare smile. I haven't forgotten that underneath the jovial fatherly mask is a cold-blooded Charter President. I look to Ruby, who is far less amused. She wears a sad smile. Next to Ruby, Ian smirks, his cheek pulling up, showcasing his facial scar in the process.

"You think I'm going to let some fucking guinea take you after all the trouble we went through to get you?" Ian says. I flinch at the word *guinea*. I hate that word.

"Hey, you do know I'm Italian-American, right?" I say, pointing at my chest. Ian just laughs, making my temper flare. I may not have much of a temper compared to everyone around me, but it's not entirely non-existent. You just have to push the right buttons. "Non insultare gli italiani se non vuoi che insulti il tuo club," I say, telling him not to insult Italians if he doesn't want me insulting his club.

"Oh no. Don't you start speaking WOP to me." He breaks out in a full smile now. He's always so serious and quiet, fading into the background, when I'm around. I can't help the smile that overtakes my face at the sight of Ian so relaxed for once. "You're talking to me," I say, a little surprised.

"Don't think this means we're best friends or something."

Rolling my eyes at him, I try to keep the mood playful, even if the nerves in my stomach feel like they're about to go Chernobyl on me. I might need to sleep for a year after the day I've had. "Don't worry, the position's been filled."

"So I've heard. Just don't go taking any cues from her. I don't want to have to kick a brother's ass for fucking around with you." Biting my lip, I look down, and the entire room goes silent. All of the shame and guilt floods to the surface in this moment. Ian's laughter dies immediately, and Jim clears his throat. I can't see them, but I can feel all of their eyes on me.

"What's going on here?" Jim asks. Pushing off the counter, he comes to stand beside me. Gently lifting my chin, he says, "What happened?"

I fight to keep the tears at bay, and succeed, but just barely. "Nothing. Ryan doesn't want me. You don't have anything to worry about," I say. Jim's gaze is cold, not even remotely surprised. Of course, what an idiot I am—Jim knows damn well that Ryan would never trade in his patch for some stupid little girl.

Squeezing past Jim, I cross the kitchen and rush down the hall to my bedroom. Just as I cross the threshold, I shut the door behind me, leaning against it. The pressure on my chest weighs heavily, and my heart beats loudly in my ears. Sliding down the door, my butt hits the floor, and I curl into myself. A rustling noise alerts me to movement on my bed. PJ stands on all fours from the center of my bed and yawns. Her short, floppy ears twitch, her head tilts sideways, and her wispy tail swings so furiously her butt wiggles from side to side. Patting my knee, I welcome her over. Excitedly, she bounds forward, leaping off the bed and crashing into my legs upon landing. I wrap my arms around her wiggling body and give her a smile.

Movement sounds on the other side of the door. Curiosity gets the best of me, and I shush PJ, commanding her to lie down on the floor. Ever the obedient dog, she does as directed, but her excited eyes stay focused on me. Turning toward the door, I place my ear against the wood and close my eyes. My room is the only bedroom on this end of the house, sandwiched between the kitchen and the rec room. People rarely ever pass by my door.

"Leave her alone, babe," Jim says in a whisper.

I hear Ruby hmph and say, "She's upset, Jim. She needs me. When I see Ryan, I'm going to tear him a new asshole."

"You don't even know what happened."

"Does it matter? She's upset, and he did it. That's enough for me," she hisses quietly. I strain to hear over PJ's excited panting.

"Calm down, Mama Bear. Your cub is fine."

"She better be," she snaps and stomps down the hall.

"Fucking women," Jim mutters. "And I know you can hear me," he says a little louder. My eyes widen for a moment before I respond.

"Yeah, well, you're in front of my door," I say back, loudly. PJ jumps to attention, pressing her nose to the closed door, and whimpers at the sound of Jim's departing laughter. I give PJ a grumpy look. Her body jerks forward, tail wagging once more, and then stops.

"Kisses," I say, giving into her pathetic blue eyes. She darts forward and covers my face in slobber. Keeping my eyes closed, I giggle uncontrollably at the loving assault. It's hard to be upset about everything else when PJ gets going. I've never had a pet until now, but now that I have her, I can't imagine being without her. It's amazing how kind and loving animals can be while humans can be so cruel and heartless.

Far too emotionally spent, I decide to skip the shower and instead opt for crashing for the night. It's well past two in the morning, and my body is giving out on me. I don't even worry about changing my clothes as I open my bedroom door a crack and crawl into my bed. Kicking my shoes off and patting the bed for PJ to follow, I snuggle into my pillow and close my eyes. The weight of everything—Jim's orders, Ryan's behavior, the way he felt inside me, the way he purposefully humiliated me in front of the club—slam into the forefront of my mind. PJ crawls in beside me, and I drift off chanting in my head, *I will not cry.*

Chapter 20

Mother love is the fuel that enables a normal human being to do the impossible.
- Marion C. Garretty

MORNING COMES WAY too early. After a fitful night's sleep, I'm not ready to be up yet, but my mind is slowly waking. I try, and fail, to block the words that have assaulted my mind since the moment they were said.

Your pussy's good, but it ain't that good.

No excuse to be a rat.

Do you want me to stop?

Harsh sunlight streams through my bedroom window, covering me in its warmth. Stretching out my legs and arms, I find myself sandwiched. Blocked on both sides by fur, I blindly pat my bed mates down, finding PJ's short double coat on my left and Tegan's long coat on my right. Tegan whimpers at my assault and rustles around immediately, then settles back in. When she's awake, she's sharp as a tack, but asleep, she's useless. PJ stands immediately, looks around, barks loudly, and then rushes out of the room at warp speed.

Blinking my eyes open, I groan at the discomfort of the first sight of the bright sun. Letting out a heavy yawn, I fold my hands over my stomach and stare up at the ceiling. Classic rock blares from the other room, the bass so loud it vibrates the retro '70s light fixture that hangs from my ceiling. This isn't exactly abnormal around here. Anytime Ruby cooks, she blasts the massive stereo system in the kitchen, no matter what time it is. And don't even get me started on her music choices when she makes her *special* baked goods.

Laughter sounds down the hallway, getting nearer, then Ruby busts in, all smiles. With a spatula in one hand and an oven mitt covering the other, her caramel brown hair is shoved up in a messy bun, and flour covers her black tank top and dark blue jeans. Pulling myself up on my elbows, I give her my best smile. It isn't much after the day I had yesterday and the awful sleep I had last night.

"Today's kind of a big day, baby. But first, we have waffles, bacon, sausage, eggs, and toast." She rattles off something about burnt waffles and a flour fight between the boys, but I hear almost none of it after she says Ryan's name. My smile falls immediately, and my eyes narrow. Catching wind of my changing mood, she bounces in place before sliding into the room and shutting the door behind her.

"We got a problem here?" she asks. I shrug and look to Tegan, who's stretched out beside me, snoring. I'm just glad she's facing the other way. She's got some of the worst breath I've ever smelled.

"It's stupid," I say.

"It's never stupid if it makes you sad," she says. I roll my eyes and blow out a heavy breath. I know her well enough by now to know that she's never going to let it go if I don't just tell her.

"Your step-son is an asshole," I say with as much venom as I feel. The level of honesty I'm willing to exhibit in this moment surprises me a little. Ruby, Nic, the club, they're all rubbing off on me, apparently.

"Yeah, he is," she admits. "I tried to steer him into non-asshole territory, but his genes prevailed. That one is just like his father." She snickers and smiles sadly. I force myself to gift her a small laugh before I pull myself up into a full sitting position. Tegan finally wakes beside me, yawns, and scampers over to Ruby, where she sits at her feet.

"How do you deal with it?" It's something I've wondered since our second day in the van. Surrounded by so many men all of the time, being one of the only women in their world—still not totally inside their world. Ruby somehow manages to bring a feminine touch to the club that is at-once comforting and off-putting. If I think about it too much, I'll worry about her now that I know how awful Jim can be.

"You just gotta know your place, baby. Jim gets to yelling, and I wait for him to finish. He gets to acting stupid, and I just wait for him to stop. But you better believe that when he shuts up, it's me who has his ear. I let him be an asshole because it's who he is. Lord knows that man has cared for me and mine in more ways than I've had any right to ever ask of him."

The music is abruptly cut off in the other room, and a moment later there's two sharp knocks on my bedroom door that jar both Ruby and me out of our bonding moment. She moves away from the door and opens it. Towering over her shoulder, Jim looks between us. Flour stains his chest, and he wears a blank expression.

"Speaking of you and yours," he says, his eyes cutting to Ruby. I blush at the fact that he heard at least part of our conversation. These damn walls are paper thin. "It's time we got this over with." Ruby's shoulders sink, and she shakes her head. "Now," he says, in that baritone command I'm beginning to hate.

"Time for breakfast and a family meeting," Ruby says, her relaxed demeanor totally gone now. The last impromptu family meeting ended *so* well, I just can't wait for this one. I just wish that when Jim said family meeting, I could pretend he was going to gripe about the way the toilet paper roll was put on the holder wrong. Taking a moment to compose myself from the impending fear that he knows what happened between Ryan and me last night, I crawl out of bed, only to remember that I'm still wearing yesterday's clothes.

"Oh, yuck," I mutter. "Can I at least shower first?" Ruby's face relaxes as she says yes, but it's Jim's retreating voice from down the hall that once again says 'now' that I listen to. A painful reminder of last night aches between my legs, and my back is stiff in a way it's never been before. Even my hip, where Ryan had gripped me so tightly, aches. So this is what it feels like to be used up and hung out to dry.

Making my way down the hall, followed by Ruby and PJ, I spot Ian and Ryan on the loveseat in the living room, neither looking my way. My steps falter before I suck up the courage to keep moving.

I'm going to fuck you out of my system.

And I suppose he did. The dirt and grim I feel on my skin and in the fabric of my clothes is one thing. I can handle feeling a little dirty. It's the disgust and shame you can't see that makes me want to pistol whip Ryan— maybe Jim, too. Ruby places her hand on my back and gently guides me into the living room, all thoughts of waffles and bacon forgotten. Ryan's eyes snap to mine, then dip down to my clothes. Same jeans, same top that I was wearing when I did the walk of shame out of his bedroom last night. The moment of recognition hits and, very slowly, his eyes travel back up to mine. I can't get a good read on him, but this is neither his angry face nor his sad face. Not that it matters.

"Sit with me," Ruby says, bringing me to the sofa. We sit down, and Jim pulls a chair in from the dining room, setting it down on Ruby's other side. "I need to tell you a story, and I need you to listen. Okay?"

I barely manage to nod. The way Ryan won't stop staring at me, Ian won't even acknowledge me, and Jim looks so sad is unnerving. Ruby angles her body toward mine and places a hand on my knee. Tears fill her eyes as she visibly fights to keep them at bay. She hasn't even started her story yet, and I already feel nauseated.

"I've fucked up a lot in my life. I've been selfish and mean. And the person I hurt the most was the one person who never did a cruel thing to anyone, not ever. My sister, she was always so quiet and kind, ya know?" Losing the battle with the tears, Ruby lets them stream down her cheeks unabashedly. None of the men in the room dare to move.

"I've always been reckless, never thinking how I hurt her. And I didn't mean to hurt her, please believe me. You have to believe me. I just wanted better than I had, that's all. I shouldn't have been so horrible to her." Her voice breaks. Jim reaches a soothing hand out to her shoulder, calming her shaky tears. I don't know what to make of this conversation and the message she's trying to convey. She keeps talking, though it's jagged. She talks about her relationship with my mother. Eventually, the tears slow, and her breathing regulates some.

"Your Aunt Gloria was my best friend. We used to get in so much trouble together." Memories flood my brain, of that last night Gloria and I spent together. She sat me down and had a similar conversation with me. Nothing makes any sense. Gloria talked about my mother like she had this spirit, this whole charming personality that just radiated. She said my mother was her best friend, but the woman Gloria described is nothing like the mother I knew—even before the cancer made her so frail. The woman Ruby describes is exactly as I remember my mother to be—quiet, obedient, kind.

"Gloria used to take me around her neighborhood, showing me off to all the men she knew. They were always older, married. It wasn't a big deal for these guys to take a goomah. She thought one of them could help me out. I had Ian, no education, and in that neighborhood, being some guy's mistress was a couple of steps up from the welfare line." An awful sickness churns in my gut. My father's taken a few whores that I know of over the years. I know how it works. All of her apologies about my mother, and now this—I just want to block it out. If she's going to tell me what I think she is, I'd rather not hear it. I respect her too much to hear that she was my father's whore.

"Did you have an affair with my father?" I bite out, shrinking away from her. A moment of regret washes over me. Curling into the corner of the sofa, I try to create as much distance between the two of us as possible. Her lip juts out as she covers her mouth and lets out a sob. Anger flashes through my limbs. My caring Aunt Ruby is a slut. I scrub my face with my hands, not even wanting to think about the way she betrayed my mother. Minutes pass as I try to process this information. Eventually, Ruby's shaky voice breaks through my bubble of denial.

"I was an awful sister. I was also a single mom with a kid I couldn't afford. I made a horrible choice, but I need you to listen. Even if you hate me, this is something you need to hear." My eyes shoot to hers, and I nearly crumple under the visible weight of her pain.

"I got pregnant. I… wanted to keep my baby." The world spins around me, my limbs shake, my lungs strain to pull in an adequate amount of air, and I'm beginning to wonder if I'm imagining things. "Your father pushed for an abortion until the babies were born. He'd been married to Esmeralda for a few years at that point, and they weren't having any luck."

"What are you saying?" I shriek, unable to control my volume. My muscles tense in a painful contraction. "Why are you saying this?"

"I am so sorry, baby. I loved you from the moment I knew you existed. I named you, I talked to you, I wanted you." A hollow sob escapes my lips as my entire body begins to tremble. I choke out a cry, and then another. Somewhere in the distance of the destruction of my entire world, I see Jim move closer. He wraps his arms around a sobbing Ruby.

But she's not just Ruby, is she?

She's my mother.

And I want to deny it. I want to call bullshit and tell her she's done a few too many recreational drugs over the years, but somewhere in a dark recess of my heart, I believe her. Choked sobs turn to panicked cries as I wrap my arms around my legs and curl into myself. Every stupid fucking thing I used to care about ceases to matter. My ears pound, my face heats, my arms and legs go numb, and my chest strains under the heartbreak.

My mother didn't die in my father's bedroom seven years ago. No, my mother abandoned me nineteen years ago. *Michael*. Why didn't she save Michael from my father, too? Does she not love him? Is he not important to her? Revulsion sets in as I disentangle myself and move to stand on shaky legs. I have to catch myself on the arm of the sofa so I don't fall right over.

"You left me there," is the first thing that comes out of my mouth. I let my voice rise, strangled and more painful the louder I get. "You left me in that house. You left Michael. Oh my God, Michael!"

Ryan and Ian, who are both watching me like hawks with matching sorrowful expressions, dart their eyes away when I look at them. "How could you let me grow up in that? Never having a choice? No chance to ever go to school? Nothing!"

My anger is diluted only somewhat by Jim's hulking frame rising from the sofa. With narrowed eyes and a firm expression on his face, he comes to stand before me. I try to back up and find I've hit the fireplace.

"You gotta be mad, fine. Be mad," he says. Wrapping his big hand around the back of my neck, he turns me so that I'm facing Ian. "But if you want to be mad at someone, be mad at that bastard you call a father. Look at your brother's face. Look at it!" Jim gives me a slight shake, and despite Ian's obvious discomfort, he doesn't break from his position on the sofa, facing me head-on. Hearing Ian being referred to as my brother makes me want to freak out all over again, but I don't dare. Not with Jim's grip on my neck, gentle or not. Sniffling, I stare at Ian, wondering what he has to do with any of this. He moves just slightly, giving me a better view of his scar. The rolling sickness swings back into full force, and I have to count my breaths so I don't get sick all over the hardwood.

"What kind of sick bastard cuts a six year-old's face open and threatens to kill him in front of his mother if he sees her again? Tell me, what choice do you think your

mother had? You and Michael were safe. Ian wasn't."
Turning me to face him and holding me by my upper
arms, Jim crouches down to my level.

"Have you ever asked yourself why I risked the life
of every one of my men to get you out of there safely?
Because there is only one thing that woman—" He jerks
his head to Ruby. "—has ever asked of me—to promise I
would make sure her children were safe. And after
watching her spend fifteen years raising my boy, crying
herself to sleep on your birthday, and waiting desperately
for Gloria to call once a year for an update on you—the
only thing she ever asked of me was to keep you safe. If
that's not being a mother, I don't know what is."

My legs give out on me, and just as I think I'm going
to sink to the floor, Jim wraps his arms around my waist
and pulls me into his chest. I'm no longer angry with
Ruby, but now with my father, with Gloria—with all of
them. Every ounce of misery makes me kick at Jim and
try to push him off of me. But he holds tight, hugging me,
propping me up. Screaming into his chest, my lungs fight
to keep up, my voice cracks, and my eyes feel swollen
from the dramatics of it all. The combination of the
sorrow, betrayal, and even the guilt at the relief of having
a mother, when I've been without one for so long, boils
over. Jim lets me cry into his chest as the panic suffocates
me and every emotion I've tried to keep in check over the
last two months escapes. All of the fear, outrage,
confusion, and anguish over feeling lied to and protected,
used and loved and so very out of place leaves my body
and, in its wake, all I'm left with is this all-consuming
feeling of being numb that I can't shake.

RYAN

Chapter 21

*How often it is that the angry man rages denial of
what his inner self is telling him.*

- Frank Herbert

I'VE BEEN WATCHING her for days. When she
speaks, it's barely above a whisper. It's been days that
she's walked around like a zombie. Days that I've
watched her like some sick fuck who's been recently
paroled.

Rolling my shoulders, I grunt at the discomfort. I've
been standing in the same fucking spot for the last five
hours. I could move around—it's not like I can't sit or
something. I just don't want to. Twisting a little to the
left, I have a perfect view of Alex through her open glass
door. I don't think she even realizes we're out here, and
we've been out here since Ma's call with Gloria.

Pop ain't fucking around with security. We didn't
have much time to prep before leaving for New York.
Gloria's call shook us all up. Fucking imagining you'd
never see your kids, then finding out you gotta head out
and save one of them? That shit will knock anyone on
their ass—even Ma—and she's tough as nails. Turning
back to the right, I see Ma in the kitchen, making a
sandwich, with Pop hovering over her. She hasn't been
the same since Alex got here. She's been more guarded,
gentle, and even forgiving.

Looking back to Alex, I see her sitting in the middle
of her bed, surrounded by every photo album Ma has.
Alex pours through captured memories of a life she
missed out on. Her legs are folded and crossed in front of
her. With an album open on her lap, she drags her index

finger slowly down the center of the page. Her hair is up today, so I can actually see her face. Yesterday she had it down, which was good, because she cried almost the entire day. I had to do a line just to deal with that shit. Fucking tears. Give me some bitch screaming and freaking out, but tears? Screw that. Even Pop can't handle that shit. Thankfully, there have been no tears today.

Her bedroom door opens, and Pop walks in, carrying a tray with a 7-Up and a sandwich on it. From my vantage point on the front deck, I can easily see both Ma and Alex. Ma is in the kitchen, chewing on her bottom lip. She's prepared every one of Alex's meals the last few days so Alex wouldn't have to leave her room. She never brings the food in, though—she makes Pop do that. I wish she'd just suck it the fuck up already and talk to her. This avoidance shit is driving me nuts.

"Thanks," Alex whispers, lifting her head and clearing her throat. She forces a small smile, which Pop returns. He hasn't seen me yet, but he will soon.

"This, uh, standoff you two got going is turning me into a waiter. I'm not a waiter," Pop says. His eyes travel over Alex and meet mine, making me uncomfortable. He told us to keep watch. I don't think this is what he had in mind. Feeling the lingering effects of the coke, I flash him a smile and raise my eyebrows. His face doesn't register the taunt.

"It's not a standoff. It's just a… I don't know what it is," she says. Back when this was my room, I used to hate how thin the walls were. There was absolutely no privacy. Now, I'm grateful for it. I'm not very skilled at reading lips.

"Well, work it out. Just hug her or something. I don't know. All this crying crap is turning my balls into a pair of fucking ovaries." For the first time in a while, Alex bursts out laughing. She covers her mouth with her hand and smiles up at Pop. These two are forming an unexpected bond. I only wish Ma would get her ass in there to see it.

Pop cracks a smile and clarifies that his comment wasn't a request, but a demand, to which she nods. Just as he leaves the room, PJ rushes in. She circles the perimeter of the bed—twice—jumps on top of a few of the albums, and then jumps down again. Smiling at her, Alex shoves the albums aside and pats the bed. With a wagging tail, PJ jumps up and plops herself down, rolls over, and sticks her legs in the air, whimpering. Damn dog. Ma ruined her. She was supposed to be a scary beast. Alex spends a few minutes rubbing PJ's belly before the dog has had enough and jumps back up and looks around the room.

Catching sight of me in the doorway, her wispy tail maniacally swings from side to side, and she barks, runs at me, circles my feet, and then runs back to the bed and jumps back on, repeating the process two more times. Alex's smile falls when she sees me. We haven't spoken since that night. And I'm sick of it. Even when shit's fucked up, I'd rather talk to her than not.

"If you're going to stand there watching me, you might as well come in," she says. Her voice has an edge to it when she talks to me. With Pop she's much softer; with Ma she's less mature. With Ian she's something else. With me, she always seems pissed off or nervous. But right now, I don't give a fuck. She's talking to me.

Abandoning my post, I step inside the room. Her fallen smile morphs into something a little angrier. Her eyes narrow, brows pull together, and her jaw ticks.

"How long have you been out there?"

"Awhile. Somebody's got to be on guard since you've turned into a zombie."

"How dare you," she snaps. Her eyes are focused on PJ as the dog rushes over and whimpers at my feet. I crouch down and rub her behind her ears. "What do you want anyway?"

"Stop acting like a baby. Talk to her," I say. It's not what I want to say, but it doesn't fucking matter. She glares, turning to face me.

"Who are you, my fucking therapist?"

Her attitude takes me by surprise, setting off my temper. I came in here to be nice, at least I think I did. I don't need this shit. "Well, you fucking need one."

Clearing a space on the bed, I plop down with my right leg bent out in front of me. PJ follows and jumps up between us, her sharp little claws digging into our flesh. I grit my teeth, trying not to show that it hurts. Alex looks down at her lap as PJ settles in on her side.

"Well, I'll tell you what I don't need—another brother. I have a brother back in Brooklyn, and apparently I have Ian, too. I don't need you taking on the role as well."

The last thing I want her to see me as is her fucking brother. Christ, I've been in her pussy. The idea that she thinks of me as her brother is more troubling to me than I'd like to admit. I just shake my head and look down at her fidgeting hands. "I don't think of you as a sister."

"No, I guess I'm just a Lost Girl then, huh?" I try to fight the way that comment makes me feel—like a real bastard. I hate feeling shit, and it seems like that's all I've been doing lately. I was not prepared for this shit with Alex. She's pretty much everywhere, and the places she's not, people are fucking talking about her. The last thing Alex is, is a Lost Girl. She's not a club whore.

"You're not a Lost Girl," I say. Why she gets me talking, I don't fucking know. I just need her to know that she's nobody's whore, not even mine.

"Then why did you treat me like I am?" Her shoulders are slumped and her brows are tight. This is the last thing she needs right now. She's still struggling with the Ma thing.

"You want to do this now?" I ask, hanging on the hope that the harsh tone I use is enough to deter this conversation. I know why I did it, I'm just not ready to face it. Pop was right. All the fucking tears going on in this house are going to make my balls sprout eggs.

"Might as well get all the ugly out of the way," she says, jutting her chin out. I've seen this before, her trying to be brave. She's so naïve. She doesn't have a fucking clue how ugly shit can get. This isn't the ugly, even though she thinks it is. This is just an aftershock of the ugly, if even that.

"We fucked. It was fun." I shrug it off like it's nothing, like it's the truth. "What, you want a diamond 'cause I got in your pussy?"

The comment makes her flinch and look away. I lock my jaw in place to keep from apologizing. Isn't that what the other night was about—hurting her? I'm supposed to be pushing her away, not pulling her closer. Letting her know that I feel sorry for treating her like a whore isn't an option.

Just when I think the tears are going to come, her face hardens and she faces me once more. "You're a bastard."

"I know," I say, my eyes trained on hers. She's finally getting it.

"Are you even going to try to change?"

"No."

"Fine," she says, throwing her hands up. "Don't change, that's fine. But we're in each other's worlds. We have to find a way to be civil around each other." She pushes her hands into the bed beside her, pulling herself up straighter.

"I don't want to be civil around you," I say, forcing myself to shut my mouth before everything else spills out. I don't want to be civil around her because civility requires an emotional distance. I don't feel distant when I'm with her. I don't feel civil or nice. I feel on edge, needy, manic. I'm way too deep into this chick to feel fucking civil. Maybe I could have been civil before I fucked her, but not now. Being in her pussy was good and all, but that's not what's fucking me up. I know she didn't enjoy it. It hurt her, and I didn't want her to enjoy it. And what kind of fucked up bastard does that shit? Not anybody she should let fuck her, that's for sure.

"You're an impossible asshole!" she screams.

"Don't you think I know that? Maybe you didn't hear me the first fucking time—it's you or my patch. What is it going to take to get you to hate me?" I reach up, hanging onto the back of my neck with my hands, and blow out a breath. I shake off bitches on the regular— why this is so hard, I don't know. Every time I try to push her away, she fights me on it.

"You say you don't want me, you act like you hate me, but you keep coming around." She shakes her head in disdain and wrings her hands together in her lap.

"I never said I didn't want you," I say and turn away from her, leaving the room the way I came in. I don't know when I turned into Mr. Fucking Chatty, but this shit has got to stop.

I have to get the hell out of here. This chick is fucking with my head again, and it's making it impossible for me to do my job. I just need some distance.

Giving Squat, whose real name is Rob, a nod, I cross the deck and take the stairs into the grass two at a time. I take a quick look back to see he's taken my position at the sliding glass door and has his piece in hand. I trust him well enough—for a prospect—but just in case, I decide to give him a reminder.

"Hey, Squat," I shout. His grip on the rifle tightens as he turns to face me. "What happens if you fuck this up?" Nervously, he straightens his shoulders and gulps. He and I barely talk, and that's how it'll be until he's patched—if he's patched. I can only train him to properly do his job if he fears me. His face distorts uncomfortably, likely remembering the conversation we had the first night we stood watch.

"You think you can handle this?" I ask. The sun has long since set, and the notorious cold Mendocino nights are in full effect. We've been out here for nearly five hours now, just feet from Alex, who's holed up in her room. If I strain to listen, I can hear her exhausted whimpers and cries as she processes what it means being Ruby's kid. Part of me wants to hold her, the other part of me wants to use my .38 on myself and just put an end to the misery.

"I got it," he says, confidently. His chest is puffed out on his short frame, and his chin juts out. He's verging on cocky, and arrogance leads to mistakes. This is one job he doesn't have the luxury of messing up.

"Okay then, get this. There are severe consequences if you fuck this up. I'm not going to kill you. I'll make you suffer instead." Closing the distance between us, I peer down, crowding him. His eyes are wide, but he doesn't move. "Your mom that you love so much? I'll fuck her until she begs me to stop, until she cries. And then I'll fuck her harder. And I'll do it while you watch."

Rage fills his eyes, but wisely, he doesn't respond. I've never taken a woman by force before, and if he fucks this up, I'll just kill him instead. But the threat to his mother is just the thing to make sure he's on his A-game.

Shouting over the chirping of the crickets, he says, "There will be serious consequences if she gets hurt, Sir."

"Who?" I shout right back.

"Cub," he says, using the nickname I gave Alex months ago, before Duke started calling her Princess—that stupid fuck.

I round the back of the garage and come up to the front of the house where I parked my bike. The afternoon sun is hidden by a wall of clouds, and the temperature has dropped dramatically. Despite it being the middle of July, the cool air is not abnormal. Mendocino County doesn't experience summer the way everything south of us does; our climate more akin to the Pacific Northwest than California.

I swing my leg over my bike—a beautiful custom Harley—and affix the helmet to my head. Popping up the kickstand and starting her up, I peel out of the driveway, creating as much physical distance as I can. Pop has four guys—five if you include me—on the house, not including prospects. Tonight, we'll be down to three prospects on the house because the rest of us have Church. But he's also got local law enforcement to keep an eye out for any out-of-town visitors who might be heading our way. Alex is safe, that's what's important. Because as much as I want to ignore that shit, her safety matters to me. She matters to me.

The cool night air hits my knuckles as I coast through town. There's a speed trap between Pop's house and the club house, but the cops in this town wouldn't dare pull over a Forsaken. Passing by the partially hidden squad car, I give it a nod. I may not be able to see who's inside, but I know they can see me. My bike is hard to miss. Not only is she loud, but the glossy lettering of FORSAKEN gleams against the matte black finish in the fading sun.

Chapter 22

I am not ashamed to say that no man I ever met was
my father's equal,
and I never loved any other man as much.

- Hedy Lamarr

FORSAKEN CUSTOM CYCLE is dead, as usual.
Pulling into the parking lot, I let my baby growl as she
crawls across the pavement. The shop is closed up for the
night, not that we're turning customers away. In a small
town like Fort Bragg, so far away from any major cities,
there's not many people who can afford a custom order
that starts at an easy twenty-five grand. Most people
around here are lucky if they don't have to choose which
bills get paid each month.

The fourteen-foot high chain-link gate with black
vinyl privacy slats swings open, providing me entrance. I
lift my chin at the prospect, Tall, who's on the other side.
His real name is Aaron, but I'm half to forgetting that
since we only ever call the prospects their nicknames in
front of Cub. It drives her nuts that every time she asks
them what their names are, they've been ordered not to
tell her. The guy looks thin and much too gangly to
handle his shit, but he's a mean motherfucker. I roll in, to
find that Tall and I are not alone.

Grady, our Sergeant at Arms, fought Pop on leaving
the clubhouse unprotected. He eventually proved his
point, and we've had at least one prospect here at all
times since. At least now I don't have to open the gate
my own fucking self. Pulling up between Tall's brand
new Sportster and Duke's Softail Convertible, I cut the
engine and give the kickstand a nudge, then swing off my

girl. She's the longest relationship I've ever had because she's never bitched I've been riding her too long. I take off my helmet and set it on her handlebars, then follow Tall into the clubhouse.

The short amount of time I was able to relax from the house to here does nothing for how fucked I feel about Alex. Every time she asks me questions I can't answer, it just pisses me off. Every time she asks me to explain or apologize for something I've done, or haven't done, there's this pit in my stomach that I think might eat away at my soul. It's so fucking lame to think about it, but that's all I've been doing. This stupid chick who Ma's been crying over ever since I met her turns out to be Alex, who isn't the sweet, kind, little girl Ma's been passing her off to be.

Thoroughly pissed off, my shoulders tense, and my fists ache to hit something—anything. Inside the clubhouse, the walls are a mixture of exposed brick, wood paneling, and painted gray sheetrock. Industrial-sized fluorescent lights hang in long rows overhead, half the bulbs cracked or burnt out. The main room of the clubhouse is dimly lit with old, tattered furniture scattered around the space. Straight ahead is the bar, a two hundred-square-foot space that's sectioned off by a change in flooring from the basic concrete slab of the rest of the space to a faux-wood finish.

I grit my teeth at the sight before me—Duke, his left elbow resting on the bar with a beer in hand. One of the Lost Girls, one I think I've fucked, stands between his legs, her hands rubbing his jean-clad thighs. Her trashy bleached-blonde hair hangs over her shoulders, spilling down her bare back to her absentee bra line. One look at her bare tits, rounder than normal and defying gravity, and I remember that we had a go a month or so back. I never forget a decent pair of tits.

Duke turns his head toward me and takes a pull of his beer, completely ignoring the bitch in front of him. Noticing his diverted attention, she faces me with a smile. Her lipstick has half worn off, and her eye makeup is smudged. She's one of the nastier bitches I've had around my dick, but she was so persistent. I'm a gentleman—I hate to turn a lady down.

"Ryan," she says with a purr, turning to face me. She places one hand on her hip, just above the top of her jeans, and cocks her head. Her tits still look like something I'd like to suck on, but she's one stupid bitch. She already tried to convince me to ride her bare once. I ain't going down that rabbit hole again. Still, looking at her, I think I'm going to need to find a way to release some tension.

"Who's here?" I ask her. Her smile falls, likely realizing I'm not up for fucking her a second time.

"Chel's in the palace," she says in irritation. I grin at her, feeling like it's my lucky day. As I pass, I gently give one of her tits a pat—a show of appreciation for the work she's had done—and veer off to the right, down the main hallway to the palace, which is the second door on the left. Inside, the walls are painted black on three sides with a floor to ceiling mirror covering the entire fourth wall. Two long couches face three evenly spaced stripper poles which are bolted in place.

Curled up on the corner of one of the couches is Chel. As per club instruction, she's wearing as little clothing as possible—cut-off jeans shorts, a midriff-bearing tank, and sandals. Her fake tan looks fresh, but the dye job she's got on her bright red hair needs a touch-up. Without thinking twice about it, I pull two hundred dollar bills out of my wallet and toss them on the book in her lap. A screech flies out of her mouth as she looks up at me. Her face is free of make-up, with the exception of the cherry-red lipstick that's painted perfectly on her lips. The lack of make-up makes her facial piercings—a nose stud and an eyebrow ring—less obvious against her pale skin.

"Ryan," she says with a smile on both her face and in her voice. She gathers the bills in her hands and waves them at me. "What's this for?"

"Get your hair done." I hate when she does this shit. She knows I don't give a fuck what she uses the money on. "Or your nails. Buy a dildo. I don't fucking care." She lets out a heavy sigh and shakes her head at me.

"The club does enough. You know how I feel about the extras." She reaches her hand out, offering the money back. I shake my head and bend down, tossing her textbook on the floor. She always does this, and I always persist, so I don't know why she keeps fronting. We've told her time and time again that the club takes care of our own, and as far as we're concerned, she belongs with us. After the shit she's been through, and with a kid no less, Forsaken makes sure she gets what she needs.

"If it makes you feel better, I'll let you suck my dick as a thank you," I say, smirking. She purses her lips and crawls forward. With her legs tucked underneath her ass, she grasps the front of my jeans and pulls me closer. Her expert fingers work the button of my fly and then slide down the zipper. She takes her time rubbing her hands along my hardening shaft as she kisses the V between my hips. I throw my head back and close my eyes. In my mind her bright red hair darkens and grows longer—

RIDE

down to her mid-back. Her green eyes become dark brown ones, and her flat, button-nose morphs into a sweeping curve. She frees my hard dick from my boxers and just as the rush of having her lips on my cock overtakes me, she's no longer the willing Lost Girl. She turns into my Cub, all spitfire and sass. In my head, Cub tells me she's sucking my dick because she wants me to feel good, but not because she has to.

Just as Chel takes me in to the back of her throat, my fantasy is cut-off by the disturbingly loud alarm ringtone coming from my cellphone. I try to ignore it as Chel works her magic, but I can't. It's Cub's ringtone, and she might be in trouble. Worried, I pull my phone out of my pocket with my right hand, and use my left hand to keep Michelle where she is. It's just a phone call; I can multi-task. I slide the bar on the screen and bring it to my ear.

"What's up?" I ask, almost calling her Cub. She has no clue, nor does she need to know that we call her that. She'll just get all girly and start thinking it means shit it don't.

"Where did you go?" she asks, huffing. Suddenly, I can see a future I might have had, had Pop not laid it out for me. I leave the house, and she huffs. It doesn't matter how hot and sassy she can be, she's a chick just like the rest of them—wanting to chop off my balls and carry them in her purse. I should probably buy Pop a fucking beer for saving my ass from that shit. Had things gone on long enough, I might have chopped 'em off and given 'em to her myself.

"We got Church tonight. What's wrong?" My tone is icy and I know it, but I'm not fucking around. If Squat fucked up, he'll be dead by midnight.

"Nothing," she whispers, her voice cowering under my snap. I look down, realizing that Chel's stopped her ministrations, which just aggravates me further. I tighten the grip I have on her head, but her hand comes up and taps out on my hip. I blow out a heavy breath and let her go.

"What do you mean, nothing?" I say. "Do you got a problem or not?" I mouth 'what the fuck' at Chel, who just shakes her head and sits back on the couch, wiping the spit off her lips. My dick is still hard as hell, and it's got nowhere to go.

"Everybody left," she says, using that small voice I can't stand. "I mean, Ruby's here. Squat's outside. But Jim and Ian—they left." Fuck. She sounds helpless and scared—both of which flip some kind of switch in me and simultaneously piss me off and freak me out.

"You're not alone. We got Squat, Dunce, and Rink on the house. You're fine."

"What if they come while you guys are gone?" she says. This clingy thing she's doing is new. I'm conflicted—one on hand, I feel needed; wanted even. On the other hand, I don't know what to think.

"They're not coming while we're gone. Shit, you're safe. You're fine. Ma's got more years' experience with a gun that I have on this planet. If you're scared, go talk to her. Spend time with her. It won't kill you. Promise."

A muffled sob breaks out on the other line. Rubbing my temple with my left hand and gripping the phone tightly with my right, I count back from one hundred. I have Church in a few minutes and can't be running off, but something has her freaking out, which is making me worry. The last thing I need to do when my dick is trying for some relief is to be worrying about Cub.

Snapping my fingers, I motion for Chel to hand me her phone. When she does, I type in Ma's number and wait for her to pick up.

"Hey Chel," she says on the third ring. In my other ear, I can hear Alex sniffling and blowing her nose. At least she's calming down.

"Ma, it's me," I say.

"Your dad just left for Church."

"So I've heard. You hear your kid? She's in her room fucking panicking that Mancuso might show up while we're gone."

"What?" she says, her voice alarmed. Her footsteps sound in the background, followed by the creaking of a door.

"Alex?" Ma says, her voice echoing in both ears. Alex's surprised gasp is high-pitched in my right ear, but barely a whisper in my left. I feel like a damn fool standing here with two phones to my head.

"You got this, Ma?" I ask into the phone in my right ear, realizing a second too late that Alex is on that line.

She hmphs and says, "Traitor," then the line goes dead.

In my left ear, Ma says, "Thanks, Punk," and hangs up the phone. Tossing Chel's cell at her and shoving mine back in my pocket, I look down at my half-hard dick.

"Girl trouble?" she asks, smirking and resuming her position. The thought of discussing Alex with her makes my dick want to deflate.

"No, now blow," I say, pointing at my dick.

"Fine, don't talk. It's not like word hasn't spread around the club anyway," she says, reaching into my boxers and cupping my balls. I close my eyes once more and try to drown out the subtle judgment in her tone. The shit that's been flying around here hasn't come from me, but between the Lost Girls and my brothers, word has spread. I wasn't exactly subtle that night I fucked Alex and sent her packing. Half our charter was in the room when she walked out, looking so fucking used. It's not like I knew anybody was there, but even if I had, what did she expect me to do? Escort her to the door? Pop made it pretty fucking clear at Church last time that Alex was off-limits to the club. It's one thing to fuck her—my brothers won't rat on me for that—but it's another to claim her.

It takes me longer to come than I'd like, but when I do, I come down quick. Before Chel can even finishing swallowing, I'm zipping up my pants and I'm out the door. When I make it to the end of the hall and into the chapel, all of our members in good-standing are in the room. The long, rectangular table stretches out over ten feet in length. At the very back of the room, Pop sits at the head of the table with our Sergeant at Arms, Grady, to his left, and Wyatt, our Vice President, to his right. Next to Grady is Ian, our treasurer, and across from him is Duke, our secretary.

I cross the room and sit in my seat beside Ian and across from our patched members who don't hold officer positions—Diesel and Bear. Chief and Fish sit next to me and at the end, respectively. Over all, we're a fairly young charter. We have to be, for the shit we do. As members age, they tend to uproot for Nevada or Oregon, maybe Arizona. The oldest of the old usually put themselves out to pasture like Rage has, in the Nevada desert. But out here, in the middle of Mendocino County, where we grow the finest fucking bud on the planet, we need the younger guys—more for their brawn than their brains.

Tall comes to the doors and shuts them, closing himself off from the patched members of the club, and Pop thunks down the gavel as Church begins. He starts off by going over old business, getting up to date on our grow houses, and making sure we're set up for runs into Wilks as scheduled. Then we finally get to the important part of Church: Cub.

"Ruby got a hold of Gloria last night, found out a few of Mancuso's guys left a few days ago. Low ranking," Pop says.

"Not a problem," Grady grunts out from Pop's side. But Pop waves a dismissive hand in the air.

"There is a problem," he says. "Ruby's boy is with them."

"Fuck," I grit out and slam my fist down into the solid wood table. I knew about the phone call with Ma and Gloria, but not about Michael.

"Where do we stand on the boy?" Grady asks.

"Same rules apply as with Cub. Can't touch him," Pop says. Wyatt shakes his head and leans his elbows on the table, looking around the table for our reactions. My body vibrates with anger at this turn of events.

"We don't know what side of the fence the boy falls on. Don't think we can risk finding out," Wyatt says. While I'm inclined to agree, the boy belongs to Ma. If the club votes him dead, I can't be the one to do it. Neither can Ian. Even though they've never met, they're bonded by blood. Pop sure as fuck can't carry that burden with him. Looking around the table, I don't know who can. Each one of these bastards loves Ma like she's his own, and for some of them—like me—she's the only mother they've ever had.

Ian's steel-toed boots tap into the concrete floor to my right. His frame is hunched over the table, his elbows resting on the edge, his arms steepled, and his forehead resting on his fists. He can't be the one to say it, or our brothers will give him shit about loyalty. Fuck it, I'm already on their shit lists.

"We can't touch him," I say. The entire table turns to look at me. Ian turns his face just slightly, giving me an appreciative glance. "Not if we don't have to."

"And if he hurts Princess? You willing to risk that, Trigger?" Duke asks, speaking up for the first time.

"He won't," I say. "She's protected."

"We can have a man on her 24/7, and shit can still go sideways," Pop says, straightening in his leather chair. "I'm calling a vote—yea, we kill the boy on sight; nay, we pull back if we can." If Ma knew Pop was here, taking this vote, she'd castrate him in his sleep and take out every last one of us who dared hurt one of her kids. Every man at the table looks to Pop, then to Ian, and finally to me. As the vote moves around the table, Wyatt, Fish, Chief, and Grady vote yea. Pop, Duke, Diesel, Bear, Ian, and I vote nay. I breathe a sigh of relief that for the moment, Ma's boy's execution is off the table.

Moving onto the game plan to protect Alex, Pop assigns prospects to the roads that lead into town on a rotating basis, and Fish and Diesel and Bear to supervise. We're probably going to have to pull from a nearby charter for full coverage, though. Wyatt, Ian, Grady, and Duke will be making a run to Nevada for firepower. The rest of us will be working out the in-town logistics.

"I got Cub," I say, while Pop is working out who's going to be where.

"Son, I thought we talked about this," he warns, his voice edgy. I grit my teeth and try to avoid a fight, but the thought of someone else—anyone else—being at her side through this shit makes me want to vomit. "I don't like that idea. You're getting fucked up over this girl."

Tired of denying it and backed into a corner, I shake my head. "Can anyone in this room tell me they care more about Cub's safety than I do? If any of you bastards can tell me to my fucking face that you give a bigger fuck than I do about her, then I'll step back. This isn't about family bullshit, or being a rat, or even protecting the club. This is about keeping Cub alive. Is that okay with you guys?" Nobody protests, and for a moment, I feel victorious. I hadn't intended to volunteer for the position, but now that I have, I'll fight any of my brothers who try to take it away from me. They know I'm right. I won't let anything happen to Cub. I'll bet my life on it, and I'm the only fucker in this room who will.

I'm not leaving her side until this shit gets squared away.

Chapter 23

My Father had a profound influence on me. He was a lunatic.

- Spike Milligan

ON MY WAY out, I try to avoid my brothers and my father. They eye me warily as I pass, unsure how to handle the shit I just pulled. Can't blame 'em. I don't really know how to handle that shit, either. If I didn't have to be coherent tonight, I'd do a couple lines, drink a few beers, and pass the fuck out while I try to jerk myself off. But that's not an option tonight. It is something to look forward to, though.

"Trigger," Pop shouts across the lot. I turn and face him, in the back corner of the lot with Grady and Wyatt flanking his sides. Behind them, painted into the black vinyl slats of the chain link fence in white paint is FORSAKEN.

"Yeah?" I say. He bridges the gap between us and places his hands on his hips.

"That's stunt you pulled in there. I don't like it."

I don't say anything, but don't shy away from him either. I knew he'd have something to say about it. Not that I really give a fuck. We've been through this already.

"I see the way you're looking at her, Son."

"I don't even know what you're going on about."

"You and Alex. Can't happen."

"Why the fuck do you care? Did Ma put you up to this?"

I take a second to look around the shop, making sure nobody's listening in. Pop hasn't talked to me about girls like this since I was a kid. Last thing I need is one of these fuckers overhearing and thinking I'm having feelings and shit. Ma talks about how much the bitches at the salon gossip, but I'd be willing to bet they ain't got nothing on the guys here.

"Ruby thinks it's cute. I—I don't think it's cute. I think it's dangerous."

"Why are you so interested in where I stick my dick?" I huff. Leaning over the pull, I flip the wrench I've been holding in my grease-stained left hand.

"Your dick's not what I'm worried about. I know that look and I—" he says, but I cut him off.

"Don't like it, I know," I say, pushing off the pull and tossing the wrench in its open drawer, turning, and walking away.

I cross my arms over my chest, standing with my legs shoulder-width apart, and level his glare with my own. "We got a problem here?"

"Do we?" he parrots, leaning in. His jaw is locked, his eyes wild. My blood boils, my muscles tense, and my chest strains. I lean in, meeting his stance with my own and gritting my teeth. I force myself to take one deep breath after another so I'm calm enough that I can speak. I'm fucking sick of this shit. So fucking sick of him getting in my business. Doesn't he think—doesn't he know—if I could force myself to not care, that I would?

He lifts his right hand to my face, pointer finger nearly touching my nose. He's way too close for comfort. I remember this shit from when I was a kid. Less than half the size I am now, he'd crouch down, let his weight rest on the balls of his feet, and he'd clasp his hands together. He'd make sure I was sitting and then he'd lecture me. Every explanation he could come up with as to how I fucked up this time—grades, attendance, attitude, drinking, drugs, bitches, fights. Anything he could think of, he'd rail me for it. Until I was a teenager, he'd ask me if I wanted him to hit me, like I had a fucking choice. If I didn't like pussy so much, I'd consider putting a bullet between my ears just so that I could make one decision he didn't have a chance to disapprove of first. I thought this motherfucker owned me back when I was a kid, but I had no fucking clue what wearing the same cut as him would do.

"Whatever you got going on in your head about this bitch, shut it down," he hisses. I fight the angry jerk of my limbs, forcing myself to stay still. If Ma could hear this shit right now, I wouldn't have a chance to lay him out. She'd do it for me.

"Any other sage advice you got for me, Mr. President?" I ask, smirking. Because if I don't do something, I'm going to slam his face into the pavement.

"You're unfocused—you're missing shit. You're going to get yourself killed over pussy you won't want in a week anyway. Your brothers can't trust you if they can't trust your woman. This family has worked too long and too hard, and sacrificed too much, to let this cunt destroy that."

Something in me snaps. Maybe it's the word cunt. Maybe it's my own fucking father calling Alex a bitch one too many times. Maybe I'm just pissed off that he's right, and I'm looking for a fight. Maybe he's just frustrated and looking to piss me off so I can start a fight. Fuck if I know what it is, but I lose focus for a brief second before his face becomes crystal clear.

Like a missile, my right hand clenches into a fist, rears back, and slams into the side of his jaw. His right arm grabs me by the back of my neck while my left grasps at his throat. Toe to toe, nose to nose, we're locked in place. Neither of us is going to give before we're ready.

"Call her a cunt again," I sneer, tightening my grip. His hand on my neck clamps down, violently pushing in on my nerves in a painful way. I welcome the pain. This needs to happen, and I need to feel it.

"This is what I'm talking about," he rasps out, sucking in as much air as he can. "I love Alex like she was my own, but this is about the club." Pop's a tough mother fucker, I'll give him that. I've seen men's necks snap under less pressure than I'm giving. His words register, but they don't faze me. For all his talk and bluster, he's no different than I am. He's no less immune to feeling shit he doesn't want, no matter how fucked up he gets.

"You want to put it to a vote, put it to a fucking vote," I scream. With one last squeeze of his throat, I shove him off, watching him stumble half a step. The brothers have gathered around us in silence. Each one takes a fighting stance, ready to throw down or break it up. I avoid meeting their eyes as I walk to my bike, strap on my helmet, and pop up her kick-stand. Walking her backward, I find they're all focused on me. Part of me feels like I should tell them all to go fuck themselves. Since when do we give a shit where a brother sticks his dick? It's fucking juvenile. The other part of me wants to get off my bike and throw my fist into the nearest fucking face. But I don't, because I've got shit to do. Instead, I start her up and peel away once Tall opens the gate.

Making a quick stop by my place to grab a few changes of clothes and some other personal things, I debate on whether or not I should be packing the condoms. For a strange moment I find myself in an unfamiliar place, worried that I might somehow offend a chick just because I brought condoms with me. Like it fucking matters what she thinks and if she's worried all I want to do is fuck her. There's nothing wrong with fucking and not feeling shit after. Angrily, I shoved a few rows in the bag before zipping it up and getting back on my bike.

The ride is simultaneously way too short and way too long. I need to clear my head of some of this shit, but I don't have time for that. Every minute I waste trying to sort my shit is a minute that Alex is missing part of her security detail. As fucked as it is, I just don't trust my brothers are going to pay enough attention that Mancuso Jr. isn't going to get to her.

Pulling up to the dirt road that leads to the house, everything is near black. I slow the bike, remove the .38 from the waistband of my jeans, unclick the safety, and place my hand back on the handlebar. My head pounds and my mouth goes dry. The house is never this quiet. Junior and crew probably wouldn't be here this quick unless they flew in. I don't know how stupid they are, though. Flying commercially leaves too many records.

Suddenly, I'm basked in a blinding white light. The intensity of it kills my vision, and I'm left blinking relentlessly as I bring the bike to a stop. The hand with the gun in it itches with the need to do something, but with zero visibility, there's nothing I can do.

The lights dulls to a warm yellow, loud popping rings out, and the only light left are the lights from the front deck and the side of the garage. My eyes take a moment to adjust, but when they do, I see Chief less than thirty feet in front of me, his homemade assault rifle pointed at my chest. Chief and I have never had a problem before, and typically lean the same way on club matters, but in this second, I'm not so sure we're on good terms. That's the thing about club life. No patched members say it aloud, and outsiders don't usually bear witness to it, but violence between brothers is a very real fucking thing.

Then he lowers the gun, turns around, and walks to the house. I breathe a sigh of relief that I had forgotten about the flood lights Ma insisted Pop install before we headed out to Brooklyn. Behind him, standing on the side of the garage, is my father. Shaking away my paranoia, I rev the bike and roll up to the garage, where I park her and climb off. I pull the duffle out of one of my saddle bags and head for the front door. The shuffling of rocks and dirt sound behind me. I turn around to find Pop catching up to me.

"You planning on staying?" he asks. My muscles tense at the question.

"Junior's on his way. Not gonna fuck around."

The front door swings open, and Ma stands in the doorway. She looks lighter than she has in a long time. I walk up to her and give her a kiss on the cheek. Craning her neck, she smiles.

"She's in her room, baby," Ma says. Moving around her, I see the glare she gives Pop. Fighting off the laugh that threatens to escape, I make my way into the house and through the kitchen, down the hallway to see Cub. Stopping at her open doorway, I take a moment to see how she's fucked up my old room.

The once-white walls are still the light beige Ma painted them right after Gloria called, worried for her niece's life. It's the rest of the room that she's put her feminine stamp on. Her bedspread and throw pillows are a dusty purple, and so are the frames of the reproductions of the paintings she has hanging up. The bed frame is a solid oak and cost a fucking fortune, according to Pop. I poke my head in, seeing her in the closet, hanging up a jacket.

"You fucked up my room," I say. She jumps in place and spins around, scowling.

"No," she says slowly, "I fixed up my room." I grin at her attitude and slowly enter the room, tossing my duffle down on her bed. Her eyes slide to the duffle on the bed, and she crosses her arms. "What the hell do you think you're doing?"

"Getting comfortable," I say, walking to the bed, sitting down, and kicking off my boots. I can almost hear the wheels turning in her head. Her nerves are on edge, and she doesn't know what to do with herself, being invaded like this. Shaking her up is becoming a favorite of mine. It almost gets me off as much as getting off does.

She swings around the bed, grabs the duffle, and tosses it on the ground. Her dark brown hair is down now, falling over her shoulders. I let my eyes travel from her bare feet up to her yoga pants and the pink T-shirt she's wearing. Just as my eyes reach her tits, her arms lifts in the air and her hand comes down hard on the side of my head. Reflexively, I stand, towering over her, and back her into the corner. Her arms reach behind her, finding purchase of the wall. Her lower lip trembles, and her eyes are wide.

"Now you did it," I grit out, trying to control my temper. My chest vibrates with a mixture of rage and desire. I run my index finger down her neck and ghost my lips along her hairline. She stays very still as I place my hands on the wall, boxing her in. My head is swarming with a hundred things at once, but the only thing I can focus on is Cub.

Chapter 24

Falling in love is the best way to kill your heart because then it's not yours anymore. It's laid in a coffin, waiting to be cremated.

- Ville Valo

I LIFT HER chin and crash my lips down against hers. She's stiff beneath my touch. I let my lips glide down her temple to her cheek where I place a gentle kiss. I'm so fucking out of my element, so far into my own head, with this tunnel vision, that won't let the fuck up. I could keep lying to myself, saying I don't know what's wrong with me. But I know damn well what my problem is.

My problem is standing right in front of me, stiff as a board and seemingly terrified. Angry, quiet, dismissive, flirty. None of it matters. She's a fucking temptress no matter what mask she's wearing. Pulling back from her lips and whispering in her ear, I say, "Relax, Cub."

"Cub?" she says, lifting her head. Fuck. I could rip my own goddamn balls off for letting that one slip. Something about her knowing the name I call her makes me feel oddly exposed. It's uncomfortable and disarming. I can't really make out why. And instead of letting her make it into a big deal, I push her up flat against the wall. Just thinking about fucking her gives me half a chubby.

"Why did you call me that?"

"It's just a nick name. We all have them, remember?" I say. It's lame, but it's all I've got. It's the same lame excuse I gave Pop and the club when I said it in front of them for the first time.

"What does it mean?"

"You're really fucking pushy tonight, you know that?" I say, backing off, irritated by the inquisition. Sure, it's a simple question, but it has one hell of a complicated answer. Her jaw locks, and her eyes narrow in anger.

"You're a fucking bastard," she hisses. Something's pissed her off damn good, but fuck if I know what it is. All I did was come in here to spend a little time with her, maybe make her come a few times, and here she is losing her fucking shit over it. She's fucking lucky it gets me hard when she gets pissed like this. Otherwise, I wouldn't have this complication in my life.

"What is your fucking problem, huh?"

"You keep doing this. You just can't keep doing this," she whimpers, crossing her arms over her midsection as tears spring to her eyes. She lifts her chin, refusing to crumble completely, despite the tears on her cheeks. "You're hot and cold. You want me and you don't. What are you, bipolar?" She's screaming now. Her arms fly up in the air as her shouts break up, half in Italian and half in English. I hear certain words that tip me off that she's pissed at me, but for what, I'm still not sure. I have a feeling if she were screaming at me entirely in English, I still wouldn't fucking know.

My entire body feels hard and tight, and I just need to pound something—preferably Cub. I've always been a go-getter. So fuck it.

I close the distance between us and cup her face in my hands. She lowers her voice, but keeps chewing me out in two different languages simultaneously. As hot as she is when she's cursing in English, she's fucking smokin' when she's pissed and cursing at me in Italian. I can't make out the words, but I know better than to assume she's praying for my soul. I lost that a long fucking time ago. When she finally calms down and stops crying, I kiss her on the forehead. When Ma's pissed, Pop does it to calm her down. Sure enough, she stops bitching and lets out a heavy sigh. With her eyes focused on mine, she looks so defeated; consumed, even.

"Tell me you want me," she says. For a brief moment, it's a reminder of how fucked up our first time was, but I play along anyway. I'm too tired, too needy to get into this with her.

"I want you," I blurt out and bring my hands to her hips. A shy smile breaks out on her face.

"You said it," she says so quietly I almost believe I'm hearing things. I don't even know what the fuck she's talking about now, which seems to be today's theme.

"What are you going on about?"

"You said you want me. Earlier, when I—" she says, but I cut her off by kissing her. This time she's responsive and eager. Her lips slide against mine. She's so soft in every way, and if I remember correctly, every fucking place. If I just focus on the physical, I can block out this shit that's running through my head.

"Tell me you want me," she says.

"I want to fuck you," I say.

With frantic movements, her hands claw at my shirt. Never one to disrespect a lady's wants, I reach down and peel the shirt over my head, breaking contact in the process. The smile on her face is blinding as I toss the shirt across the room. She's so young and so innocent in ways I can't ever remember being. Not virginal, and maybe not as naïve as I thought, but when it comes to this shit, she lets it matter. And it doesn't have to fucking matter. But I guess to her it does. And even if it doesn't matter to me, I don't stop myself anyway. Because I'm a selfish fucking bastard, and I want her.

Leaning down, I swoop one of my arms beneath her legs. She yelps as I stand erect—in more ways than one—and she wraps her legs around my waist. With one arm around my neck for support, she uses the other to cup my chin. I walk us to the bedroom door, closing is quietly. I don't give a fuck if Pop knows what we're doing in here; I just don't want a goddamn audience, and I don't want any fucking interruptions. I lock the door then walk us to the bed. We don't break eye contact, and even though I know this is the worst goddamn idea imaginable, I let it happen. There's honesty in her brown eyes I wish I didn't see. She's not a Lost Girl. She's not jaded like the rest of them. Chel knows the score. She knows exactly what we are to one another. As long as we keep shelling out the cash, she'll keep being pliable. It's a mutually beneficial arrangement. But this is different.

Bringing us to the bed, I bend at the waist, laying her down. Her eyes dance in anticipation as I lie down on top of her, my dick uncomfortably bound by my jeans and her paper-thin yoga pants. I rock into her, and she bites her lip trying to stifle a moan. She lets me lead. I begin by running a hand up her shirt, over her rubs, and sneak a finger underneath her bra. I didn't allow myself the pleasure of exploring her body the first time we were together. This time, I'm going to make damn sure I memorize every fucking curve of her flesh.

I try to give myself time and undress her slowly, but I'm anxious. She keeps looking at me and touching me in ways that no woman does—without expectation. It's fucking me up. I tear her shirt off then wrestle with her yoga pants. I get down to my underwear, and she's in her panties when I unsnap her bra. She gulps, her hands shake slightly, but she doesn't say a word. I've been here a hundred fucking times with as many broads, and none of them act nervous like this. At least, not since high school when virgins still existed—at least they did until they met me.

Using one hand, I bring her arms above her head and run my nose down her neck, kissing along the way. She purrs under my touch, shivering as I remove her bra. Her tits are fucking perfect—teardrops forming a mound. She can't be more than a B-cup at most. My hand closes around it, fingers pinching at her nipple. It's enough to make my dick twitch. As an apology for last time, I bring my other hand down to her panties, dragging a finger up the center. Her back arches; she moans under my touch. We're just fucking around, but there's no reason I can't make this enjoyable for her.

Tensing for a brief second, her body goes lax when I dip my hand inside her panties, finding her slit. She's not shaved, but she is manicured. It's been a while since I've been with a chick who didn't wax her pussy. It's pretty much a requirement of the Lost Girls. Sliding in and out of her wet lips, the tip of my finger is coated in her juices.

"You like that, baby?" I ask. She murmurs an incoherent yes, tossing her head back as I slide two fingers into her. She's so slick and wet. I lick my lips in anticipation.

"Yes," she chokes out as I slam my fingers into her wet pussy and hold them there, watching the shivers that take over her entire body. She sucks in a deep breath and says, "Again."

I pull my fingers out and push them back in between her folds. She gasps, her eyes turn into saucers, and her lips part.

"Again," she mouths, unable to speak. I'm only too fucking happy to oblige, pulling out and ramming back into her. A strangled whimper escapes her mouth as it parts, and she tosses her head back in a beautiful fucking arch. Her pussy clamps down on my fingers like it's a fucking vice. My dick is immediately fucking jealous, and I pull my fingers out. Slowly, her spasm ceases, and she looks down at me, breathing heavily. Her eyebrows pull together in question.

Reaching over and grabbing a condom from my duffle, I shove my boxers to the floor and strap on the rubber. Sliding back up her legs, I kiss her inner thigh and then her hip bone, traveling up her stomach to her ribs. Covering her naked frame, and looking into her nervous eyes, I reach down with one hand and part her legs even further. She bites her lip as I guide myself to her entrance. Very slowly, I enter her, and the feeling is fucking amazing. Hot and tight and slick.

I move out slowly, then draw back in. Her body quivers under mine. Gooseflesh springs up across her tits and her thighs. My muscles tense, and I can feel it fucking coming soon. She reaches up, cupping my chin, her eyes fixated so intently on mine. The way she looks at me just fucks me up—so trusting, so caring, so fucking stupid. It's like she's seeing someone who's not here, someone who died the day he earned his cut. Lifting her head, she brings her lips to mine and kisses me with just as much care. I've never been one for kissing while fucking, but I let her do it anyway. I guess I owe her this for that shit from the other night.

She slips her tongue into my mouth, and I eagerly welcome it. Just as I consume her mouth with my own, her body tenses beneath me, her pussy clamps down, and I can't stop myself from coming with her. She pulsates around me in a frantic rhythm, never breaking our kiss. I fight through my own orgasm, as the warmth envelopes me, sweat drips onto her forehead, and my eyes fly back into my head.

When I finally come down from the best fucking orgasm I've ever had, I open my eyes and study her. Her brown eyes are wide, and she's panting heavily. She opens her mouth and, with a breathy whisper, says, "Holy shit."

Moving off of her, I slide out of fucking wonderland and roll off the condom, tossing it into a nearby trash can. My lips turn up into a smile at her appreciation of my dick and his skills. He is pretty fucking impressive, if I do say so myself. Standing in her room, watching her scamper under her covers, I'm struck by a sudden awkwardness. This is why I don't normally fuck chicks at their place. It's too awkward when I give their ass a pat and walk out the door. Especially because the last thing I want to do right now is walk out the fucking door.

Before I can make up my mind about what the fuck I'm going to do now, she throws the covers off her beautiful naked fucking body and rushes past me to her closet where she throws on a robe. Keeping her head down, she leaves the room muttering something about needing a shower. Frustrated because I don't even know what the hell just happened, I grab my sweats from my duffle and throw them on then leave the room and walk down the hallway to the kitchen.

Just beyond the kitchen, in the living room, is Ma, curled up on the couch, watching a movie. Her eyelids are half-closed and her lips are parted. Smiling, I cross the room and pull down the throw blanket from the back of the couch. She stirs and opens her eyes, yawning.

"Hey Punk," she says, cuddling into the throw blanket. Her eyes travel down my damp frame and take in the change of clothes. Her eyes narrow and her voice comes out much harder when she says, "Don't hurt her."

I give her my classic smirk to cover up the onslaught of paranoia that's settling in. I'm not used to dealing with this shit. The chicks I fuck don't have their friends or moms coming to me, asking why I'm not calling the bitch. This shit doesn't happen to me. But I guess when she's Ma's kid, it does. Without anything good I can say, I walk away, striding down the other hallway that leads to Ma and Pop's room. Passing Ian's old room, I duck into the hall bath where I turn on the shower. Dropping my sweats onto the floor, I catch sight of a rim of bright pink around my dick. I rub my thumb over it and the pink smudges. On closer inspection, I see it's lipstick. Chel's lipstick.

Stepping into the shower, scrub the lipstick off furiously until my dick is bright red and stinging like a bitch. This isn't the first time this shit has happened, but it shouldn't have happened now. Not with Cub. This is the shit Ma was talking about. Fuck. Once my dick is clean and so is the rest of me, I turn the water off, pat myself dry, and pull my sweats back on.

Back in Alex's room, she's curled up on her side with her covers pulled to her shoulders. I crawl in the empty side of her bed, fighting for my share of the comforter as I stare at her back. "Will you share the damn covers?"

She flops over, scowling at me. Her eyes are red like she's upset, but trying to hide it as best she can. Ma's words ring in my head for the hundredth goddamn time. Don't hurt her.

"You deserve happily ever after," I say, for no other reason than I'm a fucking moron.

She clutches the blankets to her chest and hisses, "I don't want happily ever after. I want fucked up and mean."

"You don't want me," I say. "I'm a bastard, remember?"

"Don't you tell me what I want!" she says, pulls on the comforter, and wiggles in closer to me, curling up against my side. And as much as I want to tell her that I don't cuddle with chicks, it'd be a lie. Because having her next to me is really fucking comfortable, and I'll pop a cap in anybody's ass who thinks they're moving us out of this bed.

Chapter 25

Love has its place, as does hate. Peace has its place,
as does war.
Mercy has its place, as do cruelty and revenge.
- Meir Kahane

"IT'S NOT FUNNY," she whines through a scowl, but the smile on her face is bright.

"Oh yes it is," I say, with a grin. "What kind of mafia princess doesn't learn how to shoot a gun?"

"The passive kind," she grumbles, looking at my .38 she's holding with both hands. I force myself to keep grinning, avoiding the impending anxiety that's creeping up. When I first handed the gun over to her, I was nervous as fuck. I mean, I'd never given a chick I was fucking my piece before. But Cub doesn't know how to shoot, and with everything going on, she has to learn. I don't give a fuck how difficult she's being about it. Hell, even if Junior wasn't on his way here, I'd still teach her how to shoot. Yesterday, I gave up being pissed that her fucktard of a father didn't teach her sooner.

It's been days since I've spent more than ten minutes without Cub by my side. I'm getting way too comfortable falling asleep with her curled into my side, and waking up with her half on top of me. The longer it takes for something fucked to happen, the more on edge I get. Despite spending pretty much every minute with Cub and her pussy, which I swear is made out of unicorns or some shit, I can feel the tension in my bones. She walks around acting like she doesn't really care what's going on or the sacrifices the club is making to keep her tight little ass safe. I'm trying not to let her piss me off, but damn it, she's working my last nerve. It doesn't help that I haven't had a drink or any bud since before Church the other day.

"You're doing it again," she says, handing the gun back to me. Her smiles falls, giving way to a grimace. I click the safety lock and shove it in the back of my waist.

"Doing what?" I ask, trying to keep the strain out of my voice.

"That thing with your neck. You keep tensing your jaw, and it makes the veins in your neck pop out. It's creepy."

"I'm on edge," I say and blow out a deep breath. Pussy or not, she's driving me nuts with all of her observations. The only time I seem to be able to keep from snapping is when I've got my dick inside her. "It'd be nice if you acted like you fucking got it. This shit isn't a game. It's a big fucking deal."

She puts her hands on her hips and shakes her head. Her chest heaves, straining her tits against her top, and I find myself thinking of sucking on them again. Fucking unicorn pussy, I'm telling you. "Oh, I get it, you stupid jerk. My brother's on his way to kill me. You don't think I get it?"

"No, I don't think you do," I snap back. She steps forward, narrowing her eyes and huffing. Having watched her for days now, months even, I can tell when she's about to cry. She's always about to cry. I want to tell her to suck it the fuck up and chill out, but that goes against what I'm trying to do here. I need her to clue in to the reality of the situation.

"You're an idiot," she hisses and spins around, swaying her ass as she goes. The night sky is settling in, and it's getting too dark for her to be outside anyway. The air is getting chilly out here in the field. The farther she gets away from me, the worse the tightening in my chest gets. I don't like her being so far out of reach. Thankfully, we've doubled security on the house since the boys returned from Nevada, and we have brand new firepower that came with them. As much as I'm attached to my .38, there's no denying the power from the altered semi's the boys have outside.

Walking fast to catch up to her, I get halfway to the house before I realize what I'm doing. I'm chasing some chick like a sad fucking puppy. Fuck. This shit ain't me. I've seen this shit with Ma and Pop for years. She gets upset and, no matter how tough he tries to act, he fucking follows her. Doesn't matter how much posturing goes on around the table with the brothers, I see them with their Old Ladies. Fucking pussies, all of them. It fucks them up.

We all heard about it before we were patched. Hell, even before we were prospects—the club comes first. It's always supposed to come first. But put some bitch with the right smile, a tight ass, at the exact right time in front of a brother, and he's a fucking goner. And that shit bleeds over into everything he does, inside the club, outside the club. It doesn't fucking matter. All the loyalty and promises made to the club are forgotten when a brother hooks up.

That misbegotten loyalty and fucking diversion from the club is exactly why we're in this mess right now. Pop met Ma, and as much as I'm fucking glad he did, he made promises to her that could get his brothers killed. And because those fucking morons believe in the cause and the old bastard, they didn't vote against him when it came time for his ass to cash that check he promised her so many years ago.

Storming into the house, my shoulders tense, my neck muscles ready to pop, I stop dead in my tracks at the sight before me. Ma and Pop stand in the middle of the living room, her arms around his waist and his hands cupping her jaw. He places a kiss to her forehead. Pulling back, he smiles down at her, his graying black hair tucked behind his ears.

"Love you, Mama," he whispers. I've seen him look at her like that more than a thousand times, but never thought much of it. When they hooked up, he was a single dad raising his whore's kid, and she was a fucking mess with a kid of her own and a whole lot of baggage. And he took her on, made her a home. He protected her, promised to protect what matters most to her, and has held up his promise. Even after nearly two decades together, they're still in love. It's so sweet, I think I might have to fucking puke.

Leaving the room unnoticed, I turn and head down the hall to Cub's room, but before I can make it very far, I stop. Standing in the hallway, Cub has her arms folded over her chest and she's giving me a soft and dreamy smile. Fuck. This can't be good.

"What are you looking at?" I ask, walking toward her and taking the sharp detour into her room where I flop down on her bed and place my hands on my knees. She comes to stand before me, wiggling in between my legs. Lifting my chin, she cups my jaw. It's so fucking similar to Ma and Pop and I don't want any of it. She looks down at me with a look on her face that I hope to never see again. She's not just smiling. She's glowing or some shit.

"I see you," she says softly.

"See what?" I ask, knowing damn well this is a conversation we shouldn't be having. It's too real, too fucking raw. She needs to stop.

"I see you even though you don't want me to. The way you watch them—Jim and Ruby. You want what they have. I know you do." I huff and go to stand up, but she pushes me back down on the bed with a strength I didn't think possible. I knew this conversation was a bad fucking idea. Once again, my dick's got me into one hell of a bad situation.

"Why are you fighting this?" she asks, practically begging for an answer.

"I ain't fighting shit, Cub."

"You call me Cub, and that means something. And no matter how much you want to tell me you don't care, I know you do." Tears spring to her eyes, and the grip on my jaw tightens. "I believe in us."

"There is no us," I say. Fighting off the gnawing panic in my gut, I steel my body like it can protect me from her words. Everything I've been fighting since I first saw her feels like acid in my veins, destroying every defense I have. "We're just fucking around. Don't read into it."

The look on her face morphs from hopeful to gut-wrenching sorrow as she holds my jaw tighter. Her hands feel like a clammy vice around my mouth, making it hard to talk. Her scent, cool and airy, engulfs me. Just like it's been for the past three days, there's no escaping her. Only now is the first time I've wanted to. My chest constricts like I can't suck in any oxygen.

"You're a liar," she says.

A long silence stretches out. Leaning down, she places a soft kiss to my cheek. "This is my respect."

My mouth waters, my jaw tenses, and my hands ball into fists. I let my eyes close, trying so fucking hard to block everything out. But it's impossible. She's everywhere, consuming me. She raises up and places a kiss on my forehead and says, "And this is a promise of protection. I'll protect your heart because I love you."

The words rattle in my brain before they sink into my soul—what's left of it anyway. The panic consumes me. This wasn't supposed to happen. We were supposed to fuck around, have fun, rebel a little. She wasn't supposed to start spouting bullshit about loving and protecting me. She has no fucking clue what I've done in the name of the club, and she has no fucking clue who she's promising to protect.

Without thinking, I push her off me and move to storm out of the room. Her finger catches mine as she slams into the wall behind her, wide-eyed and shocked. The tears trailing down her face are too fucking much to take. Crazy fucking woman. Walking out of the house and into the field, I let out a frustrated scream. Two of my brothers come running before they see what's going on. I'm just losing my shit—again. It's nothing to worry about. Really. It isn't until Grady threatens to shoot me in my dick that I stop screaming and kicking at the ground.

When I think I have my wits about me, I make the walk back to the house. I need to have Duke sit with Alex in her room while I stand guard outside. I can't look at her right now. This is all way too fucked up. Stepping onto the back deck, I spot Ma sitting on the porch swing near the front door. She gives a loud, overly dramatized sigh and pats the seat next to her. In her lap is the hand gun Pop gave her for Christmas one year. I go to pass her when I hear the cocking of her gun.

RIDE

"Sit down, Punk," she says. Turning around, I see her gun pointed at me.

"You won't shoot me," I say, shaking my head.

"Alex is in her room crying. Try me."

Feeling defeated, I sit down beside her and raise my hands. "What do you want, Crazy?"

"Do you love me?" she asks. I go to stand up when she smacks me with the hand holding the gun. I don't care how good she is with a gun, a woman waving around a firearm is never a good thing. My heart skips several beats.

"You know I do," I say. Just like Pop, this woman has me fucking whipped. No matter how painful it is to talk about this, I try to give her the respect she's due for every night she stayed up late to help me with my homework and for every dinner she fixed up, and every time she's the mother my own didn't want to be.

"So, why's it so fucking hard to say it to Cub?" she asks. I don't answer, because whether she's my mother or not, fuck her. "You think you don't love her, but you do. You're just too fucking stupid to see it. Now grow a fucking pair and stop hurting her."

"I'm going to hurt her just by being with her," I mutter. Giving her a brutal glare, I tap my foot on the ground beneath me. "I'm an asshole, and she's too fucking stupid to let herself see it."

"One of you is fucking stupid, Punk, but it ain't her. She picked you, and you picked her. Let yourself enjoy it. You father, the club, they'll get over it."

"Whatever," I mutter. "You're just nuts."

"You want to know what love is? Love is that thing that happens when you least expect it. Love isn't about changing who you are, it's about being a better version of yourself. I see you with her, and it's like looking at your father twenty years ago. Cub makes you a better person. I didn't like it at first, but I see it now. She's good for you."

Leaning forward, I shove my head into my hands and yank at my hair. I don't want to listen to this, but I don't know how much more fight I have left in me. It's like she's been yanking away at every defense, at every hardened piece of me, fighting her way into a place I long ago thought dead. Relentless, determined, and even stupidly, she made me feel. I scrunch up my eyes and jam the balls of my hands into my sockets, trading one pain for another.

Loud shots ring out at the back of the property from behind the trees. In an instant, Ma and I are both standing, guns at the ready. My brothers rush toward the shots, keeping their guns up, trained on the tree line. I trail behind them, alert as ever. Ma rushes to the fuse box beside the front door and flips the switch just below it, basking the field in the flood lights. Whoever's back there won't get far with so much light on them.

I follow the sound, realizing only too late where I'm supposed to be. All of the fucking feelings bring thrown around screwed with my head. In a split second, I turn around as high-pitched screams ring out from the house. Lowering my gun, I take off in a sprint. Ma's nowhere to be found. More shots ring out, this time from the front of the house. My heart drops. Cub.

Out of nowhere, PJ shows up, running beside me. She pants, sprinting through the tall grass. She's so focused and trained—the perfect dog for protection. I was her pack leader once, but now it's Cub. As we sprint toward the house, I'm not sure who's more determined to get to Cub—me or PJ.

Leaping onto the deck, we rush into the house, turn right and run through the kitchen then down the hall and into Cub's room. The framed pictures on the wall have either fallen off or are in disarray. The bedspread is half off the bed, and all of Cub's valuables are tossed on the floor. A sick feeling washes over me as I eye the open sliding glass door. PJ whimpers from the corner, but I ignore it and rush out the door.

The flood lights are on, basking the front yard in a harsh light. A figure lies in the grass, coughing. It's a deep cough. I race across the deck and into the grass. Taking long strides, I reach the figure in no time. Sliding down beside the figure, I breathe a sick sigh of relief that it's not Cub.

Chief lies in the grass, coughing, his chest pooling with blood. His eyes are swollen shut, and there's a bullet hole in his stomach. His lungs wheeze and his frame shakes. "I'm sorry, Brother," he says. Letting out one more cough, his body shakes, and then he goes limp. I want to grieve for him, but I can't bring myself to. This is exactly the shit I was talking about earlier, priorities changing when a brother hooks up.

Snapping to, I rush back into Cub's room to PJ's incessant barking. I trained her to only bark like this when there's trouble. On the other side of the bed, PJ is barking and whimpering. I round the bed and drop to my knees. There, lying in a pool of blood, is Tegan. Her chest heaves in shallow breaths. Blood slowly drips from the cut across her neck. PJ's cries tear me apart as I watch the life slowly drain from Tegan. Scrubbing my face to hide the onslaught of tears from everything that's just happened, I let out a scream and vow to kill every fucking one of them. Those fucking bastards took my brother, they took my dog, and they fucking took my girl. I better find her in one piece, because I have plans for her—for us.

They're going to fucking suffer.

Alex

Chapter 26

Being deeply loved by someone gives you strength,
while loving someone deeply gives you courage.

- Lao Tzu

Earlier that day...

BEING WITH RYAN, in whatever capacity we've been
together these last few days, has been amazing. He's so
good at distracting me from the hell that's about to be
brought down on my life, and even worse—those around
me. My family. I catch him watching me, just like he
watched Jim and Ruby the other day. There's a longing in
his eyes that he doesn't want me to see. And I don't
really understand it. I want to know what screwed him up
so bad that he shut himself down. It won't last for too
long though, I can tell. I've been prying past his
protective armor. Maybe I should have warned him that
I'm persistent.

But right now isn't about Ryan and me, and it isn't
about Ryan's issues, either. Looking in the mirror, I take
stock of my appearance. For the first time in days, my
eyes aren't red with sorrow. There's so much to be sad—
even scared—about, but Ryan's right. Avoiding Ruby—
my mother—will only make the waiting that much more
difficult.

I look down at Tegan, who's lying by my feet, and
snap my fingers. She sits up, chest puffed out—confident,
in control—and waits for another command. I'm envious
of her confidence. This is really damn pathetic, being
jealous of a dog who sniffs crotches as a way of greeting.

"I guess we have to just do it, huh?" I ask. She
doesn't move until I snap my fingers again and pat my

leg twice. Leaving my room and walking into the kitchen, slowly, with Tegan at my side, I can't help but fidget. I spent two months with Ruby, growing to love her, willing up the courage to ask her about my mother. All the while not knowing, never really suspecting. Looking back, I suppose there were myriad clues, had I been paying attention.

I round the corner of the fridge and come into view, and wait to be noticed. It's an old nervous habit from life with my father, a man who didn't like to be interrupted unless it be absolutely necessary. Ruby stands at the peninsula, chopping carrots and tossing them into a commercial-sized pot beside her. Her hair is up in a butterfly barrette, and her face is free of make-up. She looks tired, worse than I've ever seen her. Selfishly, I hope she's worried about our relationship and not the impending threat. I hope she wants to be my mother as much as I want to be her daughter.

I can't kid myself though. I don't envy her position. She has three children—four if you count Ryan—and one of them might have to hurt another one in order to protect me. What might happen isn't something I can process, so instead, I avoid thinking about it.

"Hi," I whisper, praying like hell she hears me. Then when she stops the knife in mid-air and slowly lifts her head, giving me a soft smile, I almost want to disappear. It's so different now, knowing who she is, knowing what she did. She's still Ruby, but now she's something else, something bigger. And I'm—I don't really know who I am or how I fit anymore.

"Hey," she says back, just as softly, setting the knife down.

"Do you need any help?" I ask, pointing to the pot. It takes her a moment before she nods her head and waves me over. I cross the kitchen and get to work chopping celery after she hands me a knife. Standing here like this reminds me of Gloria and how much I miss her. I shut the thought down immediately, knowing I won't come back from that place if I let myself slip into those kinds of thoughts.

"The guys eat like pigs," she says. "I don't know when was the last time I cooked something that didn't feed an army." The evening after Ryan and I made love for the first time, six more guys showed up. Jim has a total of ten men on the house. The only change since they arrived was that now Ryan has the man who was on my sliding glass door down in the grass. It was my decision. I told him I wouldn't be able to be intimate with him if somebody could hear us.

Trying to lighten the mood and to move past this awkward place we're in, I force out a small laugh and nod my head. "Yeah, Ryan eats like he'll never be fed again."

She—my mother—lets out a laugh and shakes her head, saying, "Sex will do that to a man."

I freeze and keep my eyes trained on the countertop. She'd told me before we even got to California that Ryan was off-limits. Jim told me—and Ryan—more than once that we were to stay away from one another. Going against her wishes isn't the best way to build a relationship with her. Perhaps I can blame my age for my poor judgment. But no, that won't do. I think I can be good for Ryan, and apologizing for being with him goes against what I'm trying to accomplish.

"I'm not mad. Please look at me," she says, setting her knife down and wiping her hands clean on a nearby dish rag. Finding the will, I look her in the eye and wince.

"It's that obvious?" Shame creeps up my spine and washes over me. My father would have smacked me around a good bit if I'd had sex under his roof—if he knew I'd ever had sex at all. There was never, ever such a thing as equality in that house.

"No," she says with a smile. "But I suspected. Why do you think I've been watching my programs at such a high volume?" I blush under her knowing eye.

"I'm sorry. You asked me to stay away from him, and I should have respected your wishes," I say.

"I don't blame you. That boy has his father's looks and attitude. You didn't stand a chance. Besides, Jim knows nothing. He's been staked out at the barn."

"He really doesn't know?" I ask, nervously.

"I think this is one of those don't ask, don't tell situations. At least that's how I'm treating it until I can knock some sense into the club." She huffs out a deep breath and taps her long fingernail on the countertop.

"Will Ryan really lose his patch over me?" I ask. I hate having this conversation about Ryan, especially when there's so much history I wish I could bring myself to ask her about. But right now, I need to know she's okay with me and Ryan being together. I need to know what I might cost him and if I'll have to let him go.

"No," she scoffs. "Men, they're all a bunch of blowhards. This will pass, you just wait."

"Is there anything I can do to show them I won't hurt the club?"

"Loyalty and time, baby. They'll see. You just take care of him and don't let him push you around. Sooner or later they'll see," she says.

MY HEAD THROBS and my eyes can't focus. I think I can hear Michael's voice at a distance, but I'm not sure. It's a deep bravado that escalates into angry shouts. Footsteps slap against concrete, growing louder, getting closer. Rusty hinges squeak, bathing me in florescent light. It's only now that I realize I'm sitting up. My frame is held secure to the chair by rough rope, binding my legs, feet, waist, wrists, and torso. My mouth is dry, but when I try to open it and let out a dry cough, I find it's bound by tape.

I would be afraid right now, if I could bring myself to focus long enough to understand what's going on.

"Alex!" Michael shouts. His deep, familiar voice doesn't fill me with the warm fuzzies it once did. Cold fear washes over me. Michael's here, and that means my father's men are here. Michael's one of his men now, I guess. His soft hand lifts my chin, shaking it a little. The room comes into view. Concrete walls, concrete floor, no windows that I can see, and one dull bulb swinging from a string overhead.

"Where are they, Alex?" he asks, viciously ripping the tape off my mouth. It stings, but takes away from the pain in my head, so I don't curse him for it. His voice sounds nearly as cold as my father's right now. He's so distant, and emotionally removed from the situation. The only thing that gives him away is his hands—they're smooth.

"Who?" I ask, confused.

"The club," he says, tightening his grip on my chin. "I need to find them." I can't figure out in my head what he wants with the club. He has me. Isn't that what he came for, to kill me? Or does he want to make them watch?

"The house," I say. It's something he already knows, but if he's asking, that must mean they've left the house. Tegan. She tried to protect me and one of my father's soldatos killed her—a knife to her throat. A painful cry escapes me at the memory. I tried to stop them, to lunge in front of her, but she was faster, and he cut her then knocked me out for my trouble.

"Shut up and focus," he snaps. His command shocks me into silence. Despite the circumstances, I didn't expect to hear him talk to me like this. He's never talked to me like this. But then, he's also never had me tied up to a chair like this, either. Reaching around my head, he grabs a chunk full of my hair and pulls back on it. My chin points to the ceiling, my neck muscles ache from the position, and it's hard to breathe like this.

Leaning in close, he whispers, "I'm trying to get you out of here, okay? If dad thinks you're dead, he won't send anyone else. You'll be safe. But you have to trust me. Do you trust me?"

I want to trust him. I want to believe that he can keep me safe. But pretending to be dead means leaving the club behind. It means leaving Ryan behind, and leaving my mother behind. If I leave them, where will I go? Panic seizes my chest, and I shake my head. A firm hand comes down hard on my cheek. The painful sting Michael leaves behind is nothing compared to the blow to my soul.

"Let me help you."

"Let me go," I beg. He isn't having it. Rearing back, he brings another hard slap down to my other cheek. My neck jerks under the pressure, sending an ache up the back of my skull. Still, I try to right myself. When I do, he delivers another blow—this time higher up and across my right eye.

"Why do you want the club?" I choke out, pushing through the pain in my throat. He grabs the back of my neck, pulling my flesh hard against my binding, straining my neck to reach. Our noses touch, and our eyes lock.

"I'm going to kill them," he says, a smile creeping up on his face. Without losing eye contact, I muster the ability to hash this out. I won't give up the club, but maybe I can reason with him. Maybe he isn't so far gone that he won't be agreeable to a compromise.

"Why? They did nothing to you."

"Sis, listen, please," he pleads in the voice I'm used to, telling me that somewhere deep in there is still the boy I once knew. The boy I love and worry that I'll never see again. But we've made our choices, haven't we? We're not allies anymore. "If I can kill them—all of them—and burn the clubhouse, and tell Dad you died in the fire, he'll leave you alone. Don't you see?"

His eyebrows raise, hopeful, naïve. Stupid fool. Our father will want proof. It's not that easy, and Michael will never be able to pull it off. I have to believe that if he were to kill me, that it would tear him apart. Otherwise, if my own brother can kill me in cold blood, I'd rather already be dead.

"I'm not going to let you hurt them," I say. Rage fills his eyes, and he pulls back, then slams his fist into the side of my head. The chair tips to the side, sending me to the concrete. A new flash of pain emanates from my elbow, and I grit my teeth to stop the tears that spring into my eyes.

RIDE

"You would turn your back on your family for them?" he shouts.

"No, I'm protecting my family," I shout as he kicks me in the stomach. His undiluted anger pours out of him with every kick he delivers my abdomen. The first few make me queasy and send my eyes rolling into the back of my head in agony. Every inch of me hurts so bad, I'm almost numb. It's like I can feel everything and nothing. I feel delirious, and the world around me is hazy. I catch myself dozing off, only to snap to, confused. Then I remember where I am and wish I hadn't, and I pray that I'll lose consciousness.

Finally, he stops after what feels like a couple dozen or a couple hundred kicks. I widen my eyes, trying to focus on the world around me from this vantage point. Michael towers over me, cursing in frustration. Deep in my heart, I know he's trying to help me. Once the anger dissipates, I can see the fear. The only reason he could possibly be here is because he volunteered to either kill me or bring me back so someone else can kill me. And if he doesn't deliver, then he's in danger, too. A horrible sorrow engulfs me, and, for the first time since I talked to that stupid cop, the gravity of my choice really hits me. I was trying to help my brother back in Brooklyn. But I was also angry and spiteful. I couldn't have predicted what's happened, but maybe a piece of me was looking for a way out.

Through Michael's legs, I see dirty black boots in the distance through the doorway. Forcing myself to focus, I'm able to make out several pairs of dirty boots, and then I spot them—worn black steel-toed boots—Ian's boots. I've never seen him without them. Relief floods my system, then fear takes hold. If I tell Michael the club's here, he could hurt or kill one of them. I can't bear to lose a single one of them, even the ones I don't know. If I don't tell Michael, they could hurt or kill him.

"Please pick me up," I whimper. He spouts a few curse words in Italian then leans down and picks up my chair with one hand. The other holds a gold Desert Eagle gun all my father's men own. Any lingering doubt or hope I had that my brother wasn't officially connected flies out the window.

"Are you going to tell me where they are?"

"I love you," I say. And I mean it. It doesn't matter how much pain he's inflicted. I may have chosen the club, but I still love him. I'll always love him. "No," I say in defiance. Before I can get the word out and take a breath, he slaps me across my temple again. Then again, and again until I lose count. I can't even tell where the club is now. I've lost all sense of my surroundings.

"Keep hitting me," I say as loud as I can, but it comes out as a mumble. My jaw isn't quite working right. I'm slurring words, and my tongue keeps getting in the way. "I won't hurt them."

Michael's smooth hands wrap around my neck, squeezing so hard I lose sense of place and time. "Tell me where they are!" he screams into my face.

But then a second later, they're gone, and he's gone. A loud crash sounds across the room. A figure kneels in front of me, and a sharp blade closes in on my skin. Shouting ensues with so many voices going at once, I can't even make out who's who or how many of them there are. Internally, I panic at the very real possibility of being sliced up just like Tegan. Only, the blade yanks and pulls at my rope binding, and suddenly I'm free. My body slumps into the one crouching in front of me. Strong arms reach out, holding me. And it only takes a moment to know from his scent and his touch, that it's Ryan.

"I got you, baby," he whispers in my ear.

"My brother," I cry out.

Holding me close, he says, "He's alive."

It's not much, but it's something—the best I can hope for. I have no right to ask them not to kill him, even if I want to. With one arm beneath my knees and one supporting my back, he scoops me up. Moving into a standing position, he walks us out of the room, though to where, I can't tell. As he walks us to safety, he whispers his apologies in a strangled voice. "I'm so sorry, baby. Please be okay. Please be okay."

But they're not the words I want to hear, so I tell him. Or I try to. Through the steady thumping of my heartbeat in my ears, I can't make out much else besides his voice. With a raspy voice, I mumble, "Are you done fighting it?"

"I'm done, Cub," he says without hesitation. "Let's not make a big deal of it, but I love you, too." It feels good to hear it even if I knew it already. It's just a little confirmation that he's willing to go to the mat for me— for us. And once I'm healed up and I can think clearly, we'll get this mess sorted out with the club. Once everything settles down, I'm going to dig into his commitment issues. Because I'm determined to make this work with him.

As we slide into the back of a SUV, someone else crawls in to our right. Panic swells in my chest at the arrival of another person until I hear the deep, familiar voice. "It's just me, Princess," Duke says. Ian slides in to our left, also confirming his presence. The SUV fills with men I can't identify.

"You're okay, kid," Jim says, his voice breaking in-between words. Ryan's hand reaches out for mine and he slips his pinky around mine. And for the first time, despite the mild confusion and inexplicable pain, I do feel like I'm okay. More than okay, I feel protected, and whole.

"It's just a scratch," I say in a slur. The men around me laugh, all except for Ryan. He remains perfectly still and solid beneath me. I let myself drift off despite Ryan's attempts to keep me awake. Lost in thought, I think back to all the ways my life has changed these last few months. I'm not that same girl I was back in Brooklyn. I'm braver, stronger, and maybe even a little less co-dependent. But more importantly, I belong somewhere—to someone.

They came in leather and jeans, whisking me away from everything I knew—everything that was about to get me killed—all of the Armani, and bullets, and death. They made me one of them, a part of a family in a way I never had been before. Beyond gratitude and obligation, I chose them. I chose them because they love me, because they accept me, and maybe because they're wild and rowdy. Maybe because they brought me to my mother. And I still choose them. They brought me to him, and for that, they'll always have my loyalty. Because he was my salvation.

Epilogue

*Now this is not the end. It is not even the beginning
of the end.
But it is, perhaps, the end of the beginning.*

- Winston Churchill

SNUGGLED DEEP INTO the covers with Ryan at my back, I let out a heavy yawn. He pulls himself up and peers over me, moving my hair out of my face.

"You okay?" he asks, for what I swear is like the hundredth time today. I bite my bottom lip to keep from telling him that he's being annoying with all of his questions. I may pout or even give him a dirty look when he does it, but deep down, I live for these moments when he's all paranoid. I just wish he didn't have reason to be paranoid.

"I'm okay," I say and give him a soft smile. He's got almost a week's worth of stubble on his chin, as he hasn't shaved since the morning of the day I was taken. I had a bath yesterday, and that was interesting—he insisted on crawling in there with me. I'm not sure how clean I am, as my skin's a little filmy, but I couldn't bring myself to tell him he did a poor job.

"Are you sure? Because if you're not, Nic can go fuck herself," he says. His eyebrows pull together as he looks me over.

"I'm fine," I say a little stronger this time and pull myself up into a sitting position as best I can. Ryan's hovering makes it difficult, and I have to elbow him in the stomach to finish the task. "And I asked Duke to bring her by. He says she's been worried, and apparently it's a big deal for her to come to the house, and she's willing to do it to see me. So yes, I'm sure."

"Don't like it," he mutters and crosses his arms over his chest. In the days since the club found me in that warehouse, so much has changed. Jim's been nothing but kind, my mom's finally stopped crying, and now she just walks around with a big, stupid smile on her face when I can see her, but I have it on good authority she's worried about Michael. Despite everything, so am I. He's my brother, and even if he was a serious asshole and I'd like to return the favor one day, he's my brother. For the longest time, before I had the club and Ryan, and Nic—before I knew my mother—and before I found out Ian's my brother as well, all I really had was Michael and Gloria. I have no idea what's going on with Gloria, and the club's got Michael locked in a safe house somewhere nearby. I'm just not allowed to see him.

"You don't have to like it," I say for about the tenth time today. The moment I told Ryan that I wanted to hang out with Nic—alone—he practically blew a gasket. I had to hold his face and kiss him for five minutes straight before he calmed down enough to be spoken to in a rational and calm tone. "You've been great, you really have. But I need a little girl time. I have a lot to talk about that I can't say with you playing helicopter."

"I'm not a fucking helicopter, and if you're sick of me, Cub, just say so. You don't need to play these fucking games like you need girl time or whatever bull shit you're coming up with. Just tell me if I'm being annoying," he says in a rush of words that are half mumbled. Throwing the covers off himself, he crawls out of bed on the other side and stomps around the room in his boxers.

"You're being annoying," I say plainly while trying to keep a straight face. It's not so much that he's cute when he's like this as it is that he's starting to drive me crazy. If I don't choose to think it's funny, I'll have to ask my mom come to in and paddle the attitude right out of him. Because damn.

"Thanks," he snaps and bends down, picking up his jeans and sliding them on. "I'm just trying to help, you know. You're all clingy and shit, but whatever. It's fine." He plops down at the foot of the bed and starts shoving his feet into his boots. Very slowly, I lean over, ignoring the pang of discomfort in my ribs. Doctor James said it would be a couple weeks before I was back to normal, but I'm impatient. I'm not a cripple, but I might as well be with how little Ryan lets me move. Even when we make love, he demands that I don't do much of anything. He's totally turning me into a pillow princess, but if he's willing to live with the consequences of his actions, I think I can live with being pampered.

Crawling up behind him, I wrap my arms around his neck. "Don't be mad," I say and give his neck a kiss.

"Get your ass back in bed," he mutters and pulls away from me. I sit on my legs and pout at him. A dull ache gets stronger in my side, and, without thinking, I rub it softly to numb the pang.

"Now you're hurting yourself," he says and shakes his head. His eyes are narrowed and his pitch black hair is falling in his face. He pulls the covers back and points at my spot in bed and says, "Now."

"You are so damn bossy," I say and move too quickly. A sharp pain explodes in my knee and travels up to my hip.

"And you're a horrible fucking patient. If you can promise me you're not going to get up and start moving around like you just did, I'll promise to leave you and Nic alone for the entire fucking hour you put the request in for," he says. Carefully, I climb back into my spot and watch as Ryan pulls the covers up over me.

"And you just have horrible patience," I say and fold my arms over my chest. He's just grouchy because when I mentioned the idea of spending time alone with Nic he shot it down, telling me no way in hell was he leaving his room. Which is another thing. Since I'm not ready to move out and he's not ready to leave me alone—and to be honest, I'm not ready to be left alone, either—he's taking over my room. After he fixed up the mess my father's men had made when they grabbed me out of bed, he then told me the room wasn't working for him. The next day when I was sleeping, he took down my photographs of the pretty flowers that are out by the barn and replaced them with two posters of half-naked women draped over Harleys. I had to stare at those stupid bimbos for four days before I was able to yank them down, rip them up, and throw them in the trash. I can't say he was happy when he found them, but I wasn't exactly happy when he took my photographs down, either. As of right now, we're at a decorating stalemate.

He just glares at me as he walks over to my—our—closet and pulls out a clean black tee shirt that my mom hung up there this morning. He's grumbled a few times about being back in his parents' house, but with all the attention he's getting, I think he secretly loves it. When he's not in here with me, he's in the kitchen with my mom, and when he's not in there—his words, not mine—he's "taking a shit."

"Come here," I say as kindly as I can, but his expression doesn't change.

"Why? So you can tell me how much I suck up close and personal?"

"Shut up and get over here," I snap. I should know by now that being sweet doesn't work as well as being bitchy does. For some strange, twisted reason, he responds to bitchy. He walks over and sits at the edge of the bed, scowling down at me.

I give him my best smile, bat my eyes, and say, "Say it again."

"Uh uh," he says, shaking his head. He moves to stand, but I put a hand over my ribs and let out a soft moan. His eyes dart down to my hand, and he covers it with his own. His eyes are pained as he looks to make sure there's no additional bruising and the swelling's gone down. "What's wrong?"

"You pain me," I say with a pout. It's really unfair to pretend to be hurt to get my way, but if he's going to act like a child, so am I. I tried being the mature one in this relationship and all it got me was bimbos on my wall.

"That's really not fucking funny," he gripes and pulls back. I catch his face in my hands and pull him down to me, placing a kiss on his cheek.

"Come on, baby. Please," I whisper. His body drops to the bed, and I know I've won.

"Scoot over," he says, and I do. I move over another foot so he can stretch out beside me. I wiggle down the bed and turn to face him. He huffs and then purses his lips. When he's done fighting it, he smiles down at me and cups my face with one hand and pulls me flush against him with another. With his breath washing over my face and his arms around me, I almost rethink asking Nic to come over. Maybe Ryan's right and I don't want to spend an hour away from him. But I need girl time, I remind myself. I want to keep Nic as a friend, and that means letting her in—especially since word around the house is that Duke's been sleeping in her bed almost every night—and O.M.G.— that's something I have to talk to her about.

"I love you," he says and kisses the ridge of my brow. "I love you," and this time it's a kiss to my closed left eye. "I love you," and it's a kiss to my cheek. More kisses follow all with more "I love you's," and I melt into him. I don't let him see me wince when his lips trail over one of the bruises that hasn't healed yet. My stomach flutters, and I lose my breath for a single second. It never lasts as long as I'd like for it to, but it's worth all the begging and pleading I have to do in order to get my way. Because there's nothing on this planet like hearing Ryan say he loves me. There's nothing that comes close to him showing me that he loves me with every annoying question and every moment he spends hovering over me. When he's done, there's a smile on his face that tells me that he enjoys that almost as much as I do.

"I love you," I say and place a kiss on his lips that slowly turns to something more carnal than I had intended for it to. I don't hear my bedroom door as it opens, but I do hear the throat clearing that makes me pull back from the kiss. Ryan's head shoots to the door, and he glares at Nic, who's standing there in front of Duke. Her nose is turned up, and she's shaking her head.

"Ew," she says. "I thought you said you were nobody's girl." The comment is intended for me, but she's glaring and shaking her head at Ryan. Behind Nic, Duke lets out a heavy sigh and shoves her into the room, stepping in behind her.

"Right back at'cha," I say. My eyes dart between the two. They look good together, even if she won't admit it. Her eyes finally land on me, and while I'm smirking at her, thinking nothing of the fact that she hasn't seen me since before everything that went down, I've totally forgotten about the bruises on my face. Her face falls, and she scowls. She crosses the room at a quick pace and crawls onto the bed on the other side of me. I turn her direction and, with Ryan's help, I pull myself up.

"I knew you were hurt, I just didn't know how hurt," she says quietly as she gets comfortable with her legs crossed in front of her.

"I'm okay," I say and look back at Ryan. Reaching out, I give his hand a squeeze. "Really, everything's okay." Ryan hops out of bed and greets Duke at the doorway.

"Sixty minutes," he says with his eyes trained on Nic. She rolls her eyes, but smiles at him.

"Gosh, you really do love her, don't you?" she says. His playful smile disappears, and he huffs as he leaves the room.

"Yeah," I say. "He really does love me."

Thank you for taking the time to read Ride. I hope that you will take a moment to leave a review for the novel on Amazon and Goodreads. Positive or negative, your opinion matters.

BONUS CONTENT

RYAN

Ryan's point of view
from Chapter 6 of Ride

I LEAD MY brothers off the highway and into the dirt parking lot of a small gas station—the only structure for miles around—and thank a God I don't believe in that I can finally take a piss. My back is killing me, my ass is numb, and my nerves are shot. I won't feel better until we make it home.

I turn off my bike, push down the kickstand, and dismount. Our charter, the Fort Bragg Forsaken, pulls up beside me. Our Detroit charter, led by patch president, Rig, trails behind the van that carries Ma and her kid. But she's not really a kid, now is she?

Barging into her bedroom back in Brooklyn took me aback. I knew going in that she was nineteen, but there's nineteen and then there's nineteen. Even free of makeup, with a braid running down the back of her head, and with her body covered up, she not a little girl. She's on the verge of womanhood. I guess it's been longer than I thought since Ma got a picture from Gloria. And fuck if it ain't screwing with me. Now's not really the time to think about getting my dick sucked, but it's not like I've got much else to think about on such a long ride.

I weave through my brothers and head toward the black van, parked at the gas pump. Ian and Pop stride up behind me, stretching their tired muscles as they walk. The front doors of the van swing open, and Bear and Diesel climb out and head toward Rig's crew is filling up the bikes. Reaching the van, I grab hold of the sliding door and pull it open.

Sitting on the long seat in front of me is Alexandra. Seated next to her is Ma, who looks like she's in serious need of a drink and some bud. Alexandra's eyes are wide, and the exhaustion from the situation shows on her face. In this moment, they look so much alike. Neither one is well rested, nor do they appear very comfortable around each other. I hate it when bitches are sad. They end up crying and shit.

I give them both a wicked smile and say, "Anyone who has to piss, come with me." I turn around and walk toward the side of the gas station's tiny store where the bathroom is. I don't get far when Alexandra rushes up beside me. The faint scent of perfume wafts off of her, infiltrating my nose. It smells kind of like roses. Not too strong and fairly pleasant. You know, for a chick's perfume.

"Hey, Trigger," Ian says from behind me. I stop immediately. He never uses that stupid fucking nickname unless he's trying to piss me off. Turning around, I give Ian a flat stare.

"Yeah?" I say. Ian's frame is tight, and his hands are on his hips. Something's pissed him off. But then, he's been in one hell of a mood since we left Mendocino County. He doesn't talk about it, but I know he has some fucked-up memories of Mancuso. Back when we were kids and my dad started hooking up with his mom, he used to have nightmares about how he got the scar that run from the tip of his left ear up to his eyebrow. He may be one disturbed bastard, but he couldn't be more my brother than if the same blood ran through our veins. I hate that this shit is so fucking personal for him.

"Where are you going with the kid?" he asks. I shoot Alexandra a look, wondering what the difference is between him and me that he sees her as a kid. Then I remember that important little biological connection. By the time Ruby was pregnant with Alexandra and her twin brother Michael, Ian was old enough to know what was going on. My gut twists at the realization.

He loves her. He may not even think of it like that, but I see it in the worry lines around his eyes and the way he carries himself. She has no idea who he is, but he's always known her. Every year that Ma lit two candles on Alexandra and Michael's birthday, every Christmas that she pulled out those ornaments with their names on them, every time someone asked her about her kids...

In a way, we all love her. There has never been a Ruby without an Alexandra and a Michael. In that way, thinking of the weight of her presence in our family, I get why Ian looks like he can't decide between barfing or starting a fight. We're in the middle of nowhere and we have over two thousand more miles to log before we can chill out a bit. This somber shit has got to fucking go.

"Around back," I say with a smirk. Ian's expression darkens. Alexandra gasps, her wide brown eyes shooting up to mine. Her cheeks are beet red. She lowers her head back to the ground in obvious embarrassment.

"You're not funny," he responds. Ma scoffs from a distance and walks up to our small group. She gives me a light shove and turns, giving Ian a glare. Her face softens minutely as the pain in his features registers in her mind. Sometimes, when you know people well enough, you just know what they're thinking. Mancuso, the scar on Ian's face, the sacrifice she made so many years ago. It's like I'm witness to the most excruciatingly painful moment either has ever experienced.

"You," Ma says to Ian, "fill up the tank." Wheeling around, she slaps my bicep. "I ought to rip your ear off for that comment, Ryan," she says. And just like that, she's back to being the woman who raised me—tough as nails and ready to take on anyone.

I walk away to check my phone for messages. So far, so good. The prospects know to call one of us if there's a problem, and as of right now, I don't have a single message. Shoving my phone in my pocket, I look up to see Ma waving me over to her. I close the distance between us, toss an arm over her shoulder, and bend down, kissing her cheek. Pop got it right when he hooked this one. She's the only woman I think I'll ever love.

"And this punk is Ryan, my step-son," she tells Alexandra.

"Don't let her tell you nothing," I protest. "She lies." Ma laughs loudly as Alexandra looks shocked as all hell. What kind of bubble has this chick been living in?

"See? A punk," she says and jerks her thumb at me. "No respect." For the first time since I saw her for the first time, Alexandra looks relaxed. A small laugh escapes her, and she shakes her head ruefully. Her laughter dies down quickly, and she shuffles her feet in the dirt before she spins around and rushes into the now vacant bathroom.

Ma's smile falls as her eyes suddenly fill with tears. She wipes them away quickly. I can't help but envelope her in a tight hug. With her head against my chest, I give her back a pat and kiss the top of her head. Sometimes I forget that this is hardest on Ma. I think we all do. She's so fucking tough it's easy to gloss over the reality of what's happening here.

"Chill out, woman," I say. "She's real. She's not going to fucking float away." Ma sniffles then pushes me away with a clipped laugh. Pop walks up, and I happily hand her off to him. He married her, he can take care of this weepy shit. If he weren't here, I'd do it, but being in Ma's arms makes me feel like I'm ten years old all over again.

A hard object rams into my back, sending me toward the dirt floor. Pain radiates from my shoulder blades and shoots down my spine. I catch myself before my knees hit the ground, and spin around to see Chief—whose real name is Charles—grinning at me. Once recognition dawns, I throw my fist at his face, connecting with his jaw. It's barely a second before he flies at me, fists wailing and excitement in his eyes. I fly backward from the impact and hit the ground with a heavy thud, this stupid bastard on top of me. I manage to throw him off only to move the wrong way and end up in a headlock. I need this shit. The adrenaline keeps me awake, and aware.

Pop shouts, getting everybody's attention. I shove Chief off me and stand, brushing the dirt off my arms. Rig's crew and the rest of our charter stop what they're doing and form a loose circle in front of Pop, ready to hear what he has to say. As usual, his speech is short, it's just not short enough. "We're making good time. We need to keep it up. If anybody can't keep up with the hours we're pulling, turn in your fucking patch. We didn't get this far to fuck up now. Straight through to Nevada, boys."

I let my attention wander from Pop to the men surrounding me. They're all silent and respectful enough. Despite the bored looks and tired eyes, they remain silent and keep their focus on Pop. Off in the distance stands Alexandra. Her eyes travel through the crowd with a sense of wonderment on her face. After all of the change she's endured the last few days, it's a wonder she can stand there with such a look of both curiosity and confidence.

Over the years, we've done our fair share of recon missions through the club. Everything from pulling hookers out of crack dens to helping a brother out of a sticky situation he's found himself in. My brothers are always grateful for the assist, but the bitches we help usually act so fucking entitled that it's almost not even worth it if I don't get my dick sucked afterward. I mean, Christ. We've had our fair share of divas over the years.

But looking at Alexandra as she looks over the club with such intensity, and not an ounce of detest, makes me wonder what else is going on inside of her head. Finally, her eyes land on mine. She flinches in surprise then her expression warms. I can't quite figure her out, but I'm going to try. She's not someone I should be fucking around with, I already know that. And I don't want to fuck anything up. She is family, after all. But damned if I'm not fucking baffled by her behavior. Her eyes widen and her plush lips part. Dick-sucking lips if I'd ever seen 'em. Her eyes dart around before coming back to me.

A faint smile covers her face as she mouths the words that will be etched into my mind for months to come. She says, "Thank you," like I've done something for her. The show of appreciation takes me aback, forcing me to break the stare for a moment before I regain focus on her face. And I can't look away. Women don't thank me much, even after I've fucked them just the way they want it. They don't thank me when I do nice shit for them. But this chick thanks me in a way I'd have expected the least and I can't look away until Ma exits the bathroom, walks up to her, and starts chatting her up. I force myself to go back to paying attention to Pop, but the only thing I can think about is this stupid girl and her gratitude. It makes me feel like I've done something worth doing, which I haven't experienced in a long time. And I'm not sure I'm going to recover if she keeps appreciating shit.

Ryan's point of view
from Chapter 13 in Ride

FUCKING DUKE. HE thinks he's paying me back or some shit. We go back all the way to elementary school. He was my brother even before we shared a patch. We've been through some shit, he and I. I got his back in anything. Anything but this.

"Princess wants to have fun," he says, leading Cub down the hall with one arm slung over her shoulders and a "fuck you" grin on his face. It doesn't matter how many times I've heard him call her Princess, both to her face and when she's not around, it still grates on me. I know damn well he doesn't have a thing for her. His dick's too wrapped up in wishing Nic would acknowledge his existence to develop any fucking feelings for Alex.

This chick—Mary, Melanie, Ellen, fuck if I know—continues to rub herself up against my dick. I'm barely at half-mast. The frustration builds inside, making me restless. Alex moves to pass me, her arm dangling at her side. Unable to help myself, I reach out and hook my index finger around her pinky. She's so soft. Everything about her is soft, even the sass she throws on the rare occasion that she speaks to others. She doesn't know I see her, but I do.

A rush of excitement builds in my gut, making me gasp. This chick—the one who's sucking so hard on my fucking neck, I think she's going to leave a bruise—takes it as a sign that she's doing something right, and she runs a hand down my stomach and cups my dick.

Despite our connection, she continues to create a distance between us. It's probably karma or some shit. I'm a dick to her, and she leaves me. But all I can do is stand here like a fucking tool, latching onto her pinky for dear life. Ever since I met her, that's how I've been feeling. I'm off balance, and the club's figured it out. I try to play it off, like I'm not desperate to get into her pussy or something, but they know better.

Just before we lose contact, her head spins around. She's scowling. Her brows pull together, and her bottom lip juts out. But damned if it doesn't feel good to have her look at me. It's been months since I've spent any time around her, and even then it was brief. But she won't go away, and I don't know why. She's everywhere and it's fucking insufferable. Her dark brown hair falls around her shoulders, and she looks so young and yet so determined to grow up at the same time. She's like a baby bear—a cub—little, but already so very fucking lethal. At least, that's how it feels when she tears her eyes away from mine and passes through the kitchen by Duke's side.

I strain to keep my body in place, but the need to follow her is overwhelming. Finally, having enough of the fucking vacuum at my neck, I give the bitch a gentle shove. I just need some distance. She's gorgeous as shit and fucking stacked with some of the perkiest natural tits I've ever seen, but she's also just too fucking eager. It used to be my thing, but not now. Now, I'm all kinds of fucked up with ideas of a gentle touch and a soft smile, and coy flirting. It's the worst fucking thing I could be getting into, and yet I am.

"What's wrong, baby?" the chick asks. Blowing out a frustrated breath, I practically spit a string of curse words at the wall before me. She blinks rapidly, and her face falls. Shit. Bitches who look like that aren't as eager to ride my cock. I really don't want to have to start over with another bitch. This one's mostly ready to go.

"Nothing. Come on," I say, grabbing her wrist and moving toward the kitchen. She doesn't budge, and I stop in place. Looking back at her, I raise my eyebrows.

"Where are we going?" she asks, her eyes shooting to Cub's bedroom door. An irrational flash of anger shoots through me at the thought of her in that room, on that bed. She has no fucking business being in that room.

"Do you want me to fuck you or not?" I ask in a harsher tone than I intend, but she gets the point. I've seen her around the clubhouse and in the palace. She's got a thing for attention, and she's taken some raunchy dick to get it. So she relents, just like I knew she would. I keep her wrist tight in my hand and lead her out of the house. It's a typical party, maybe even a little tame. People are fucking around in every corner of this house. I find myself stumbling around drunk fuckers left, right, and sideways. It's ridiculous and I love it. I miss this shit. Ma's been low-key since she brought her cub home, probably worried she'll think we're all just a bunch of heathens—which we are.

It's no coincidence that as we leave the house, Duke and Alex are a hundred feet or so in front of us. Walking through the backyard, I make sure not to lose them in the crowd. Up ahead, in the large red barn, it looks like some of the party guests are hot boxing the fucking thing. I pull the chick around the corner of the barn, shielded just enough so neither Duke nor Alex will see us.

She leans against the side of the barn and immediately goes to work on the button of my jeans, and then the fly. Pulling my jeans down just below my ass, and then slowly lowering my boxers, she gently pulls my dick free. I haven't even come yet and I'm already over it. She licks her lips and smiles at me as she lowers herself to the ground. "You're so big, baby."

"Shut up," I snap, unable to stop myself. "You wanted my dick, you got it." Ignoring my attitude, she lets her tongue glide against my tip, and finally I'm starting to feel something.

On the other side of the barn, Alex presses herself up against Duke—my fucking brother. This fucker and I, we share a patch, and that is supposed to mean more than fine pussy. I place my hand against the bar to keep myself steady as this chick works her magic on my dick while her hand cups my balls. It's starting to feel pretty fucking euphoric, but then his hand moves to her hip, sneaks around to her ass. And I'm numb.

I barely feel her lips on my dick as I watch his tongue shove into Alex's mouth. My hand aches from the way I'm gripping the aged wood of the barn. The way Duke touches her makes everything else in the world fade away. He's seducing her, just like he's done to so many others. Lowering her to the grass, I feel a twinge of anger start to build. This is so wrong—all of it. Him doing her, me watching him do it. I've seen brothers run a train on some bitch I didn't even know, and it didn't faze me. But this is different. I know Alex, and I don't think she can handle what he's about to do to her.

Suddenly, my dick is cold. I look down and see the chick has stopped doing her thing. Instead, she's standing up, and pulling a condom out of her pocket. I shake my head and pull one of my own out. Call me paranoid, but I'm not about to knock some chick up. Especially one whose name I don't even know.

Making quick work of the condom, I roll it onto my dick and spin her around, pushing her front up against the side of the barn. Eagerly, she discards her clothes and kicks them aside. I don't know why she bothered with her top. I'm not in the mood to motorboat her tits or anything. She tries to turn, but I place my hand between her shoulder blades to keep her in place. I use one hand to keep her steady and the other to guide myself in. She moans loudly, irritating me. All I want to think about is her pussy, but all I can think about is Cub's. She's got to be tighter than this; sweeter, too. I bury myself in this used up cunt, then pull out, and ram myself back in. She murmurs something unintelligible. She's enjoying this way too fucking much, and I'm not enjoying it at all.

Duke shifts just enough, providing me a clear view of Alex as she lies, with her jean shorts unbuttoned and peeled open, on the damp grass. Above her, Duke trails his hand down her stomach, and then over her underwear. I can't see the top of her panties, but I know that move. Sure enough, he hooks a finger beneath the fabric. Everything I've been feeling, and everything I've lied to myself about feeling, boils to the surface. Blind rage takes over, and I push this chick up against the barn. Her only response is to moan in delight as I batter her with my dick.

Alex squirms and then lets out a breathy moan. My stomach clenches and my visions hazes over. This stupid bitch whines and tries to shove off the barn. Giving her a firm, but slight, push, I wrap a hand around her hair and tilt her head back just a bit. "Enjoy it. This is the only time you're getting my dick," I say.

"You're being too rough," she protests, but I ignore her and tighten my grip on her hair.

"Ow. Careful," she whimpers, but it's not enough to make me stop what I'm doing. Again and again, I pummel myself inside of her. Watching Alex writhe under Duke's touch crosses signals in my brain, makes my chest pound, and makes my mouth go dry. Like the sick fuck that I am, I fine-tune my movements in time with his. If I zero in on the arch of her back and the sounds of her orgasm as it builds, I can pretend it's my dick inside her and this bitch and Duke are nothing but a fucking memory.

"It hurts," she says in a harsh tone, but it doesn't matter. Alex tosses her head back and she grips the grass beside her. Watching her fall apart like that forces my own orgasm out. My head pounds as I come, still ramming into her pussy, but letting go of her hair.

Barely coming down off of her high, I have to watch as Duke stands, and licks her juices off of his finger, and then walk away. I still myself and pull out, then toss the condom off into the grass and pull my pants up the rest of the way. But I don't move. The chick turns around and tries to kiss me like we're a fucking couple now or some shit. Barely able to manage it, I say, "Go."

And she does, and I'm left to watch Cub as she cries in silence in the damp grass.

THRASH

A BAYONET SCARS NOVEL

Releasing January 9th, 2014

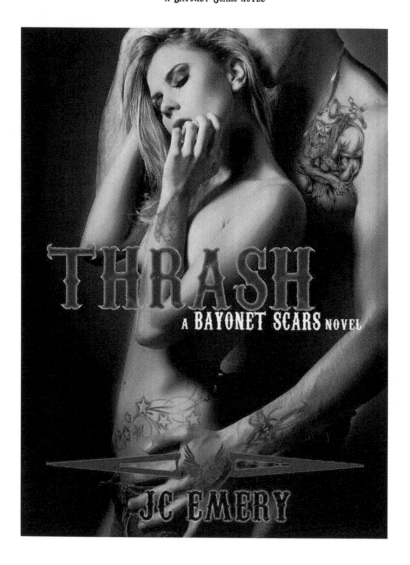

THRASH

A BAYONET SCARS NOVEL

JC EMERY

LONELINESS SUFFOCATES THE HEART.
ACCEPTANCE BREAKS DOWN WALLS.

As a Lost Girl to the Forsaken Motorcycle Club, Nicole Whelan knows how to party. She's not cut-out for relationships and her life is way too complicated for anything more than casual encounters. But one night when she falls into Duke's bed at the clubhouse, he sees something in her that he can't let go of—no matter how many times she tries to run.

Having been left to raise her teenage brother, Jeremy, she's already got her hands full and isn't looking for anymore complications. But Duke's just watched his best friend fall for the only girl he couldn't have, and then almost lose her so shortly after, shaking him to his core. Faced with his own loneliness, he's more determined than ever to break down Nic's walls and show her that he can be good for her; but he's got a bad track record and she's got a bad temper. Changing his ways isn't easy when he's not sure what he's even changing for.

The violence and turmoil are at an all-time high, and Forsaken is in a vulnerable place when a twist of fate breathes new life into the club. It's a much-needed beacon of hope for the embattled biker family, even if everyone's not exactly on board. With Duke and Nic's relationship already on shaky ground, and something even more important at stake, the Forsaken Motorcycle Club will fight like hell to keep their family together and whole.

Love is never more precious than when it's new.

RIDE

MAY

Prologue

EVERYTHING IS FUCKED up. The room tilts slightly—or maybe it's me—and the edges of everything around me is fuzzy. Maybe I drank too much this time. No, scratch that, I *know* I drank too much this time. Being here, with him, should be my first clue that I fucked up and went too far. I promised myself I wouldn't do this, not with him. This is what happens when I drink too much. I make poor decisions. This time my poor decision has an all-too-familiar name: Duke.

He's been trying to fuck me for years and I've always lied through my teeth and let him think that I wasn't interested. If he knew about the stupid crush I've been harboring for him after all these years, I wouldn't have been able to keep him off of me for this long. He's persistent, I'll give him that.

It doesn't matter what-- or who-- he's doing. Every night we're both here, we hang out for a while. Usually, it's me sitting in silence drinking my beer, and it's Duke telling me I should suck his dick-- to which I decline. But he's here and it's a routine I've come to appreciate. It's not much, but it's something. And until now, it's always been enough.

Maybe just for one night I want to let myself indulge in the fantasy.

He holds my hand in his, atop his bent knee. I'm leaning into him, an arm on the top of the bar to hold myself upright, my ass is scooted to the edge of the barstool. Duke's blue eyes are bloodshot and hazy. Small lines appear on the sides from the smile on his face. I try to smile back, but I probably look like a stroke victim. Everything keeps tilting. It's really not fair because it makes it harder to really *see* him. He's all thick neck and goatee and short blond hair and sex. And I've seen him make other Lost Girls come. They scream their brains out as he fucks them hard. And tonight it's my turn. Tonight, it's like Christmas and I'm about to get a present that is going to make it hard to walk for the next two days.

I try to focus on the beer bottle as he brings it to his lips. I can't quite read the label on the side. It's less than a foot away, but everything I look at seems backwards, but not backwards at the same time. Damn, I'm fucked up. He tips his head back, and gulps down what's left in the bottle. Sitting the empty on the bar, Duke licks the beer off his lips. It's almost like he's teasing me with every part of his body I've fantasized about for so long, but have never given myself the right to have. I don't realize I'm biting my lip until it hurts. He smirks and pulls my lip away from my teeth.

We've never been here before. This close. It's unnerving.

"You've been a hard one to catch," he says. I purse my lips and smile at him. Duke has always been the kind of guy that people are just naturally drawn to. Ever since the first time I saw him freshman year of high school, I've had a thing for him. But Duke likes to fuck around and play mind games and that's a surefire way to get my heart broken. So, no thank you.

But right now he's all muscles and goatee and smooth talking, and I'm all drunk and relaxed, and up for anything. So, yes please.

"Let's go," he says, standing from his position on the stool. He gives my hand a slight tug, encouraging me to move. I'm not sure it's such a good idea. I list myself off the seat and move to step down, but somehow lose my footing and slip toward the floor. A strong arm catches me on my way down, pulling me against a mass of warmth wrapped in leather and jeans.

Holding me up, Duke leads us through the main room of the Forsaken Motorcycle Club's clubhouse, and down a long hallway with doors on both sides. At the very end of the hall are the double doors to the chapel. I've never been in there. If there's anything sacred to an outlaw motorcycle club, it's the chapel. On the left side is the palace, which I admit with no great amount of pride, that I've danced half naked in a time or two. The other doors lead to bedrooms which serve as crash pads for club members, and I know exactly which rooms belongs to which brother. All Lost Girls know that.

We stop at the third door on the right which Duke was gifted when he earned his officer patch as SECRETARY. He reaches out, twists the handle and lets the door swing open. The room is dimly lit and reeks of body odor, which is not uncommon. With his hand on my lower back, he encourages me into the room with a gentle push. I blow out a deep breath and walk in, shrugging off my reservations.

This is what we do. It's nothing really. The club, the girls. We drink, and fuck, and pass out. But Duke and I have a history, and I told myself I wouldn't do this—not with the man who used to be the boy who I once thought hung the moon. But now I know better. He'll be all about me for a minute before he tosses me aside, just like he's done to every girl who's come before me.

As the door clicks shut behind me, I decide that all of this overthinking is bullshit. I knew what I was doing when I showed up tonight. After the bullshit with Jeremy at school today, I needed the release, so I showed up at the clubhouse. This was the whole point of coming, wasn't it? To fuck and forget—to let the entire world dissolve into a vacuum of feeling devoid of worry?

Fuck it.

I spin around to face Duke, giving him a smile that's a total goddamn lie. After all this time, the idea of being with Duke puts my nerves on edge. I've thought about this moment for so long that I almost can't believe it's really happening. He lifts his chin just slightly, making his goatee look longer than it is. Before I can stop myself, I lunge at him. Leaping into the air, my hands latch onto his shoulders and as smoothly as I can, I wrap my legs around his waist. Immediately, he grabs at my ass, keeping me in the air. Now firm in his arms, I move my hands to the sides of his neck and pull his face to mine. I press my lips to his, and don't have to wait for him to catch up. If there's one thing I've heard about Duke, it's that he knows how to fuck.

A jolt of what I can only describe as pure electricity runs through me at the touch of his lips on mine. He presses down, relentless in his pursuit. His lips are rougher than I expect, but not entirely unwelcome. I open my mouth, inviting him in. Just like I knew he'd be, Duke takes every invitation I extend. Pushing my pelvis into his, a low growl erupts from deep in his throat as his hands clamp down on my pliant flesh. A moan escapes me at the contact.

A frenzied mess of limbs, we tumble onto the nearby queen-sized bed, bouncing into the air and completely disregarding of the noise we make. For even a brief few hours it's nice to be so free and so out of control. All the jostling makes it difficult to breathe for a minute. The mattress protests in squeaks beneath us as Duke covers my body with his, trailing a hand down my side. He's going so slow, and I'm just not used to it. I can't tell if I like it or not, but I know better than to step out of my place.

I bring one of my arms up and beneath my head, and prop my head up on it so I can see exactly what he's doing. His tattooed hand grips the top of my jeans before deftly flicking the button loose and pulling them down with one strong, commanding tug. I've spent years watching his moves, but it's an entirely different thing when the focus is on me. No stranger to the palace and all the debauchery that goes on in that place, I've seen Duke take women out in the open. He's never been shy, that's for sure.

"What's wrong?" he asks. Realizing I've been staring off into space, I shake my head and look down at him. My pants are around my ankles, his hand still around the bunched material as if he stopped in mid-pull. His blond hair, shorter than he normally keeps it, falls into his piercing eyes as he stares me down.

"Nothing," I say and buck my hips up to him in encouragement. For a moment I think he might argue, but he doesn't. Pulling off my jeans the rest of the way, and tossing them across the room, he lets out a heavy sigh. His mood's changing for reasons I can't even fathom. If I thought he was moving slowly before, I was wrong. Now he moves at a turtle speed as he kisses his way up my legs, alternating between the two, but staying toward the middle. Finally, he lands a kiss on the center of my black thong panties. Having been so attentive the entire night, now he keeps his eyes lowered as he grips the sides of my thong and slowly pulls it down.

Without lifting his head, he crawls up my body, letting his nose drag along my flesh. I didn't know he would be this slow with me. He's not been slow the few times I've seen him in action, not that watching Duke have sex is something I'm prone to doing. It's just something that happens around here.

I try to pull my mind out of that awkward place it keeps going to—remembering everything he's done with other women, and thinking about how it compares to what he's doing with me. I'm such a mess, I'm starting to wonder if getting off is even worth all the trouble this shit is causing me. I mean, I told myself I wouldn't fucking do this with him for a reason. I'm way too attached. And when everything little memory and all of the worry gets too much to take, I decide to mentally check out and be goddamn done with all of the "what if" crap that I'm usually so good at pushing out of my head.

Sitting up, he scoots back to avoid getting knocked in the face with my elbow. Quickly, I pull my bra tank over my head and toss it across the room then reposition my legs beneath me and pull him up to me. Propped up on my legs, I use his heavy torso as leverage to keep myself steady. Running my hands up and down his leather cut, I try to ignore that little voice in the back of my head that reminds me how very much I am like the woman I hate so much: my mother. She always had a thing for bikers, and much less a thing for motherhood as evidenced by her departure all those years ago.

"If you're not into this, I'll get someone else," he says. My head snaps up, eyes finding his, and I give him my best mean face. He gives me a serious look and says, "But I *want* you."

"I was trying not to puke on the leather. You don't have to be a dick," I say. A kaleidoscope of butterflies erupts in my belly at that comment. The hint of a smile forms and he grips my sides, then in a surprise move, drops backwards and pulls me on top of him. I was buying time when I told him I was trying not to puke, but now I'm not lying anymore. The world spins around me as I hold onto him tight. His body shakes beneath mine and when I can see steady once again I notice that he's on his back and I'm straddling his lap. Totally naked and bared to him, I remind myself that I've done this more times than I can count. He's Forsaken, and I'm a Lost Girl. It's who we are and this is what we do. I have zero reason to be weird about this. Except that he's not just some random guy. He's charming, and he's funny. And he's Duke.

Taking the front of his cut and gently pulling it off his shoulders, a disturbingly loud cell phone rings, startling me. Duke's eyes narrow as he grumbles something about his dick and then manages to yank the offensive object out of his pocket. Flipping open the phone, he brings it to his ear.

"Yeah? Now? Fuck. Yeah, just gimme five?" he says into the phone, flips it shut, and tosses it beside us on the bed. Throwing one of his muscles arms down on the bed he curses and then bucks his hips. I grip the leather of his vest tightly and go to move off of him but his hands find their way to my hips, keeping me in place.

"We just have to be quick, baby," he says. Reaching over, he pulls a condom off the side table and sets it down beside him. Leaning back, I pop open the button of his jeans and pull down the zipper. Just as I'm freeing him from his constraints, one of his hands finds its way to my center. His thumb parts my folds and rubs me in small circles until my thighs clench tightly into his hips. The room feels so cool, every slight gust of wind that moves past me sends chills up my spine. Gooseflesh covers me from head to toe.

"I could watch this shit for days," he says in a husky voice. As much as I want to see looks of wanton desire in his eyes, I don't risk losing the building euphoria I have going on. My mind, shoulders, and soul feel a little lighter the longer he attends to me for. Breaking from the rhythm he's created, Duke speeds up his ministrations, applying more pressure and sending me to the edge. I toss my head back, my body locks up, and for a brief moment, nothing—not even me—exists. And I'm floating. When I come back down to earth, I pry my eyes open to see Duke ripping the wrapper open with his teeth and then rolling the condom down his shaft.

Not giving myself a chance to change my mind, not that with the way my body responded to just the pad of his thumb I'm doubting much, I pull myself up his body and sink down onto him. Moving at first slow and steady, then fast and relentlessly, I slide myself up and down his length. Keeping my eyes trained on his face, I watch as he locks his jaw up and his breath catches. Bringing his hips up to meet mine, he drives himself into my core, making me gasp for air. It isn't long before we're a sweaty mess. His thumb starts with the circles again and the combination of everything he's doing to my body is too much to take. I clamp down around him as tight as I can while bringing one hand behind me and cupping his balls. His movements still as his eyes fly to the back of his head and his body goes still, and his muscles turn to stone beneath me.

I give us both a moment to come down from our highs before I give his chest a soft pat and slide off of him. His eyes pop open with a cloud of confusion beneath the surface before he washes it all away and just like always he's back to being the bad-ass I know he's always had to be.

On shaky legs, I stand beside the bed, watching as he tears the condom off and tosses it in a nearby trash bin and then zips his jeans up. Blowing out a deep breath, he stands, and pulls me to him. Cupping my face in his hands, he slams his lips against mine. This time I expect the power behind his touch and his rough lips. Duke has always been like a gravitational pull that I can't escape, but knowing how his lips feel on mine is going to be a difficult thing to ignore.

"I gotta go, but when I get back..." he trails off and then shoves his hand down between us and slides one of his fingers between my wet folds. "This is mine. We clear?"

"Excuse me?" I say, stumbling over the words. A gasp escapes me as he uses his thumb to rub my swollen nub and then hooks his finger inside of me. My hands fly up to his chest to keep myself steady and my eyes fall back in my head. The only thing I can do is focus on the incredible feeling that he's creating with his hand, and not on the words he's said.

"You let me have it, and now THIS. IS. MINE," he says, and presses hard on my clit, sending a slight tremor through my body. I moan and let my head fall onto his chest. He wraps his other arm around my waist to keep me up. He unhooks his finger inside of me and slides three more in. The shock of being filled so suddenly is too much to take and I burst apart in his arms. My legs quake, my breathing stops, and my entire body spasms. I'm clutching his cut like it's the only lifeline I have and when my head finally clears and he removes his hands from my slick pussy, I realize that he's claimed me and try to process everything that that means.

Nodding my head out of stupidity and pushing off of his chest, I suck in a much-needed breath and look around slightly dazed. I'm barely able comprehend what he's said before he's out of the room.

He claimed me and then left me, and while this is something I've fantasized about many a night, while I was alone in my bed, stroking my own pussy and pretending it was Duke-- I don't want this. I only want him if it's real, and it never is real with Duke. So I don't want it.

I'm left looking for my clothes so I can get out of here. I find my pants and pull them up my legs, then find my thong and shove it in my jeans pocket. As I'm pulling the bra tank on, I start to feel myself sobering up and the reality of what I've done sneaks up on me. The only thing worse than denying myself Duke is having Duke and then losing him.

Now that I've been here, I can't go back to that place where I bury my feelings for him and pretend that he's just another member of the club.

JULY

Chapter 1

"HAVE YOU HEARD a single word I've said?" The words come out of my mouth, but I still can't believe I'm saying them. I'm way too young for this shit.

"I heard you. Just fucking chill, won't you?" Jeremy says. My brother's a good kid—or rather, he's not that bad of a kid—but he's got a mouth on him. He wasn't always so bad, but the older he gets without his dad around the more uncontrollable he gets.

"Then what did I say?" Fuck. I sound exactly like my mother, and I hate that bitch. She should be the one here, dealing with this shit.

"Look," Jeremy says, standing from his seat at the table. He's so tall now, just like his dad, Butch. Over six feet with broad shoulders and muscles that have come out of seemingly nowhere. Jeremy's as tan as anyone gets around here, and despite his size and attitude, he's still got the same smile he did when he was little.

"I get it. You're pissed that you had to leave work. Point fucking taken." Leaning over the back of the chair he was just sitting in, he lets his hair fall into his eyes as his head is tipped down. He looks like a grown man already, and he's only seventeen.

"No. Point not fucking taken. That shit job I had to leave puts food in that smart mouth of yours. Do me a favor and just don't hit anybody else after your suspension's up, okay?"

Tipping his head up slightly, he gives me a blinding smile. "Sure thing, boss."

"Don't do that," I say, letting my head fall into my hands. I'm worn out and figuring that it's just not worth the fight. As much as I want to do right by the kid, there's only so much I can do. In less than a year he'll be eighteen and my guardianship will be over. The only thing I'll have then is the roof over his head and the fact that we're the only family each other has. When Butch-- Jeremy's biological dad, and my step-dad-- went down for something club-related back when I was in high school, we ended up living with the club president and his wife. It didn't last long though and the president managed to get social services off our asses and me and Jeremy back into our own home. Now, looking at my brother, with all his attitude and arrogance, I can't remember why I wanted to take this on myself.

Rounding the table, he walks up behind me and kisses the top of my head, saying, "Love you, Sis."

"No more fighting?" I say, lifting my head and tilting it back to meet his eyes. His eyes are a navy blue that he's used to melt the panties off more than one of his female peers.

"No more fighting," he says, backing up into the living room and then turning and walking into his room. I know it's bullshit, but it's better than nothing. If I can just keep him off the principal's radar for the remainder of summer session, he might be able to graduate on time next spring.

Pushing up from the table, I cross the kitchen to my purse atop the counter by the stove, and pull out my small compact mirror. Checking my makeup for signs of wear, I make sure I don't look half as much of a mess as I feel. I powder my nose and then shove the compact back in my bag and rush out of the house. I'm a total disaster with my bleached blonde hair as messy as ever and my makeup half worn-off. The only thing worse than the way I look right now is the way I feel.

RIDE

Jeremy's going to be home for the rest of the week doing God only knows what, but I don't have that luxury. I have to get back to work and explain to my boss why I had *another* family emergency.

I lock up the small ranch house Jeremy and I share and take a look up at the sky overhead. The cool air hits my exposed skin, leaving faint droplets of condensation behind. Rushing to my car, an old Toyota Corolla, I yank the driver side door open and slam it behind me before I get too wet. It can't be above sixty outside and I'm wearing a low-cut black tank top and tight ripped jeans. I'd grab a sweater, but business has been slow this week and I need the tips, especially after missing half of my shift this morning to deal with damn teenage shit.

The engine grumbles to life as reluctant as ever. She's on her way out, I can tell, but she's got to hang in a few more years until I can figure something out with my brother. I make a mental note to take her by the shop in Willits. Hopefully she makes it that far without issue. Backing out of the driveway she practically wheezes, then makes a grinding sound as I cut the wheel. I grit my teeth at the thought of having to take her to the shop in town— the only shop in town— Forsaken Custom Cycle.

I haven't been on Forsaken property in almost two months— not since the night I decided it would be totally cool to act like an idiot and sleep with Duke. Not since he all but claimed me, something most Lost Girls pray for, and then totally disappeared. Not that I give a shit-- or rather-- not that I'm trying not to give a shit. He's been back in town from wherever he went for weeks now. I've seen him ride by Universal Grounds enough times just like he always has. He never stops in, never checks on me. I spent weeks making up excuses for why he's been

RIDE

absent-- weeks where I let myself think that bullshit where he claimed my pussy was anything more than punishment for making him wait so long. But now I'm done and fuck him.

He knows where I live, and he knows where I work, and still-- nothing. Like a moron, me believing him, and him being Duke and being untrustworthy, I should have seen this coming. But no. Like a moron I avoided the clubhouse because the Old Ladies don't spend much time at the clubhouse. It seemed like the right thing to do, if I was going to take myself off the market. And even though I knew it was going to hurt when he eventually got tired of me, I set myself up for the prospect of spending more time in Duke's bed, and maybe even a little time on the back of his bike. But he never showed up and now I'm left with a bad case of embarrassment.

I make the drive through the straight-up blue collar residential side of town and into downtown in less time than I'd like. I've tried to consider the best course of action in explaining my continual disappearances to my boss, but so far, I've got nothing. It's not easy having to apologize for your fuck ups again and again.

Pulling up to Universal Ground, I check my red lipstick in the rear view mirror, gather up my purse, and pull my tits up high as I can in my bra. Downtown is pretty much dead today, which doesn't bode well for the next few hours. With my purse over one shoulder and my long blonde hair pulled over the other, I pull open the heavy glass and wood door to the front of Universal Grounds. Inside, the air conditioning is on at a lower than comfortable temperature— all a ruse to encourage patrons to drink more overpriced coffee— and the place is spotless. Courtesy of the two patrons inside and my coworker Mindy, there's light chatter being thrown around keeping the shop from sinking into a dead silence.

Leaning over the counter with a rag in hand, Mindy nods her head full of strawberry blonde curls toward the back room. She knows exactly why I'm here because she's the one who was cool enough to cover for me this morning when the principal of Jeremy's high school called to ask me to come pick him up. Mindy's cool and totally anti-Forsaken, so I'm thinking we might be able to be friends which is totally up my alley at this point. But then she's also kind of a prude, so I don't know what we'd even do if we did hang out.

"Thanks, Min," I say, crossing the shop and squeezing behind the counter on my way to the office that's in the back. I blow out a few heavy breaths and psyche myself up for the conversation, but don't have much time. As I round the corner, I see the door to the office is open. Universal Ground's owner, Eileen, is at her computer, typing furiously. I give a soft knock on the door frame before stepping into the small office. It's more of a broom closet, really, but it serves its purpose.

Eileen looks up, her natural gray hair is pulled back in a low ponytail and she wears a sad smile on her face. She waves me in and I close the door behind me. I don't even have to ask. We've been here before.

"Nicole," she says as pleasantly as her mood will allow. "I assume you're here to talk about why you left your shift early?"

Inwardly, I cringe. Setting myself in the chair across the desk from her, I nod my head and say, "Yes." She waits as I collect my thoughts to present the most compelling argument for not writing me up.

"Principal Beck called, asking me for an immediate meeting and to pick Jeremy up for the day," I say, figuring she'll find out eventually. It's near impossible to keep anything a secret in this town, and it really doesn't help that Eileen's youngest son is in the same grade as Jeremy. She'd likely find out by dinnertime even if I didn't tell her.

Thoughtfully, she nods her head and leans back in her chair. She's dressed in her usual attire— clean cut khakis and a colorful polo shirt. My eyes dip down to my ripped jeans and tight blank tank for only a moment before I stop myself from comparing us any further. She's the epitome of class in a soccer mom uniform, while I'm… not. She's always been good to me which is one of the reasons I hate ditching out on her so often.

"I'm sympathetic to your family situation, Nicole. I understand that occasionally things will come up when you care for a child. I'm not interested in making you feel any worse than you already do, but we need to figure out a way to limit the number of times you have to run off for a family emergency."

"It won't happen again," I blurt out, knowing it's a lie. Eileen knows it, too. I always tell her it won't happen again, but then it does. Jeremy hits some kid in the hallway, or he's been caught cheating on a test, or even worse, he's at the police station for truancy. It's one thing after another and no matter how hard I try to keep him in check, it's useless.

"Okay. Let's let Mindy finish out this shift. You can resume the rest of the week as scheduled," she says in a kind voice. I mumble an incoherent "thanks" and stand from my chair and slink out the door. I'd thought I would ask if I could finish my hours this afternoon, but it doesn't seem like a good idea to push it now, especially since she's made up her mind about it already. Sympathetic or not, she kept the conversation short and to the point. Plus, I'm not in any position to be asking for favors right now.

Heading out of the backroom, I run into Mindy as she's turning the corner. With a perky smile on her face, her eyes widen, and she gives a giggle-laugh. Between my boss, the soccer mom, and Mindy, our resident Barbie doll, I'm ready to just throw in the towel. Mindy ducks around me, mumbling something that has the words "silly" and "goose" in it. I try to ignore her despite the fact that her quirks are really fucking cute. What grown woman actually calls herself a silly goose-- Mindy, that's who. I sort of envy her. Anyone who says shit like silly goose can't be all that fucked in the head.

I'm almost to the door when the bell chimes and it door swings open. A man of average height and build stands in the doorway looking around. I can barely see his face, but I already know who it is: Darren Jennings. We used to date back in high school, and things had gotten pretty serious until it all went to hell. He eventually upgraded to some chick I didn't really know, but I felt bad for her all the same. He's got a little scruff on his face and a ball cap pulled over his brown hair. For just a second, I freeze. I can practically feel my face paling. Before I can duck around, recognition covers his face and he smiles at me. It's never been an evil smile. It's pleasant in that unsuspecting way.

"Nicole," he says. "It's been a while." Checking out his khakis and polo shirt, I can't see much change from high school.

Acting surprised, I say, "Darren Jennings?" as if I hadn't already made the connection in my head. He swoops down and wraps his arms around my torso, pulling me into a what probably looks like a friendly hug. My lungs feel like they're shrinking down to nothing as a swell of panic overtakes me. I stay perfectly still and wait for it to end. I pause, then try to hug back, but my right arm is crushed between our bodies. I pat his back softly with my left and hope he lets go any second. I hate people who are huggers. It's like they have zero sense of boundaries. And Darren has always been a hands-on kind of guy.

"How have you been?" he pulls back, holds me at arm's length, and asks with a huge smile on his face. It's a challenge to stop myself from telling him that I feel like puking all over his loafers because he's touched me. I want to tell him that despite whatever was fucked up in my life before this moment, that shit just got a whole hell of a lot worse. I really just want to gouge his eyes out.

"Listen, I gotta go," I say, refusing to have this conversation with him. I mean, if I tell the truth, it's a pretty gloomy story-- and it's half his fault-- and I'm not about to go down that road with him. Last time it didn't end well. He narrows his eyes slightly at my response.

"So, I just graduated from USC," he says like I've forgotten our long-lost plans or something. Darren was always supposed to go to the University of Southern California, as he did. He's a legacy, meaning his dad graduated from there, and now he has too. I wasn't ever going to get into USC, but I was shooting for a school nearby there. But that was before everything fell apart and I decided that I'd rather rot in this place than to spend anymore time in his presence than absolutely necessary.

RIDE

I try to offer my congratulations as he continues. "I'm back home for the summer. We should hang out. We have a lot to catch up on." The mere thought of hanging out with Darren turns my legs into Jell-O.

"I've just been really busy," I say in an attempt to end the conversation without really pissing him off, not that there's a formula for keeping him calm or anything.

"You were wild back then," he says, a gleam of mischief in his eyes. It almost makes me sick.

"She's wild now," a deep, masculine voice sounds from behind me. I practically jump in place at the intrusion. Darren's eyes jump from mine over my shoulder to the man behind me. Turning around, I see the person I least expect standing in Universal Grounds: Diesel. He's tall and thick in every way imaginable; a little more portly than most of the club members, but he wears it well. His shaved head has a short black buzz growing in and he's scowling at Darren like he's a piece of shit that dared make its way to the bottom of his shoe. He may be a serious bad-ass, but I've always had a soft spot for Diesel.

Living in a small town like Fort Bragg, California, with a local motorcycle club like we have-- the Forsaken Motorcycle Club-- you're either their friend or their enemy. There is absolutely no in-between, especially if you're like me and you're the daughter of one of their incarcerated members. It's wise to make good with the club, and for lack of a better social scene, I've made *real* good with the club.

"Hey," I say. Inside, I'm screaming at him to leave. Club members showing up at my work-- for the first time in as long as I can remember-- is not a good thing. I don't care that it's Diesel and we're on good terms. I guess I can at least breathe a sigh of relief that it's not Duke.

But today is *not* the day to show up at my work-- of all days. Eileen is as straight-laced as they come, and while she knows my dad's Forsaken, it's not something she's keen on acknowledging. Knowing that mouthing off to Diesel won't end well, I just bite my tongue and give him a pleasant smile while taking a few steps in his direction.

Diesel's never done me wrong no matter how many times we've hooked up, but I'm not stupid enough to think he'd treat me any better than he did Julie if I start shit with him. "You want some coffee?" I ask, hitching a thumb toward the espresso machine. *God, please tell me this man just stopped in for coffee.*

Heavy boots clunk against the hardwood floor behind Diesel and a large, familiar form comes into view despite being partially obstructed by Diesel's massive body. Wearing blue jeans, a black wife beater, and his leather cut, Duke strides up beside Diesel and place his hands on his hips. It's the first time I've seen him in about two months-- ever since he claimed me when we hooked up. He looks damn good despite my frustration, and no matter how much I hate myself for it, I can't help but let my eyes travel down to his hips where his hands rest. Those hips can perform magic tricks that would make performers in Vegas jealous.

"Where in the hell have you been?" he asks, irritation evident in his voice. It only takes a moment for my temper to rise, making me see red. He's fucking joking, right?

xxx

RIDE

Add *Thrash* to your to-read shelf!
Available for purchase **January 9th, 2014**!

About the Author

As a child, JC was fascinated by things that went bump in the night. As they say, some things never change. Now, as an adult, she divides her time between the sexy law men, mythical creatures, and kick-ass heroines that live inside her head. A San Francisco Bay Area native, JC has also called both Texas and Louisiana home. These days she rocks her flip flops year round in Northern California and can't imagine a climate more beautiful.

Find JC Emery on the web . . .

http://www.jcemery.wordpress.com
http://twitter.com/jc_emery
http://www.facebook.com/jcemeryauthor
http://www.goodreads.com/jc_emery

Made in the USA
Charleston, SC
31 December 2013